Beautiful brides, snowy settings,
decorated trees, gaily wrapped presents—
gorgeous, rich and sexy grooms.
Surely nothing is more romantic than…

Christmas
Weddings

Charming new stories by three favorite authors
to make your holidays even more warm and wonderful.

Praise for Carole Mortimer

"Carole Mortimer dishes up outstanding reading as
she blends dynamic characters, volatile scenes,
superb chemistry and a wonderful premise."
—*Romantic Times BOOKreviews* on *Married by Christmas*

"*The Yuletide Engagement*...by Carole Mortimer
is a page-turner with two delightful characters,
a lovely, emotional storyline
and just wonderful storytelling."
—*Romantic Times BOOKreviews*

Praise for Shirley Jump

About *New York Times* bestselling anthology
Sugar and Spice:
"Jump's office romance gives the collection a kick,
with fiery writing."
—*PublishersWeekly.com*

"Shirley Jump gives a thoughtful and insightful story
with *The Other Wife.*"
—*Writersunlimited.com*

Praise for Margaret McDonagh

"Margaret McDonagh writes with plenty of warmth,
charm and sensitivity."
—*Cataromance* on *The Italian Doctor's Bride*

"Complex, believable and nuanced characters
bring this tale to life, creating scenes that are
unbelievably moving."
—*Romance Reviewed* on *A Doctor Worth Waiting For*

Christmas Weddings

Carole Mortimer

Shirley Jump

Margaret McDonagh

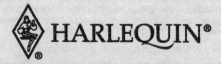

HARLEQUIN®

TORONTO • NEW YORK • LONDON
AMSTERDAM • PARIS • SYDNEY • HAMBURG
STOCKHOLM • ATHENS • TOKYO • MILAN • MADRID
PRAGUE • WARSAW • BUDAPEST • AUCKLAND

ISBN-13: 978-0-373-83727-4
ISBN-10:   0-373-83727-5

CHRISTMAS WEDDINGS

Copyright © 2008 by Harlequin Enterprises S.A.

The publisher acknowledges the copyright holders
of the individual works as follows:

HIS CHRISTMAS EVE PROPOSAL
Copyright © 2007 by Carole Mortimer.

SNOWBOUND BRIDE
Copyright © 2007 by Shirley Kawa-Jump.

THEIR CHRISTMAS VOWS
Copyright © 2007 by Margaret McDonagh.

CONTENTS

HIS CHRISTMAS EVE PROPOSAL

Carole Mortimer

Carole Mortimer was born in England, the youngest of three children. She began writing in 1978, and has now written more than 140 books for Harlequin Mills & Boon®. Carole has four sons—Matthew, Joshua, Timothy and Peter—and a bearded collie called Merlyn. She says, "I'm happily married to Peter senior. We're best friends as well as lovers, which is probably the best recipe for a successful relationship."

CHAPTER ONE

'JUST leave the coffee on the side, Donald, thanks.' Hawk called out from his bathroom to his English factotum, after he'd heard the other man knock on his bedroom door before entering. 'I'll be out in a couple of minutes,' he added, as he continued to towel-dry his hair after taking his morning shower, not expecting an answer; Donald Harrison was efficiency personified, and Hawk congratulated himself once again for having found the man ten years ago.

He continued humming to himself as, draping the towel about his shoulders, he took a couple of seconds to contemplate the view from his bathroom window, relishing the blanket of snow that swept across the whole of the foothills towards the Canadian Rockies, which he could see towering majestically in the distance.

Home. It was a stark contrast to the warmth he had left behind in Los Angeles yesterday; he'd been able to feel the biting cold as soon as he stepped out at Calgary airport last night. But Hawk had dressed with the Canadian weather in mind, his sheepskin jacket, faded denims and the boots that had seemed so out of place in Los Angeles ideal for the refreshing coldness that he'd known he would find here.

He instantly felt part of the impending festive season now that he had the weather to go with it. It was unthinkable for him to even contemplate spending Christmas anywhere else but here. No matter where he was in the world, he always flew back to what had once been the family home for the holidays.

His parents now lived in Florida, as the warmth there was much kinder to the arthritis his father suffered after years of working on the land. They would arrive in three days' time at the five acres and house that were all that remained of the family farm. Hawk's younger sister and her husband—the city slicker—would fly in from Vancouver at the weekend, with their two young children.

No doubt the scores of female fans who avidly followed the movie career of Joshua Hawkley would find his family Christmas a pretty tame affair, probably imagining him instead to be on some Caribbean island, soaking up the sun on a golden beach and drinking piña coladas with a half-naked female at his side!

The half-naked female didn't sound half bad, but the rest of it could take a hike.

He turned to study his reflection in the slightly steamed-up mirror over the sink, rubbing the dark stubble on his chin as he debated whether or not to shave. He decided not; he had three more days before the parents arrived to just wind down and relax after all the razzmatazz that had gone along with attending his latest movie premiere last weekend, and not shaving was part of that process.

No doubt his mother would have some comment to make about his longer hair, though, he acknowledged ruefully as he looked at the dishevelled damp locks that rested on the broad width of his shoulders. He was due to start filming the long-awaited sequel to *The Pirate King* next month, and had grown his dark hair in preparation for the part.

If they could find a replacement leading lady, that was. A five months pregnant female pirate captain wouldn't exactly look right, and Hawk's schedule was such that filming couldn't be delayed until after the baby's birth.

Oh, well—that was the director Nik Prince's problem, not his. Hawk shrugged dismissively to himself as he strolled through to his bedroom.

'Donald, I think I might—who the *hell* are you?' Hawk rasped. He came to an abrupt halt in the bathroom doorway to stare across the room at the young woman standing in front of the window and drawing back his bedroom curtains.

There was no mistaking that she was a woman. Her long red waist-length hair gave that away, flowing down the slenderness of her spine the colour of rippling fire against a body-hugging black sweater.

But even without the hair it was impossible not to recognise that the tall, leggy figure belonged to a female. Her skin-tight black denims were doing everything they could to prove the point, Hawk saw with a frown.

At the same time he knew there shouldn't be a female—tall and leggy or otherwise—within several miles of here!

Rosie had turned at the first sound of the unmistakable, sexily husky voice of the actor Joshua Hawkley, taking in a sharp breath as she found herself gazing upon his nakedness.

Joshua Hawkley, thirty-five years old, the most sought-after film star in the world for over a decade, was standing in front of her—gorgeously, gloriously and magnificently naked!

Her throat felt dry, her lips and tongue numb, as she continued to stare at him with wide green eyes.

She had never been the sort of teenager—had never been *allowed* to be the sort of teenager!—who'd hung posters of pop and film stars on her bedroom wall. But if she had, this man would definitely have had pride of position!

Joshua Hawkley—or simply Hawk to his friends—at a height well over six feet, had a body Adonis would have been envious of: his shoulders were wide and muscular, and dark hair grew on the broadness of his chest and down over the flatness of his stomach to—

Wow.

Gasp.

Whoa!

A sudden rush of saliva moistened her throat and mouth as she found it impossible to remove her gaze from his perfect manhood.

As if becoming aware of the avidness of her gaze, Hawk moved one hand to casually pull the towel from his shoulders before draping and fastening it about his waist.

Rosie blinked, as if waking from a spell, before dragging her eyes back up to his face. Colour warmed her cheeks at the knowing smile curving those sculptured lips in a face that could have—*should* have—been carved by Michelangelo. A face dominated by cobalt-blue eyes above a long aquiline nose, that lazily smiling mouth and the strongly squared jaw. Long dark hair, damp and dishevelled after his shower, did absolutely nothing to dispel his air of masculine perfection, only adding to his ruggedness.

'I have absolutely no idea how you got in here,' Hawk bit out impatiently as the girl continued to stare at him unblinkingly. 'But I seriously advise you to get yourself out again!' he added, with none of the tolerance he usually felt towards his more enthusiastic female fans.

This was his bolt-hole, damn it, and it shouldn't even be public knowledge, let alone accessible to some desperate woman who had got in here because she either wanted to share his bed or use a relationship with him to acquire a movie role!

How on earth had she got past Donald?

The girl—for she was no more than that, Hawk was sure, despite her height and the fullness of her breasts and those curvaceous hips—moistened the sensual softness of her pouting lips.

Her eyes, between lush dark lashes, were a deep, mesmerising green, her nose was small and pert, and covered with a smattering of freckles and her chin was stubbornly pointed in a heart-shaped face. And all of her elfin beauty was surrounded by that long flame of pre-Raphaelite-style hair.

At any other time, Hawk knew, he would have found her untamed beauty fascinating. But not when she had invaded the privacy of his home. Not just his home, but his bedroom, for heaven's sake!

'If you aren't out of here in two minutes I'll have no choice but to forcibly remove you,' he warned her harshly, and he ran an impatient hand through his tousled hair, his previous good humour having completely evaporated, to be replaced by impatient anger at this girl's intrusion.

She moistened her lips a second time before speaking, those green eyes huge and haunting. 'If you would just let me explain, Mr Hawkley—' Her voice was throatily soft, her accent distinctly English.

'Keep your explanation and just get out of here!' he cut in irritably, his gaze narrowing suddenly as he saw the tray bearing a cafetière and coffee cups on the bedside table. She must have brought it in with her. 'Where's Donald?' he rasped suspiciously.

'That's what I was trying to explain,' Rosie answered, with some relief.

'You were?' His stance was challenging now, muscles rippling as he folded his arms across his chest.

He really was as gorgeous as he looked on screen, Rosie acknowledged slightly breathlessly, and his semi-nakedness made him more immediately so in the intimacy and privacy of his bedroom.

But it was also pretty obvious from Joshua Hawkley's comments that he was in complete ignorance of who she was or what she was doing here. That Donald hadn't told his employer that she was even staying here.

Joshua Hawkley's aggression was understandable now that she realised he had thought she was an intruder—an over-enthusiastic female fan?—in his home.

She shrugged. 'My—er—I don't know if you noticed, but Donald wasn't at all well yesterday when he picked you up from the airport...' She grimaced as Hawk gave a puzzled shake of his head. 'No? Well, this morning he woke up shivering and with a high temperature. I think he probably has the flu,' she finished.

Three things became obvious to Hawk from that statement.

First, this girl knew exactly who Donald was, and so wasn't an intruder at all.

Second, she had come to an abrupt halt after beginning her statement with 'My—'

And third, perhaps she didn't need to complete it. She had obviously been around to see what Donald had looked like when he woke up that morning...!

CHAPTER TWO

IN THE light of those realisations, Hawk re-evaluated the young woman standing beside his sleep-tousled bed.

She looked vaguely familiar to him—as if he should know her… Where had he seen her before? He knew he had never met her.

And obviously she was here to see Donald…

She had to be in her early twenties—but then Donald was only in his early forties. A twenty-year-odd age difference wasn't an insurmountable barrier.

Hawk had never found the need to discuss Donald's private life with him, but he supposed that his assistant must have one. He knew that the older man liked to listen to classical music, and that when their schedule allowed Donald took off to go to live concerts in one part of the world or another.

But, despite his cultured tastes, there was still no doubting that Donald—even with his prematurely white hair—was still an attractive guy, and in possession of all normal male needs.

Even so, Donald could have warned Hawk that he had invited a female guest to stay when Hawk had returned home last night. Donald had arrived two days earlier, so that he could prepare and warm the farmhouse for his employer's arrival.

Hawk scowled, feeling at something of a disadvantage now, after his first assumptions about this lady. 'Does Donald need to see a doctor?'

'I don't think so.' Rosie shook her head, somewhat relieved that Hawk wasn't probing for intimate details of her relationship with his long-term employee. 'I've given him some medication to bring his temperature down, so he probably just needs to go back to sleep for a while. Something he's loath to do without speaking to you first,' she added. The reason for Donald's urgent need was becoming obvious now that she knew of this man's ignorance regarding her identity.

Joshua Hawkley gave a terse nod. 'I'll get dressed and come straight through.'

'I—yes. I'll make fresh coffee, shall I?' she asked with a grimace, as she picked up the untouched tray she had brought in earlier.

Hawk felt a brandy might be more beneficial after the jolt of unexpectedly finding this woman in his bedroom, but as it was only ten o'clock in the morning coffee would have to do. 'That would be great,' he accepted briskly, turning away, eager to put some clothes on so that he could go and speak to Donald.

He pondered the fact that if Donald had relationships, then he had never brought any of his women home with him before. But at the same time Hawk recognised it was the holiday season—a time when everyone wanted to be close to somebody.

Which meant he would probably have to accept Donald's red-haired and wildly beautiful friend staying for a while.

A thought he found strangely disturbing…

* * *

The fresh coffee had barely finished percolating when Joshua Hawkley entered the cosy warmth of the open-plan kitchen, with its green and white tiles and oak cabinets.

'The medication seems to have served its purpose,' he drawled, as Rosie turned to give him a guarded look. 'Donald is already asleep,' he elaborated. 'Which means that any explanations will have to come from you,' he finished dryly, and he moved to sit on one of the stools at the breakfast bar, looking across at her enquiringly.

He was a little less overwhelming now that he was wearing a navy blue sweater, faded denims and scuffed cowboy boots, Rosie acknowledged. But only a little; the dark good looks that so captivated cinema audiences, that held millions of women in his thrall, were no less disturbing in reality, and the long length of his hair was giving him a piratical appearance.

Which was probably the idea, Rosie allowed, knowing he was due to start filming the sequel to his previous million-dollar box office hit *The Pirate King* some time in the New Year.

She deliberately turned away from his piercing blue gaze to pour his coffee into a waiting mug, playing for time, not really sure how much Donald would want her to tell his employer. The fact that Donald hadn't told Hawk anything about her at all only increased her reluctance!

'Pour yourself a cup and join me,' Hawk invited huskily, once she had placed the steaming mug of black coffee on the breakfast bar in front of him, along with milk and sugar.

After all, just because she was Donald's friend it didn't mean she had to wait on him.

Hawk watched her through narrowed lids as she reluctantly complied with his suggestion, the movements of her graceful hands economic, her slender body willowy—apart from the pert fullness of her breasts as they thrust against her sweater.

For all that he had been surprised to find her here, Hawk certainly couldn't fault Donald's taste in women!

He waited until she had seated herself on the stool opposite, her gaze not quite meeting his, before speaking again. 'Perhaps we should start with your name?' he invited mildly.

It shouldn't have been a difficult question, but nevertheless Hawk sensed her hesitation, the slightly searching look she gave him before answering.

'Rosie,' she finally told him, those graceful hands wrapped around her coffee mug as if drawing strength from its warmth.

Hawk kept his expression deliberately mild. 'Rosie what?'

'Look, Mr Hawkley.' She looked up at him, obviously seriously uncomfortable with his questioning. 'I really think you should talk to my—Donald about this.'

Again Hawk heard that hesitation after 'my'...

'My' what? Friend? Lover? What?

Hawk found himself with an overwhelming curiosity to know the answer to that question.

So he waited, knowing from experience that an expectant silence on his part would eventually bring a response. He didn't have to wait long.

'If my being here is an inconvenience, then you only have to say so and I'll leave,' she began flusteredly.

But the mere suggestion of her doing any such thing seemed to make her cheeks pale and those deep green eyes look haunted...

Why? Hawk wondered. What was this woman hiding, or running away from? More to the point, why had she chosen Donald to run to?

He regarded her with hooded eyes. 'I'm not saying so,' he drawled. 'I'm merely wondering. Have you and Donald known each other long?'

Had she and Donald known each other long? Rosie pondered. Surely that depended on what was meant by *knowing* each other?

'A while, yes,' she finally answered huskily.

Hawk nodded. 'And you're here to spend the holidays with him?'

'Possibly.' Again her answer was noncommittal.

Only having arrived in Canada herself yesterday, Hawk's imminent arrival and Donald's early flu symptoms had proved a distraction to any deep conversation she might have had with Donald, so Rosie had no idea what her short or even long-term plans were. No idea whether Donald would even want her to stay and spend the holidays with him.

The only thing that had consumed her yesterday, as she'd thrown things into a suitcase in readiness for her flight, was the thought of the white satin and lace wedding dress that hung on her wardrobe door—a constant reminder of just why she had to get away. She'd needed to go somewhere where no one would think of looking for her, hopefully where no one would recognise her either. Joshua Hawkley obviously hadn't...

Rosie had been puzzled, a few days before, when, taking her passport from the box where her mother kept all the family's papers, she'd seen a piece of paper there too, on which Donald's telephone number was scrawled. Her puzzlement had turned to shock when curiosity had made her call the number and Donald had answered. She had discovered it was his current mobile number!

She didn't know which of them had been the more surprised to hear the other's voice, although Donald had readily agreed when she'd asked him if she might fly out to Canada to see him.

Hawk was still watching her from between narrowed lids. 'You aren't being very—forthcoming about your relationship with Donald,' he finally murmured impatiently.

Her relationship with Donald? Did she have one? She wasn't sure any more. But perhaps that was part of why she had come here—to find out...?

She straightened. 'I really think you should talk to him about this.'

Hawk shrugged broad shoulders. 'He isn't up to talking about anything at the moment.'

And Donald hadn't been yesterday, actually, Rosie accepted. Donald's flu symptoms were obviously worse today, which was making this situation more difficult for her than it needed to be.

It had all seemed so simple when she'd arrived yesterday and discovered that Donald had his own suite of rooms over the garage adjoining the farmhouse. It was an arrangement that meant Joshua Hawkley didn't even have to be made aware of her presence if Donald decided otherwise.

But waking up this morning to find Donald incapacitated in his bed had changed all that—even more so when he had asked her to take Joshua Hawkley's morning tray of coffee up to his employer. A request Rosie had very reluctantly agreed to when it seemed it was the only way to stop Donald's growing agitation.

She roused herself to reply to Hawk's comment. 'Then I suggest you wait until he's feeling better.'

Hawk found himself bristling at her dismissive tone. He

was being reasonable about this, wasn't he? Considering he had found a strange woman wandering around his bedroom only a short time ago, he really thought so!

What—?

'Hawk!' A distraught, tousle-haired and robe-covered Donald staggered into the kitchen, the ravages of the flu evident in the paleness of his lined face. 'I meant to tell you—' He looked at the two of them seated at the breakfast-bar. 'I just felt so ill last night that all I wanted to do was fall into bed—' He gave a frustrated shake of his head as he swayed slightly. 'I hope Rosie has explained?' he added weakly as she stood up.

Hawk's mouth twisted ruefully as he also stood up. 'Not so far, no,' he drawled ruefully. 'But I'm living in hope,' he added, with a mocking glance at her flushed face.

Donald looked across at her dazedly. 'You haven't told him…?'

Told him exactly what? And how much? Rosie frowned.

The situation had felt so difficult last night—the gulf between Donald and herself so wide that the two of them hadn't had a proper chance to talk yet, let alone involve a third party. And that third party was Joshua Hawkley! A man who lived in the limelight himself, who once he knew her full name might add two and two together and come up with the correct answer of four!

The fewer people who knew who she was, the less likelihood there was of—

'Rosie is my daughter, Hawk,' Donald turned to tell the other man before she had a chance to stop him.

Hawk's cobalt-blue eyes widened on her incredulously, telling Rosie that this was the last explanation he'd been expecting!

CHAPTER THREE

DONALD'S daughter…

Whoever Hawk had thought this young woman might be, it certainly wasn't the other man's daughter!

He hadn't even known Donald had been married, let alone that he had a daughter of—what?—twenty-two, twenty-three?

But maybe Donald hadn't been married. Maybe this girl was the result of a brief relationship all those years ago. Whatever—it didn't make her any less than *Donald's daughter*.

Hawk had never once heard Donald mention her in the ten years he'd worked for him, let alone seen her!

But had *Donald* seen her during that time? Hawk supposed that he must have done. After all, his employee had holidays, free time, and he certainly didn't owe Hawk any explanations about his personal life.

Where had Rosie suddenly appeared from? Because he was pretty sure that Donald hadn't known she was going to join them here when he'd come ahead from Los Angeles a couple of days ago.

More to the point, *why* had she come…?

Hawk felt a little dazed. 'Perhaps we should get you back to bed,' he murmured, as Donald coughed painfully. 'Rosie can tell me anything else I need to know,' he concluded, with a narrow-eyed glance in her direction.

But Rosie had no intention of telling him anything more than she absolutely had to!

Hawk's surprise at discovering she was actually Donald's daughter, rather than the lover he had clearly assumed her to be, had been pretty obvious. But, if anything, he looked more disapproving of the true explanation of their relationship than he had of his previous assumption!

She shrugged off the movie star's disapproval impatiently. Her father might work for Hawk, and as such owe him some sort of explanation as to why she was here, but that didn't mean Rosie was answerable to him too.

Not even if she was to be a temporary guest in his home?

No, not even then, she decided stubbornly.

'Let's go and finish our coffee,' Hawk suggested, softly but firmly, as they settled Donald back in his bed. The effort of coming downstairs seemed to have tired out the factotum, and he lay back exhausted against the pillows.

'Would you like me to stay and make you some tea?' Rosie offered gently, at the same time pointedly ignoring Hawk. 'Or bring you a glass of cool juice?'

Donald gave a weak smile. 'No, I—I'll be fine. You go and talk to Hawk,' he encouraged huskily.

Not what she wanted to do at all, Rosie reflected, as she turned and preceded Hawk from the flat and back down the stairs to the kitchen in the main house, all the time thinking of what she actually needed, *had* to tell, this disturbingly attractive man.

Not that much, really, she decided. The bare bones of the truth should do it. She hadn't had a chance to tell her father everything yesterday, about her reasons for being here, and there was no need to tell Hawk either.

'Have you finished deciding how much I need to know?' Hawk probed wryly once they were seated back at the breakfast bar, knowing by the way her cheeks became flushed that he had scored a direct hit with his question.

She raised her pointed chin defensively. 'My father has already told you all there is to know, Mr Hawkley—'

'Hawk,' he put in firmly, elbows resting on the breakfast bar as he studied her across its width. 'Somehow I don't think that's true, Rosie,' he persisted. 'For instance, the glaringly obvious thing Donald hasn't told me is why I didn't know of your existence until today!'

Auburn brows rose over her cool green eyes. 'Perhaps he didn't consider it any of your business,' she dismissed.

Hawk was starting to feel seriously irritated by this woman's deliberate rudeness. She certainly hadn't looked so cool earlier, when he had strolled out of the bathroom stark naked!

If he were honest, he hadn't felt that cool himself when he'd first became aware of her in his bedroom—the tell-tale stirring of his body had been proof of that! He studied her closely now, noting the golden ring circling the green of her eyes, making them appear almost luminous, and the freckles that covered her nose, making him wonder if she had freckles anywhere else. And what it would feel like to kiss every one of them...

He straightened, impatient with his own wandering thoughts. He wasn't involved in a relationship with anyone at the moment, but he had only left Los Angeles yesterday—the land of plenty when it came to beautiful available women. Finding himself attracted to Rosie Harrison, who took the phrase 'woman of mystery' to a whole new level, was a complication he certainly didn't need. Now or at any other time.

'Are you here to spend Christmas with Donald?' he enquired tersely, the thought of Rosie sharing the flat over the garage with Donald during the holidays robbing him of some of his contentment at the contemplation of a quiet family Christmas.

'That hasn't been decided yet,' she answered noncommittally.

She brought a whole new dimension to that saying about getting blood out of a stone too, Hawk acknowledged impatiently, deciding he had had enough of this verbal fencing for one morning.

'Although the fact that he's obviously ill does rather change things, doesn't it?' Rosie suddenly opined.

Hawk eyed her warily. 'It does?'

'Well, of course it does,' she came back waspishly. 'Apart from the fact that he's ill and will need looking after, he's obviously also unable to work. As I understand it, you're expecting the rest of your family to descend on you in the next few days…?'

'Yes…' Hawk confirmed, wariness in his own tone now.

'And Don—my father,' she corrected awkwardly, 'was supposed to shop for food, put up the decorations and things?'

'Yes.' Hawk nodded, very aware of the fact that she seemed to be having difficulty actually calling Donald her father.

Damn it, why did Donald have to get the flu now? Because Hawk was pretty sure he was going to have to wait until his assistant was better before he got any helpful answers to his questions!

No matter how much she was determined not to answer Hawk's questions, Rosie was also aware that if he chose to tell Donald she couldn't stay on here her father would have no choice but to ask her to leave. And the truth was, at this moment in time, she didn't have anywhere else to go to…

In the circumstances, it wasn't in her best interests to be completely uncoopérative…

'Well, I could do those things for you instead—if you would like me to,' she offered lightly. 'If you'll just point me in the direction of the nearest supermarket and tell me where you keep the Christmas decorations…?' she prompted, at Hawk's lack of a response to her offer.

He raised dark brows over mocking blue eyes, a slightly derisive smile curving the sculptured mouth that was set so arrogantly in his ruggedly handsome face. Rosie's pulse fluttered slightly as she was once again forcibly reminded of exactly who this man was.

Only a woman who was deaf, blind or totally insensitive to blatant sexiness could fail not to tremble slightly with awareness in his presence.

But she was a woman running away from her wedding day, from a man she neither loved nor wanted to marry, which should have made her totally immune to the attractions of any other member of the opposite sex.

But it didn't…

She tried to break her gaze away from the compelling blue of Hawk's eyes. And failed. Instead she felt as if she were drowning in their dark depths, as if she were trying to swim against the tide, and the effort to resist rendered her slightly breathless and trembling.

This wouldn't do, she told herself firmly. Joshua Hawkley might be one of the most dangerously attractive men she had ever met, but he was also her father's employer—her father's over-curious employer! She would be wise to keep that in mind.

It took some effort, but she finally managed to drag her gaze away from his, staring at a point somewhere over Hawk's left shoulder. 'Unless you would prefer to do those things yourself—?'

'Hell, no! You feel free to carry on, if that's what you want to do,' he bit out as he stood up.

Rosie sighed. 'I merely offered because I'm sure my father would expect it,' she explained.

'I've already said it's fine, Rosie,' Hawk drawled. 'I still have to shop for gifts, anyway. One more to add to the list now,' he added pointedly.

Rosie gave him a startled glance. Surely he didn't mean her...?

'Please don't bother on my account,' she told him hastily.

She'd brought some cash with her, which she had changed into Canadian dollars at the airport, but those funds were limited, and certainly wouldn't last very long if she had to go out and buy Christmas presents for Joshua Hawkley and his family. She'd had no choice but to use her credit card when she booked her air ticket, but was loath to use it now. Canada was a big country, but paying with her credit card would certainly give away her location to anyone unprincipled enough—determined enough—to use that method to track her down.

Her caution would probably seem a little dramatic to anyone else, but she had come to know only too well the ruthlessness of her pursuer...

In the last few minutes Hawk had watched all the different emotions as they'd flickered across the beauty of Rosie's face. Emotions too fleeting for him to be able to fully comprehend. But he had registered her slight panic at his mention of buying Christmas presents. What was this woman hiding?

Hawk wondered frowningly, as he continued to watch her anxious features.

Because he was pretty sure from the way she avoided answering his direct questions that she was hiding something…

CHAPTER FOUR

'I'LL drive you to the mall, if you like,' Hawk told her briskly. 'You can shop for food while I go off in search of gifts for my family.' Even as he made the suggestion he could see that it didn't sit too well with Rosie Harrison. Her slender hands trembled slightly as she collected up their empty coffee mugs and put them in the dishwasher.

At least he thought it was his suggestion that was making her tremble...

It was difficult to tell what she was thinking or feeling when she continued to avoid his gaze!

She shook her head. 'I don't think my father would approve of my putting you to any trouble on my behalf—'

'It isn't on your behalf if you're going to be shopping for food for my family,' Hawk reasoned. 'Besides, I'm going into Calgary anyway,' he added firmly, feeling a sudden determination, now that he could see her reluctance, to take her with him.

How contrary was that?

Very, Hawk acknowledged ruefully. But after years of being a public figure, of being pursued by some of the most beautiful women in the world, it was something of a novelty to find a woman who was so obviously reluctant to spend any more time in his company than she had to.

That wasn't conceit on his part either, only fact; his place on the Hollywood A-list made him an easy—and possibly useful—target for any woman who was trying to make it in the movie business.

Besides, he might be able to get Rosie Harrison to open up a little more about herself if he spent some more time with her…

She gave another small shake of her head, her glorious red hair shimmering like a living flame as she did so. 'I don't think it's a good idea to just leave my father on his own when he isn't well.'

Considering Donald hadn't been well several times during the last ten years—whether with other bouts of flu or stomach upsets—and had managed pretty well without the attendance of his daughter, Hawk didn't think her being here this time was going to be of any relevance to the other man's wellbeing or recovery!

'Like all men, I know for a fact that Donald prefers to be on his own when he isn't feeling well,' Hawk assured her. 'But I'll go up and check on him while you get ready—explain what's happening if he's awake, if that makes you feel happier about going,' he assured her.

Rosie wasn't fooled by Hawk's lazily relaxed tone for a moment. She knew by the look of determination on his face that he wasn't about to accept any of her arguments against going to Calgary with him. Much better to just give in gracefully.

'I'll only be five minutes,' she told him reluctantly. 'What?' she prompted, when she saw his sceptical expression.

'If you do only take five minutes to get ready to go out,

then you'll be the first woman of my acquaintance to do so!' he explained wryly.

Rosie gave him a narrow-eyed glare. 'I can only assume that must be due to the type of woman you're acquainted with!'

'You're probably right!' Appreciative laughter glinted in his deep blue eyes as he gave a grin, his teeth white and even against his tanned skin. 'I'll go up and see Donald in a couple of minutes,' he confirmed, his gaze slightly mocking.

She hadn't taken the complication of this dangerously attractive man's presence here into account when she'd arranged to come to Canada so suddenly, Rosie acknowledged to herself as she hurried from the kitchen up to her father's flat. If she had thought about it at all, she'd have believed the actor would be too busy with his own family to even notice her. And if her father hadn't become suddenly ill, then he probably wouldn't have done.

All of which made absolutely no difference to the fact that he *had* noticed her, and that she was about to accompany him into Calgary in order to do his grocery shopping for him!

What would she have been doing if she were in England now?

Considering the time difference, she would most probably have been in bed. Although she doubted very much that she would have been asleep. Sleep seemed to be something that had eluded her more and more as her wedding day had approached and she'd realised what a mistake she was making.

But it was a mistake she had now done something about, she reminded herself firmly. Before it had been too late.

In fact, now that she thought about it, she didn't even want to contemplate what would be happening now if she were still in the UK!

She was going to take one day at a time, deal with one problem at a time—and what she had to concentrate on right now was getting ready in the five minutes she had assured Hawk that she would take!

'I'm impressed,' Hawk announced, as Rosie hurried down the stairs to join him at the front door—still with ten seconds of the allotted five minutes to spare!

He was a little disappointed that the wild flame of her hair was hidden under the black woollen hat she had pulled on over her ears. She was wearing a black coat too, which reached from her neck to her booted feet. Only the lively beauty of her face, dominated by those challenging green eyes, gave colour to her appearance.

He looked down at her assessingly. 'You shouldn't wear black,' he said disapprovingly. 'It drains all the colour from your face.'

Colour—angry colour—heightened the paleness of her cheeks. 'When I want your opinion, I'll ask for it!' she snapped, before preceding him out of the door he was holding open for her, more annoyed with the fact that she knew he was right than with his actual comment.

But almost every item of clothing she owned was black, so he was going to be disappointed if he expected his criticism to elicit any change in her wardrobe!

She drew in a sharp breath at the extreme cold she encountered as she stepped outside. Snow had started to fall some time in the last ten minutes or so, landing stingingly on her face as she turned to look up at Hawk. 'Perhaps we should wait until this storm blows over…?' she voiced uncertainly.

He grinned down at her, seeming completely unconcerned by the flakes landing in the dark thickness of his hair. 'If you stayed home every time it snowed in Canada you would never go anywhere,' he assured her as he used a remote to open the garage doors.

Rosie knew that a blizzard like this in England would bring everything—public transport and private cars alike—to a grinding halt. But if Hawk said it was okay, then she would have to take his word for it. She certainly wasn't about to let him think she was worried by a little thing like a snowstorm!

She had to admit that everywhere looked very beautiful as they travelled into Calgary. And there were lots of other drivers on the road who obviously felt the same reluctance as Hawk to have their movements dictated by the weather.

As they entered the shopping mall together, Rosie heard the Christmas carols that were playing over the public tannoy, saw the real pine tree that was at least twenty feet high, decorated from head to base in glittering red and green and lit by gold lights, and was suddenly struck by the realisation that it was going to be Christmas in a few days' time…

How ridiculous that she hadn't really thought of it before!

But she knew it was the thought of her wedding on Christmas Eve that had driven awareness of anything else from her panicked mind.

How long had it been since she had been free to actually enjoy Christmas? To listen to Christmas carols? To go to a mall like this and see all the excited expectation on the other shoppers' faces?

Too long, she acknowledged heavily.

But she was free to enjoy it now, she assured herself determinedly, at once brightening at the thought. It might even be fun to spend Christmas here in Canada with her father—

'Feel like sharing the secret?' Hawk asked huskily at her side.

She turned to give him a startled look. 'What secret?' she snapped warily.

He shrugged his broad shoulders. 'You were looking serious, and then you suddenly began to smile; I merely wondered what had brought about the transformation.'

Well, he could go on wondering!

Too many of her freedoms had been curbed these last ten years, but her thoughts were most definitely her own!

'Hey, Hawk,' a man called out in greeting as he walked past them. 'Looking forward to seeing your next movie!'

'Thanks,' Hawk returned with a smile.

It was the first of many such greetings as they continued to stroll down the mall.

It was interesting to Rosie that although people obviously recognised Hawk as the actor Joshua Hawkley, and smiled or spoke to him as they passed, he met their attention with a languid charm that, while it was not unfriendly, didn't invite further conversation either. A manner they all accepted with good humour.

She turned to give him a curious glance, feeling Hawk's hand beneath her elbow as they strolled towards the grocery store. 'Doesn't it bother you?' she questioned. 'All this attention,' she explained as he raised dark brows enquiringly. 'People talking to you? Watching you? Talking about you?'

He gave the question some thought. 'If it was going to bother me, then I shouldn't have become an actor and put myself in the limelight,' he finally replied.

Rosie couldn't help admiring his pragmatic attitude. Even if she didn't share it…

But then, becoming a public figure in the UK had never been her choice, had it?

'Are you going to be okay doing the grocery shopping on your own?' Hawk enquired as they reached the store entrance. 'If not, I could always—'

'No, I'm sure I'll be fine,' she assured him quickly. 'I just— do you have any cash?' she asked awkwardly. 'My credit card is maxed out from booking my flight, I'm afraid.' Having mulled her difficulty over during the drive into the city, she had decided this was the best excuse she could come up with.

Hawk looked at her for several long seconds before answering her. 'Just wander about for half an hour or so, picking up what you think we're going to need, and then I'll meet you at the checkout and pay for it all,' he finally decided.

Rosie turned away on the pretext of collecting a trolley so that he wouldn't see the embarrassed colour that had stained her cheeks under his probing gaze. Not feeling it was safe to use her own credit card was going to be more difficult than she had imagined if Hawk was going to look at her in that totally sceptical way too often...

'How many people am I shopping for?' she asked briskly as she rejoined him.

'Seven adults and two kids. Donald normally joins us for Christmas dinner,' he explained.

Maybe that was what Donald normally did during the holidays, but he had his own daughter here with him this year—and Rosie certainly didn't want to be included in the Hawkley family Christmas.

But standing outside a supermarket, with Hawk still attracting curious glances, wasn't the ideal time to argue that particular point!

'Traditional fare?' she enquired efficiently instead.

'Very traditional,' Hawk answered dryly. 'My mother is

British. Anything less than turkey and all the trimmings is sacrilege in her traditionalist's eyes!'

Rosie felt a little unsettled at the knowledge that Hawk's mother shared her own nationality. It made him a little less of the unknown quantity that she would have preferred him to be.

Hawk felt himself smiling with hard satisfaction as he saw that knowing his mother was British had unnerved Rosie slightly. She was far too cool and self-contained for his liking, and anything that gave him an edge had to be a positive thing.

'She will have made a Christmas pudding and will bring it with her, so don't worry about that,' he instructed.

'I wasn't worrying,' she assured him tartly.

'Do you cook, Rosie?' He quirked his dark brows.

'Why?' she countered suspiciously.

Hawk shrugged. 'It's always useful to know.'

Her mouth tightened. 'No, Mr Hawkley, I don't cook.'

'Pity.' He grimaced. 'In that case, it looks as if we'll have to put up with my cooking for the next few days!'

Rosie stared up at him wordlessly for several long seconds, looking as if she would like to argue his use of the word 'we', and then thought better of it as she snapped, 'If you'll excuse me? I'll go and do your food shopping for you now…' She moved off with her shopping trolley.

Hawk stood and watched her go, knowing a quiet satisfaction that he had managed to rattle her cool control slightly.

Rosie had been in the bathroom getting ready when Hawk had paid his visit to check on Donald. The older man had been dozing—not peacefully so, but caught somewhere between sleep and slight delirium as he muttered to someone who clearly wasn't there…

'Don't worry, Gloria… Going to America…won't be

coming back,' Donald had mumbled. 'Won't forget the money, Gloria.' Then, with startling clarity, the feverish man had bitten out, 'Don't bring our daughter up to be a money-grasping bitch like *you*!' before lapsing back into his troubled slumber.

'Our daughter...'

Rosie...?

The young woman who had felt no qualms just now at asking Hawk for cash to buy the groceries even though she must have known he was good for it—that he would have re-imbursed any money she had paid out on his behalf?

Had the absent Gloria brought her daughter up to be a money-grabber, after all?

He didn't know—couldn't fathom what sort of woman Rosie was from the little she was prepared to tell him about herself.

It was a situation that would need watching.

And for all that he didn't quite trust her, or her motives, Hawk knew he would be more than happy to watch Rosie...

CHAPTER FIVE

'HERE—let me do that.'

Rosie barely had time to register that Hawk had rejoined her in the supermarket before she felt him move to take over pushing the trolley.

Except she hadn't let go of it yet...

Hawk's hands covered hers. Big hands. Warm, protective and strong hands.

So very strong, Rosie thought, and she felt the equivalent of an electric shock run along the length of her fingers and up her arm.

She snatched her own hands quickly away. What was that? What had just happened?

'Did I hurt you?' Hawk had turned to her with concern, reaching out as if to take her hands in his so that he could inspect them.

Rosie thrust her trembling hands behind her back as she stared up at him. Hurt her? No, he certainly hadn't hurt her. She wasn't sure what had happened...

For years she had imagined that some strong, dauntless man would come along and sweep her off her feet. A man who would rescue her and take her away from a life that had become more of an ordeal than the enjoyment it had once been.

But Joshua Hawkley, although certainly strong and dauntless, certainly didn't want to rescue her! More the opposite—she had the definite feeling that since he had realised she was Donald's long-absent daughter he thought her father was the one who needed rescuing from her!

She moistened her lips before speaking. 'Just an electric shock from the trolley handle,' she dismissed, apparently unconcerned.

Those blue eyes darkened speculatively. 'Are you sure—?'

'You're back early,' Rosie interrupted brightly. 'Couldn't you find anything?' She looked at his empty hands.

The same hands that had just evoked such a strange trembling inside her…!

He grimaced. 'I made the mistake of going into a toy store first, and realised that I have absolutely no idea what to buy for a six-year-old boy—let alone a seven-year-old girl! I don't suppose you have any idea what I could get them?'

'Me?' Rosie echoed incredulously, that moment of complete awareness starting to fade. From her trembling body if not her memory!

'I guess not,' Hawk said, thinking that it had probably been a silly question; as an only child Rosie probably had no more idea of what children were into these days than he did. At least, he *assumed* she was an only child…

'You guess right,' Rosie confirmed dryly.

'I'll give Jen—my sister—a call later, and check it out with her,' he returned as he gave Rosie a considering look. 'Aren't you hot in all that gear…?' She was still wearing the thick woollen hat, as well as the heavy coat that covered her all the way from her throat to ankles, and her face was no longer pale but flushed from her stroll around the heated grocery store.

'It's easier than carrying them,' she replied tautly, before turning her attention to the rows of pasta on offer.

Deliberately? Yes, he believed so, Hawk decided frustratedly. What was it with this woman? Why was it such hard work even just trying to talk to her?

And what had happened just now when he touched her?

Because something had…

'Do you need any help putting that away, or can I go up and check on my father?' Rosie asked politely, once she had helped Hawk carry the bags of groceries from the garage into the house.

Enough groceries to feed an army rather than a family over Christmas—Hawk having added lots more things to the shopping trolley after joining her.

That was okay with her; it was his money, after all. Besides, once she had actually got inside the supermarket she had realised that, apart from buying the turkey and some accompanying vegetables, she knew absolutely nothing about feeding nine people over the Christmas period.

When she stopped to think about it, she couldn't remember the last time she had actually been at home for Christmas. She seemed to have spent the last five or six of them in some hotel suite somewhere in the world. And even when she and her mother had been at home, they certainly hadn't celebrated Christmas in the lavish way that Joshua Hawkley and his family were obviously going to.

What must it be like to be part of a big family like that? Rosie couldn't even begin to imagine—

Stop prevaricating, Rosie, she told herself firmly.

Stop pretending that nothing had happened!

Because it had. It most certainly had!

This wasn't about Christmas. This was about what had happened when Hawk had touched her in the supermarket. And no amount of prevarication on her part was going to make that go away!

That lowering of her guard—or the opening of her eyes to the joy of the people around her—seemed to have opened her up to all sorts of other emotions too.

Since then—since Hawk had touched her—no matter how she tried to deny it she had been totally aware of him, had trembled with awareness every time she looked at him.

She wanted to call a halt to the wild thoughts rushing through her brain, to make these new sensations go away. But, as hard as she tried, she hadn't been able to do it.

Maybe because, after this morning, she knew exactly what Hawk looked like beneath the thick sweater and denims he was wearing. How his muscles rippled across the width of this chest and arms when he moved. How silky the dark hair was on his tanned chest…

How much she longed to run her hands over the width of his shoulders and down the length of that muscular chest!

That was all she'd thought about since the moment Hawk's hands had touched hers in the supermarket!

In a supermarket, of all places!

She knew what it was, of course. She wasn't that naïve.

Sexual attraction.

Something she had never known before. Never felt before. But she knew she was feeling it now. Her whole body was trembling with her awareness of him, her senses singing with that same emotion, her breasts tight beneath her jumper, their nipples sensitised, aching.

Which was why she had to get away from Hawk for a while. Had to go somewhere she didn't have to look at him any more. Had to try to make some sense, gain some control, over these totally unexpected yearnings.

'Sure—you go and check on Donald,' Hawk agreed distractedly, as he began to open kitchen cabinets and put the food away, his muscles rippling as Rosie had known they would. 'It must be some time since the two of you last met up?'

He voiced the question casually, and yet Rosie knew it wasn't casual at all…

'A while,' she answered evasively.

Hawk turned to look at her, the intensity of his gaze easily holding hers. 'How long is a while?' he persisted.

Rosie's mouth tightened. 'Several years.'

'Years!' Hawk echoed incredulously, trying to put that knowledge together with Donald's fevered mumblings earlier. Although, when he thought about it, he knew Donald and Rosie hadn't spent Christmas together in the last ten years, because Donald had spent those Christmases with Hawk and his family! But still… 'You haven't seen your own father for *years*?'

Her gaze was challenging as she met his. 'No.'

'How many years?' he tried again.

'A few,' she bit out unhelpfully. 'Now, if you wouldn't mind, I really would like to go and see how he is…'

Hawk did mind. Very much. He was growing tired of this woman's guardedness, was becoming more and more convinced that her reasons for being here weren't innocent. 'I'll get the two of us some lunch when you come back—'

'I'm really not hungry,' Rosie cut in, not liking the turn

this conversation had taken—deliberately so on Hawk's part, she was sure.

She was desperately hoping it was only tiredness after their morning out that was filling her with the fanciful longing to see Hawk naked once again…

'I—think jet-lag is catching up with me, or something.' She looked down at the floor to hide her discomfort.

Hawk's gaze narrowed as he continued to look across the kitchen at her. She had finally taken off the black woollen hat and her long coat, but was still looking a little pale, and her eyes seemed to glitter almost feverishly as she scanned the tiled floor. 'You aren't coming down with the flu too, are you?' he asked gently, and he moved across the kitchen towards her.

'No!' she protested, looking up suddenly and stepping back. 'No, I'm sure I'm not,' she repeated bristly, the smile she attempted not quite happening. 'A couple of hours' sleep and I'm sure I'll be fine,' she added, with forced, bright dismissal, her gaze not quite meeting his now.

Hawk stood only inches away from her and continued to look down at her searchingly. There was a slight flush to her cheeks now, and her eyes were definitely feverish, but somehow he didn't think that was caused by the onset of flu…

Her breathing was shallow, her breasts barely rising up and down with the movement, and yet he could see the clear outline of her nipples against the wool of her sweater. Aroused nipples. Engorged and thrusting…!

His eyes returned to her pinkened face—a face she raised to his now in defiant challenge, her jaw set, mouth firm, her green eyes defying him to voice what they were both aware of.

Rosie Harrison was completely physically aware of him!

A dangerous realisation when he was completely physically aware of her too! In fact, he couldn't remember the last time he had been so attracted to any woman, and that feeling had stayed with him since their hands had touched in the supermarket—

It was madness on his part to want Rosie! Not only was she the daughter of his employee, but Hawk also didn't yet trust her, or her motives for this sudden reappearance in Donald's life. And he would need to know a hell of a lot more about her before he did!

Damn it, for all he knew her reason for suddenly popping up in Donald's life could be as simple as the fact she was just another woman on the make, using her father in order to get close to *him*. Other women had tried much more daring exploits to gain his attention—including the one who had climbed from her tenth floor balcony over to his adjoining hotel suite in an effort just to say she had met him.

Unfortunately, it went along with the territory of being such a public figure.

It was also the reason that he had never even considered marriage.

He wanted the sort of marriage his parents had. One of complete giving and taking by both parties. Wanted to know that the woman he loved wanted him for himself, and not because he was Joshua Hawkley, movie star.

A tall order, he knew, when that was exactly who he was. But he wasn't willing to settle for anything less.

And Rosie Harrison, with her mysterious past as well as her present, certainly wasn't that woman.

The sooner Donald rallied and was able to answer some of Hawk's questions about his daughter, the better Hawk would like it!

'I'm sure you will be too,' he rasped, before stepping back. 'If Donald needs anything, let me know, hmm?' he added abruptly.

'I'll do that,' she replied sharply, turning and walking determinedly away from this man who tormented as well as attracted her.

What was wrong with her? Rosie berated herself as she climbed the stairs to her father's flat and closed the door firmly behind her. A little Christmas cheer, and the previously unknown luxury that for the first time in her adult life she was free to do whatever she wished, plus the first single, sexy man she had been in contact with for longer than she could remember—if ever!—and she responded like some gauche schoolgirl.

Worse, Hawk had *known* she responded!

She had seen that knowledge in his eyes just now, as he'd looked down at her so searchingly.

She gave a self-disgusted shake of her head before going through to the bedroom to check on her father. He was asleep, his temperature down when she touched his forehead, so she quietly left him to rest.

Without thinking about it, it seemed, she took her violin from its case, cradling it to her like a precious child. Which to her it was. It went with her wherever she travelled.

She wondered how long it had been since she had last played the precious instrument and known that same singing pleasure as her body had known when Hawk's hand had so briefly touched hers? Since she'd had the freedom to express in her playing the same excitement just looking at Hawk, imagining touching him, having him touch her, had given her...

Too long, she suspected.

How long before she would play like that again?

If she ever did…

CHAPTER SIX

'COME on, sleepyhead, let's get you moved to somewhere a little more comfortable!'

Rosie felt herself being lifted up in strong arms. A part of her wanted to protest, but her eyelids were too heavy, and she couldn't seem to find the words either, so instead her arms moved up over strong shoulders and she snuggled more comfortably against the hardness of a male chest beneath her cheek.

Her father had always carried her up to bed like this when she was a child and had fallen asleep in front of the television—carrying her up the stairs before tucking her warmly beneath her duvet—

Her lids flew open, wild with panic as she remembered she wasn't a child any longer. That she wasn't at home, but in Canada! That she had been too tired earlier to do any more than change into a soft cotton nightshirt and plait her hair before pulling the duvet over her and falling asleep on the sofa.

And her father was in bed himself, in the adjoining bedroom, suffering with the flu, so he couldn't possibly be carrying her anywhere.

But Hawk was!

He gave a wolfish grin as he looked down into her wide,

startled eyes. 'Don't look so worried, Rosie. I'm only taking you to one of the bedrooms in the main house.'

Which bedroom? His own? Had her arousal earlier been so obvious to him that—

'It suddenly occurred to me that there's only one bedroom in Donald's apartment,' Hawk rasped as he easily read—and didn't appreciate—the panicked thoughts going through Rosie's tousled head.

Hell, what sort of man did she imagine he was, to even think that he might be about to take advantage of her half-naked sleep-befuddled body?

His mouth tightened. 'There's no way you can sleep on the sofa for the whole of your stay, Rosie,' he said firmly.

'I'm sure that my—Donald and I will be able to sort something out once he's feeling a little better...' She trailed off, a frown creasing her creamy brow as she looked up at Hawk. 'You can put me down now!' she exclaimed. 'There's absolutely nothing wrong with my legs!'

There was nothing wrong with any part of her that Hawk could see. And he could see quite a lot. The nightshirt she wore was only knee-length, and showed a long expanse of shapely bare legs. Long, silky legs that would wrap around a man as he—

He gritted his teeth, his arms tightening about her as he felt the stirring of his body. Great. He had just taken umbrage because she obviously thought he had less than innocent intentions towards her—and now his body had hardened with desire for her!

'We're here now,' he said tersely, and he kicked open a door and carried her inside.

Where was here? Rosie wondered anxiously, as she looked around the room.

It was a bedroom, certainly, and the lack of any personal items on display meant it was probably one of the guest rooms in the main house.

'I can't stay here,' she protested, even as Hawk laid her down on the duvet-covered bed.

'Why can't you?' he rasped, as he straightened to look down at her. 'The farmhouse has four guest bedrooms, so there's plenty for everyone.'

She looked extremely defenceless, lying amongst the gold-coloured cushions scattered on top of the duvet, her white nightshirt patterned with pink roses, her hair no longer flowing loosely about her shoulders but secured back in a single plait that ran the length of her spine.

She gave a shake of her head. 'Your family—'

'Would be disappointed in me if I let you continue to sleep on Donald's sofa,' Hawk assured her huskily, and he sat down on the side of the bed.

He hadn't meant to. He'd told himself to get out of there. Now. But his body had ignored the instruction!

She really was the most delicately beautiful woman he had ever seen, he acknowledged, even as his gaze roamed appreciatively over her face and body. Her features were so perfect, the green of her eyes so mesmerising, the gentle curves of her body softly alluring, her breasts pert, her waist tiny and her thighs shapely above those long, long legs.

Hawk's gaze returned to her face, and he frowned slightly as again he processed the feeling that *he had seen her somewhere before*.

'Hawk…?'

His dark gaze moved to meet hers, seeing the question in her eyes as she looked up at him uncertainly. He placed his hands either side of her head and he began to lower his head towards hers.

Damn it, what had happened to his not taking advantage of her half-naked, sleep-befuddled body? Hawk remonstrated with himself, and he paused with his mouth only centimetres away from hers.

To hell with that! He *wanted* to kiss her, to touch her. And Rosie didn't seem to be fighting him off either, if the way her arms had moved up about his shoulders was anything to go by!

Just one kiss, he promised himself. Just to know the feel of her lips against his. To know the taste of her…

Rosie's whole body turned to molten fire as Hawk's mouth finally claimed hers, her lips parting instinctively as they explored him the way he was exploring her.

The awareness she had felt earlier today was nothing to the heated pleasure she found now in his arms as their kiss deepened and Hawk's arms moved about her to pull her up hard against him.

Rosie melted into him, seeming to become a part of him as her legs entangled with his.

She groaned low in her throat as one of his hands moved the length of her, skimming the curve of her hip and waist before moving to cup the thrust of her breast, the pad of his thumb moving across its hardened tip.

Her body arched instinctively against his caressing hand, her lips opening wider to the assault of his tongue as it thrust in moist rhythm to the wild beat of her heart. The hardness of Hawk's body lay half across hers, telling her of his own arousal.

So this was what it was like—what it felt like to make love, Rosie realised wonderingly, in the small, joyful part of her brain that could still function.

It was more beautiful, more wonderful, than anything she could ever have imagined, and she knew no sense of denial as Hawk's hands began to restlessly roam the length of her spine, before cupping her bottom as he pulled her more tightly against him.

Rosie pushed her own hands beneath his sweater, touching him as she had so longed to do, her hands moving caressingly across the broad width of his back.

He felt good. So very good.

But she wanted more. Needed more. Wanted to feel—

She fell back against the pillows as Hawk wrenched his mouth from hers and held her away from him, to look down at her with eyes turned navy blue and a face pale beneath his tan.

Hawk breathed shallowly, moving determinedly away from Rosie even as he saw the hurt confusion in those dark green eyes at his sudden rejection.

He stood up to move across the room and stare out of the window. The same snowy scene that he had found so soothing earlier this morning did absolutely nothing to calm his chaotic thoughts now.

What was he doing?

He didn't even know her. Not that that was a prerequisite to making love to a woman. Normally. But Rosie wasn't just *any* woman. She was Donald's daughter. The daughter of the man who had been his friend as well as his employee for the last ten years.

Donald's daughter—whom Hawk distrusted as deeply as he desired her!

He leant his forehead against the coldness of the window-pane as he fought for the control that had so readily deserted him minutes ago.

Well, he knew what Rosie tasted like now: of heat and sensuality. Of a sweetness that had made him want to kiss her and carry on kissing her until his body was joined with hers and he found release inside her.

It was a need he was determined not to satisfy!

He dragged deep, controlling breaths into his lungs, tensing his shoulders before turning back to face her.

She no longer lay back amongst those pillows but sat on the side of the bed, her face very pale against the vivid fire of her hair, which was no longer confined in that plait but had come loose to swing protectively forward and cover the swell of her breasts.

Breasts that seconds ago had fitted so perfectly into his hands and had responded to his lightest touch…

His mouth tightened as he firmly closed a door on those memories. 'Who are you, Rosie?' he snapped harshly.

She blinked her confusion. 'You know who I am—'

'Donald's daughter.' He nodded impatiently. 'But that's not who you really are, is it?' he accused.

Rosie frowned across at him warily, even as she fought an inner battle to put her defences back in place. Defences Hawk had so easily knocked down only minutes ago as he kissed and caressed her…

But she mustn't think about that now—had to concentrate on what he was really asking her.

Hawk hadn't seemed to know anything about her at all this morning—not even that she was Donald's daughter. But had that changed in the last few minutes? Despite his earlier ignorance about her identity, had Hawk now recognised her as the world-famous virtuoso violinist Rosemary Harris? As 'La Bella Rosa', as the enthusiastic Italians had long ago dubbed her?

CHAPTER SEVEN

HAWK'S gaze narrowed speculatively as he easily saw the pallor deepen in Rosie's face, those deep green eyes once again taking on a haunted look.

So he was right after all, he acknowledged heavily. Rosie *was* hiding something. And with Donald too ill as yet to enlighten him—if indeed he even knew what secret his daughter was hiding—it would have to be Rosie herself who satisfied his curiosity.

From the guarded look on her face it was something he didn't think she was going to be too willing to do!

He thrust his hands into his denims pockets. 'You're— what? Twenty-two? Twenty-three?' he prompted harshly.

'Twenty-two,' she confirmed shakily.

He nodded. 'Then who have you been for the last twenty-two years, Rosie—because you sure as hell haven't been Donald's daughter!'

'Don't be ridiculous!' she came back with a derisive laugh. 'If I'm Donald's daughter now, then I must have been his daughter for the last twenty-two years too!'

The laugh had been a mistake, Rosie realised as she saw Hawk's gaze darken dangerously. But what else could she do?

She didn't want Hawk to know who she was—that in the world of classical music—a world he obviously wasn't in touch with—she was as well-known and successful as he was. She didn't want anyone in Canada to realise she was Rosemary Harris. She wanted—needed—to maintain her anonymity for a little longer.

Perhaps it would be better if she left here now?

She hadn't seen her father since he'd walked out on her and her mother when Rosie was twelve years old—had only come to him now because she had known it was the very last place her mother and Edmund—the man Rosie didn't want to marry on Christmas Eve or at any other time!—would think to look for her.

But Hawk was proving to be a complication she hadn't bargained for. And not just because of his persistence in trying to find out more about her...

He disturbed her. Excited her. Aroused her. Gave her an insight into emotions she hadn't even guessed at.

Which might be a positive thing with regard to her interpretation of the music she played, but was of absolutely no help at all to the peace of mind she was so desperately seeking.

The peace of mind she needed if she was to discover if she ever wanted to play again...

Which meant she had to concentrate on finding that peace for herself. And she couldn't find it around Hawk!

She shook her head. 'It's obvious you would rather I didn't stay on here, Hawk, so—'

'It's "obvious", is it?' he repeated scathingly. 'After the way we just were together?'

Well...no. But he certainly wasn't too pleased about his own response to her a few minutes ago, was he?

She shrugged narrow shoulders. 'I think that's something better not repeated, don't you?' she said carefully.

Hawk gave a humourless laugh. This woman really was something else. But what? That was the real question…

'Am I to take it from that comment that you're not sure, if you *do* stay on here, that you'll be able to keep your hands off my body?' he derided mockingly.

Her cheeks coloured at the taunt, her eyes sparkling angrily as she raised her chin challengingly. 'You really aren't that irresistible, Mr Hawkley,' she bit out coldly.

This time his laugh was genuine. 'Touché, Rosie,' he murmured appreciatively. 'But as for your leaving…' He sobered, shaking his head. 'I somehow don't think Donald would appreciate my driving his daughter away before the two of you have even had a chance to spend any time together.'

'This is your home, not my father's,' she replied evenly.

Yes, it was—and his stay here wasn't turning out to be the relaxing time he had expected it to be. But all the same he knew that Rosie's leaving wouldn't stop his curiosity to know more about her. Or the way he still wanted her!

'Then I'll ask you to stay on, Rosie,' he said tersely. 'I also suggest that we call a truce until Donald is feeling better.'

She raised auburn brows. 'I didn't realise we were at war…'

Not at war, Hawk conceded, but they were certainly a challenge to each other.

'Okay, Hawk. I'll stay on at least until I've had a chance to talk to my father,' Rosie decided. 'Talking of which…' She stood up, no longer looking at Hawk as she felt slightly self-conscious dressed only in her nightshirt. 'I really should go and check on him.'

'Do that,' Hawk agreed. 'Then perhaps you would like to come down and join me for a late lunch?'

Rosie gave an uncertain frown. 'I can easily get myself something in my father's kitchen…'

'Why bother when I'm cooking? Besides, I owe you something for waking you up so suddenly.'

Rosie searched his ruggedly handsome face for signs of mockery of the way in which he had woken her. But she could read nothing from his bland expression. Considering what a talented actor he was, maybe that wasn't so surprising!

Was having lunch with this man a good idea? Was *not* having lunch with him a good idea? Hawk seemed to have developed a relentless curiosity about her sudden appearance in her father's life, and he obviously felt protective towards the older man. As if he suspected that for some reason she had come here to hurt Donald.

Years ago she might have thought she would like to hurt her father, in the way he had hurt her when he had deserted her and her mother so completely ten years ago. But maturity had brought with it the knowledge of just how impossible her mother was—how ruthless she could be when she set her mind on a course of action. Who could blame her father for wanting to escape from *that*?

Hadn't she just done exactly the same thing…?

No, she hadn't come here to hurt Donald. If anything she just wanted to talk to him—to find out why, when he'd left her mother, he'd had to abandon her so completely too. But that was all she wanted. It was too late—far too late—for anything else between them.

'Come on, Rosie.' Hawk cut cajolingly into her thoughts.

'Surely it doesn't take this long to decide whether or not you want to have lunch with me?'

Or maybe it did after what had just happened between them...

Not the most sensible thing he had ever done, he thought self-derisively. But being sensible had been the last thing on his mind once he had held Rosie in his arms and touched her!

'Okay.' Rosie accepted the invitation slowly, suddenly aware that she was hungry.

Something she hadn't felt for some time—weeks, possibly months—as the wedding had loomed ever closer. Always slender, she knew she had lost several pounds in weight in the last month or so. Even the idea of eating had made her feel nauseous.

But she felt really hungry now. Her mouth was watering, and her stomach was cramping slightly as she remembered she hadn't eaten anything at all since consuming a sandwich last night after she'd arrived.

Perhaps the arousing of her sensual appetite had awakened her appetite for food too...

What a disturbing thought!

'If you could wait fifteen minutes or so?' she said briskly. 'After I've checked on my father, I would like to take a shower,' she explained, at Hawk's questioning look.

'Fine.' He nodded. 'Perhaps you would like to move your things in here while you're at it?'

Rosie looked around the room, appreciating that it would be much more comfortable than sleeping on the sofa in her father's flat. But she was also aware that if she moved in here it would bring her out of her father's domain and into Hawk's—almost as if she really were an invited guest. Not a good idea, in the circumstances.

Once her father was feeling better, and the two of them had talked, she had every intention of leaving. To go where, she still had no idea. But Hawk was far too curious about her for her to stay.

'I think I'll continue to stay in my father's flat, thank you,' she told him firmly. 'I would like to remain close while he's feeling ill,' she added challengingly, sure from Hawk's expression that he wasn't convinced by her concern for Donald.

And he was wrong to feel that way; she might not have seen her father for ten years, but as soon as she had met him again at the airport yesterday she had known an upsurge of the adoration she had felt for him as a child. It was an emotion she had quickly controlled, but nonetheless she had felt it. She certainly didn't intend hurting her father in any way. She had a feeling, from what she had come to know of her mother, that he had been hurt enough in the past.

Hawk's mouth twisted derisively. 'Your concern is touching,' he drawled. 'If a little late in coming!'

Rosie's cheeks flamed with the anger she obviously felt at his rebuke. 'Considering you know absolutely nothing of my relationship with my father, perhaps you aren't in a position to judge!' she snapped coldly.

From what he had already learnt, Hawk very much doubted there had been any relationship between Donald and his daughter for years!

But she was right. He wasn't in a position to judge. Yet. He gave an abrupt inclination of his head. 'I apologise.'

His apology obviously surprised her. Her eyes widened slightly as she eyed him suspiciously.

But Hawk was aware that he might just be wrong in his suspicions about this woman. Might be. Maybe...

'We can decorate the two trees Donald has placed in the sitting room and family room later this afternoon, if you would like?' he offered lightly.

Rosie still eyed him warily. 'Fine,' she agreed, her gaze guarded as she walked to the door.

What was it about this woman that made his pulse race and his body tighten with desire? Hawk wondered, even as he felt the renewed stirring of his body. At this rate *he* would need to take a shower before lunch himself. A cold one!

Rosie was a beautiful woman, yes. But no more so than many of the women he had known intimately over the years. Her body was willowy. But again, not startlingly so. In fact, she could do with putting on a few pounds.

So why, in spite of his uncertainty about her motives for being here at all, did he feel so attracted to her?

'Oh, and, Hawk…' She paused at the door to turn and look at him from beneath lowered lashes.

His gaze narrowed warily. 'Yes?'

A slight smile curved those sensuously full lips. 'I'm afraid I lied to you earlier,' she murmured throatily.

Hawk's wariness increased, his shoulders tensing. 'Oh, yes?' he prompted hardly.

'Yes.' She nodded, that smile widening as her eyes openly mocked him now. 'I *can* cook!' she taunted, before turning lightly on her heel and leaving him alone in the bedroom.

The little—!

That was why he was attracted to her, Hawk realised frustratedly. Unlike most other women he knew, Rosie, while obviously aware of his suspicions, had absolutely no interest in what he did or didn't think about her. In fact, she behaved as if his opinion of her was of no importance to her whatsoever.

Which, although she might not be aware of it, only succeeded in deepening his interest.

Perhaps, with Donald as ill as he was, it was up to Hawk to find out more about this previously unknown daughter of his?

Donald's mutterings about Rosie's mother earlier certainly didn't inspire any confidence in Rosie's innocence.

Yes, perhaps he should employ some other way of seeing if he couldn't find out more about her…

CHAPTER EIGHT

ROSIE continued to smile as she walked down the hallway to the door that led to her father's flat. It had been fun teasing Hawk just now, taking his suspicions about her motives for being here and turning them back on him.

Perhaps she was finally getting her sense of humour back?

About time too!

Returning Hawk's kisses, his caresses, hadn't been such a good idea, though...

Her smile faded as she thought of her response to him, of just how much she had enjoyed being kissed and touched by him. Something that had never happened to her before.

He was Joshua Hawkley, top Hollywood movie star. Of *course* she had melted when he kissed her. What woman wouldn't?

Keep telling yourself that, Rosie, she told herself, as she went into her father's flat. Maybe with time she might even come to believe that was the only reason she had responded to him so absolutely.

Maybe...

'Oh, good, you're awake.' She smiled at her father as she

entered the bedroom. He was sitting up slightly, so that he could drink some of the juice and take the medication she had left for him earlier on the bedside table. 'Are you feeling any better?'

'A little.' Donald gave a wan smile as he dropped back onto the pillows, the effort of sitting up at all obviously having weakened him. 'I still can't believe you're actually here, Rosie,' he croaked.

He reached out to grasp hold of her hand as she stood beside the bed, letting her know that his skin was hot and clammy. If Rosie had needed anything else to tell her how ill he still was, she could see how his hair was sticking damply to his brow, his face was flushed and his hazel-coloured eyes feverish.

'Promise me you won't just disappear again until after I'm better and we've had a chance to talk!' he pressed hoarsely.

Her own cheeks flushed guiltily as she acknowledged that, minutes ago, disappearing was exactly what she had been thinking of doing. If she could have thought of somewhere else she might go, that was!

'I won't just disappear,' she assured him huskily, squeezing his hand slightly before awkwardly letting go. Even this brief physical contact with the father she hadn't seen for years was opening up old wounds, filling her with questions she knew Donald wasn't well enough to answer yet. 'Hawk and I are going to decorate the Christmas trees,' she told him lightly.

He smiled at this mention of his employer. 'What do you think of him?'

She was trying *not* to think of Hawk!

She avoided her father's gaze. 'He seems—pleasant enough,' she replied awkwardly.

'Pleasant?' Donald echoed incredulously. 'That's the first time I've heard a woman call him *that*!'

Rosie felt the blush deepen on her cheeks. 'He's Joshua Hawkley, Father; what else is there to say!'

Donald frowned, a pained look on his face. 'How long have you thought of me as "Father" instead of "Dad"?' he queried gruffly.

Too long. But it had become easier, less painful, to think of him in that way than to remember the man who had spoilt and loved her for the first twelve years of her life. The man she in return had adored.

At least he had stopped talking about Hawk…

'We're strangers now—'

'No!' Donald protested. 'Never that. Not you and I, Rosie. We have a lot of catching up to do—things we need to talk about—but I've never stopped loving you. Never stopped loving my little girl. You have to believe that!' He looked up at her pleadingly.

She had never stopped loving him either. But it had been *ten* years!

'All of this can wait until you're feeling better,' she soothed, as she saw how pale he had become from the strain of talking at all.

'Yes,' he breathed raggedly. 'We have time now, don't we…?' he murmured, before drifting off into sleep once again as the medication obviously kicked in.

Rosie stared down at him for several more minutes. Apart from his prematurely white hair, he still looked the same to her as he had ten years ago. Was he still the man in whom she'd had total faith then? Whom she'd believed would never let any harm come to her?

Why had he abandoned her? Why hadn't he taken her with him when he'd left her mother? Why hadn't he tried to at least *see* her in the intervening years?

No matter how much she might know she had to get away from Hawk, Rosie knew she couldn't leave here until after she had the answers to those questions…

'We aren't going to get the trees decorated by standing around looking at them,' Hawk commented dryly, as Rosie stood staring up at the huge pine tree that dominated the sitting room.

He had taken the opportunity of her delay to come down and light the fire in the open hearth that served both the sitting room and the family room, and its warmth and flames added to the Christmas atmosphere.

Even the snow was falling again outside, to add to the festive spirit!

But Rosie seemed mesmerised by the tree.

It was a beauty, Hawk had to admit—smelling strongly of pine, at least twelve feet high, its branches lush and green.

'Rosie…?' he prompted softly.

She blinked, turning to stare at him as if she had forgotten he was even there. Once again he noticed she was wearing black—yet another black sweater, with black denims.

What was it with this woman and black?

Admittedly it brought out the vivid red of her hair, which was at the moment tied back in a ponytail. But it also made her face way too pale.

'Sorry.' She gave a rousing shake of her head. 'Where do we start? Do we put the lights on first, or the decorations?'

'The lights, of course,' Hawk answered, slightly puzzled. 'Haven't you ever dressed a Christmas tree before?'

Not that she could remember, no…

Probably she had helped her parents to decorate a tree when they were all still together, but Rosie certainly couldn't remember having done so since then.

Her mother considered real Christmas trees messy, smelly things, and preferred to buy an artificial one, already decorated, that could be stored in the attic after Christmas and brought down again each year.

With the fire burning so merrily, and the snow falling softly outside the windows, this setting was just too enchanting for Rosie not to be affected by it.

'Not one like this.' She avoided a direct answer. 'Lights first, then,' she added briskly, to avoid any further discussion on the subject.

'Lights first,' Hawk confirmed slowly, his gaze still narrowed on her speculatively. 'Why do I get the idea that you somehow haven't been living in the real world these last few years, Rosie…?'

Probably because she hadn't!

Her life had seemed so bleak and empty after her fun-loving father had left. She had retreated into herself, withdrawing from her friends to become something of a loner.

But all that had changed the day her music teacher, trying to encourage her to take an interest in music, had persuaded Rosie to pick up a violin.

From the moment Rosie had touched the instrument it had felt right, as if it were a part of her; just touching the polished wood, holding the bow, filled the empty void inside her.

More amazing was the fact that although she had started fairly late in life, after a couple of false starts she had actually known how to play it!

Instinctively.

Intuitively.

She hadn't even been able to read music at the time, and yet as she'd held that violin in her hands she had *known* how to play it.

So she had played it and played it. And that had released her from the prison of loneliness in which she had locked herself away.

And maybe if her music teacher, overwhelmed by the discovery of her amazing ability, hadn't called her mother in and told her of Rosie's natural talent—if her mother hadn't realised just how lucrative having a musical protégée for a daughter could be—Rosie's bewilderment and pain after her father had left might have been healed, allowing her to be a teenager.

Instead normal life had ended for ever the day her mother had discovered her gift for playing the violin...

'Don't be ridiculous, Hawk,' she snapped back at him. 'My mother employs staff to deal with the household tasks, that's all,' she elaborated, inwardly wincing at how snobbish she knew she must sound.

The knowledge was reflected in the flash of anger in Hawk's eyes before he masked the emotion.

He had met this woman—what...seven, eight hours ago?—and during that time she had aroused surprise, curiosity, amusement, anger and desire in him. More emotions than he had felt for any woman he had known ten times that long!

Right now he felt angry. He wanted to bring her out from behind that shield of coldness she was hiding herself with.

That it was a shield, Hawk didn't doubt. He had seen the real warmth of this woman when he'd held her in his arms such a short time ago.

She had wanted him then. As he had wanted her.

As he *still* wanted her, damn it!

'Is that how you think of your father?' he prompted softly. 'As a mere member of staff whose function is to carry out household tasks for me?'

'Of course not!' Rosie gasped, her cheeks blazing with heated colour. 'When I made that reference to staff I wasn't talking about my father—'

'Weren't you?' Hawk scorned. 'I think that you were—'

'I don't give a damn what you think, Hawk—'

'No, I know you don't!' he rasped.

'And that bothers you?' Rosie looked at him, her whole body tense with challenge now. 'Does it irk you that I don't bow and scrape before the mighty film star Joshua Hawkley?'

Add absolute fury to that list of emotions, Hawk thought, even as he clenched his hands into fists to stop himself from expressing his anger as he had so longed to do minutes earlier.

Mainly because he wasn't sure, if he touched her, that he would be able to stop there; the desire they had shared earlier was lurking only just below the surface of this conversation.

As it had been since they'd first met this morning...!

'I don't expect *anyone* to bow and scrape before me,' he grated out between clenched teeth.

'No?' Her chin was raised and she looked at him with challenging green eyes. 'But it seems to me that's exactly what everyone does!'

She was deliberately trying to annoy him, Hawk suddenly realised with calming clarity.

Why? Because he was getting too close? Because he was daring to ask her questions she would prefer not to answer?

He had called a friend of his in England earlier and asked

him to see what he could find out about one Rosie Harrison. But he didn't expect to receive a call back for some time, so perhaps it would be better if he just backed off for a while.

He forced himself to relax, his smile derisive. 'You're entitled to your opinion,' he dismissed with a shrug, before turning to take the lights from the box. 'Do you want to hold the bottom of the step-ladder while I take these to the top of the tree?'

She wanted to knock him off the damned thing altogether, Rosie realised bad-temperedly, even as she moved to steady the ladder while he climbed up it.

He was rude.

He was persistently inquisitive.

He was also wildly, ruggedly, good-looking. So powerfully sensual, so exquisitely male, that he made her legs go weak at the knees!

She didn't want to feel this way. Didn't want to want this man.

But she did. Even now she wanted to reach out and touch him, to feel the warm strength of him beneath her hand, longed to feel his hands on her again.

Why *this* man? Why—?

'Damn!' Hawk swore as his mobile began to ring. Resting the lights on one of the branches, he reached to take it out of his back pocket. 'Yes?' he barked irritably into the mouthpiece.

Rosie watched his face as he took the call, his initial irritation quickly followed by frustration. 'No, I don't have any comment to make,' he snapped. 'Jeff, just find out which newspaper has it and see if you can stop it. Then get back to me. Yes, now,' he bit out tersely, before abruptly ending the call.

Rosie eyed him warily as he looked down at her with piercing eyes. 'What?' she voiced uncertainly. 'What's wrong?' Because she knew from his face that something was.

Hawk sat down on top of the ladder, running a hand through the long dark thickness of his hair before replying. 'How do you feel about having your photograph in the newspaper?' He sighed.

'What…?' she gasped weakly, hands gripping the stepladder so tightly now that her knuckles showed white.

'That was my agent on the telephone,' Hawk bit out grimly. 'He's been contacted by a reporter to see if I have any comment to make about the woman I'm spending Christmas with!'

She gave a dazed shake of her head. 'But how——? You said something about a photograph——?'

'Apparently some resourceful soul took a photograph of us with their cell-phone when we were out shopping this morning,' he explained hardly. 'A reporter now has it, and is intending to have it published in one of tomorrow's newspapers.'

No, Rosie inwardly protested.

This could not be happening!

CHAPTER NINE

'HEY, it may not be that bad!' Hawk encouraged, as Rosie staggered back to drop down into one of the armchairs, her face pale. 'Jeff will get back to me and let me know how damaging the photograph is,' he added, as he climbed back down the ladder.

Damaging!

That there was a photograph of her in Canada at all, with or without Joshua Hawkley at her side, was more damaging to Rosie than he could ever imagine!

'Rosie...?' Hawk came down on his haunches at her side. 'It isn't the end of the world—'

'Maybe to you it isn't!' she came back heatedly, her eyes stormy in the pallor of her face.

She shook her head. Hawk didn't understand—couldn't understand—that any photograph of her that appeared in the newspapers now was sure to bring repercussions. She was supposed to be in England, taking time off to prepare for her wedding. Not in Canada, with the charismatically sexy actor Joshua Hawkley!

Hawk looked at her searchingly, obviously confused. 'Aren't you overreacting a little?' he attempted to cajole.

'The speculation about the two of us will be a nine-day-wonder, and then—'

'Nine days?' she repeated, stricken.

In four days' time, as far as the general public was still concerned, Rosemary Harris was due to marry world-famous conductor Edmund Price!

Edmund knew she wasn't going to marry him, of course. She had told him so three days ago, when she'd given him back his ring. The point was, her mother would know it too now. But there had been no announcement of the wedding's cancellation made in the newspapers yet, and any photograph of her with another man—let alone the wildly handsome Joshua Hawkley!—was sure to be more than a nine-day-wonder!

She shook her head. 'You don't understand...!' She buried her face in her hands like a child, as if not being able to see Hawk would make all of this go away.

Once she'd realised her father's employer was the famous actor Joshua Hawkley she should never have stayed here. She should have just gone to some discreet hotel on the other side of the world and made herself 'disappear', until the supposed wedding day was over and the speculation that was sure to follow had died down.

Instead of which she had now been photographed shopping for food in a Canadian mall with Joshua Hawkley!

'Look, Rosie,' Hawk reasoned softly. 'I would be very surprised if your own mother would recognise you, covered up in the way you were!'

How unintentionally ironic—when it was her mother she didn't *want* to recognise her!

Gloria would be over here on the next plane if she knew which province Rosie was in. Of course her mother couldn't work out exactly where she was staying in Calgary. But Rosie, of all people, knew how tenacious Gloria could be when she got an idea in her head…

For example, the idea of Rosie's marriage to maestro conductor Edmund Price…

Rosie should never have allowed things to get as out of control as they had, of course. But her mother was like an express train when she decided on a course of action—she had absolutely no hesitation in knocking down anything that got in her way, including Rosie's own reluctance about the marriage!

As far as Hawk was concerned, he felt Rosie was overreacting to this. Okay, so it wasn't very pleasant, having an innocent excursion like this morning's shopping expedition taken out of context and blown up into something it wasn't. But it really wasn't the end of the world.

At least, it shouldn't have been.

Except to someone he suspected was hiding something…

'Rosie, why don't you tell me what's wrong?' he encouraged huskily. 'A problem shared is a problem halved, and all that…'

She gave a humourless laugh. 'You have no idea!'

'Then tell me, damn it.' His voice hardened in his frustration with the situation.

She looked at him for several searching seconds before shaking her head. 'There's nothing to tell,' she bit out tightly.

Hawk's frustration deepened as he realised that Rosie had obviously looked at him and decided he couldn't help her. 'We both know that isn't true,' he returned scathingly. 'It's been obvious from the first that you're running away, or hiding from something. If you tell me what that something is, maybe I can help…?'

Rosie swallowed hard as once again she looked at him searchingly.

Could she tell Hawk the truth? Could she tell him—explain how her life had been during the last ten years? How her mother's single-minded pursuit of fame and fortune for her daughter, and ultimately for herself, had made Rosie's life so restricted and lonely? Could she tell him of the wedding she had fled from so urgently because she had known she simply could not, *would* not, marry a man she neither loved nor wanted to be with, but who her mother saw as yet another step up on the ladder of Rosie's already meteoric musical career?

Could she tell Hawk any of that and have him understand…?

How could he, when she knew from her conversation with him earlier at the mall that he accepted the public adulation his career attracted, the invasion of privacy that accompanied being in the public eye. He would never be able to understand why she didn't.

As for her broken engagement to Edmund Price, a man years older than her, goodness knew what Hawk would make of *that* after the way she had responded to him earlier!

She gave another shake of her head. 'There's nothing to tell,' she repeated firmly.

'Damn it, Rosie—' Hawk broke off his angry outburst as his cellphone rang for a second time. Frowning his irritation, he stood up to take the call. 'Yes?' he barked, turning away from her.

Rosie didn't doubt that the call was from his agent. With more news on the photograph, no doubt.

How had that happened?

Why had it happened?

Wasn't it enough that Hawk was over-curious about her presence here, without someone actually taking a photograph of the two of them together?

She still couldn't believe that someone had done that and then sold it to a reporter, who in turn had no doubt sold it to the newspaper who would pay the most.

She stood up and moved over to stand in front of one of the windows, staring out at the snow-covered landscape. It was so beautiful here. So quiet. Like stepping out of time—stepping off the world for a while.

Except that reality—first in the form of Hawk, and now with the existence of this photograph—kept intruding!

'Rosie…?'

She turned back to Hawk, her expression deliberately bland as she looked at him enquiringly.

'It's already too late to stop the photograph being published in tomorrow's newspaper,' Hawk explained with a grimace. He easily guessed that her calmness now was only a pose, that the dismay she had exhibited earlier wasn't far beneath her surface coolness. 'Jeff is e-mailing a copy of it over for us to look at, so that at least we'll know what's coming,' he finished heavily.

She didn't look reassured, he acknowledged ruefully; her face was starkly white against her black clothing and the fiery colour of her hair.

'Let's hope that at least they haven't caught me pushing the shopping trolley,' Hawk joked, in an attempt to lighten the situation. 'That would do nothing for my swashbuckling image!'

Rosie's mouth tightened. 'I'm glad you find all of this so funny!' she cried.

He didn't. Not the fact that the photograph existed, nor Rosie's reaction to it.

But it wouldn't be the first time he had been photographed

when he would rather he hadn't been. And he doubted it would be the last either.

He sighed, pushing his hands into the back pockets of his denims. 'Maybe if you explained—'

'I don't owe you any explanations, Hawk,' she countered emotionally. 'A few kisses—totally unwise on my part—do not entitle you to my life story!'

Hawk's hands again tightened into fists in his pockets, even as he breathed deeply in an effort to control his temper. Because he was sure she was doing this deliberately—that she wanted to antagonise him by deliberately belittling their time together earlier. And he wasn't about to give her that satisfaction.

Rosie wasn't going to succeed in pushing him away that way!

And she *was* deliberately pushing him away.

Why? Because he had got too close?

Well, she had got too close to *him*—had somehow succeeded in getting in under the radar that had always alerted him before to the dangers of getting involved.

And he *wanted* her life story!

He wanted to know what she had been like as a little girl. Whether she had found her teenage years as awkward as he had. Wanted to know what her hobbies were. What food she liked. What she liked to do. What work she did. Whether there was anyone special in her life...

Most of all he wanted to know the latter!

Rosie Harrison had seriously got under his skin, Hawk acknowledged, slightly dazed. He had known her only a matter of hours, but already he wanted to know everything there was to know about her.

Contrarily, Rosie didn't want to share any part of herself with him.

'The e-mail, Hawk?' Rosie reminded him tightly, having no idea what he was thinking right now, but pretty sure her efforts to annoy him and so put him at a distance had succeeded.

'Yeah.' He sighed resignedly. 'My lap-top is in the study.' He gave a half-smile before turning and striding from the room.

Rosie resisted the impulse to follow him, knowing she had already betrayed her anxiety enough without that.

If the photograph was as damning as she thought it would be then she knew she would have to leave here before its publication tomorrow—with or without that conversation with her father.

She would have to leave Hawk too.

Something, she realised with sudden consternation, that she was already loath to do…

CHAPTER TEN

'It's a good photograph of you, isn't it?' Rosie spoke brightly as she tried to hold back her relieved laughter now that Hawk had downloaded a copy of the photo.

Her own face was shown only in profile, totally unrecognisable beneath the black woollen hat pulled low over her ears—as it had been meant to be!—whereas Hawk's worst fear had been realised: he was indeed depicted pushing the shopping trolley!

He looked at the photograph on the computer screen disgustedly. 'The PR team for Prince Movies are going to love this!'

Rosie wasn't so out of touch that she didn't know of the famous movie company owned and run by the three Prince brothers. The same movie company that was due to start filming the sequel to *The Pirate King*, starring Joshua Hawkley, in the New Year...

'As you said—not exactly the swashbuckling image required, is it?' She smiled.

Hawk closed down the computer file, then turned to look at her. 'You're enjoying this, aren't you!'

Considering that only minutes ago she had been worrying about the repercussions that might follow the publication of this photograph—an anxiety she now knew had been totally unnecessary—yes, she *was* enjoying Hawk's obvious discomfort!

Her eyes glowed with laughter. 'The only thing that could have been less macho would have been if the shopping trolley had been a baby buggy!' She grinned, soon dissolving into full laughter as Hawk gave her a reproving look beneath raised brows.

She was lovely when she laughed, Hawk acknowledged. Twin dimples appeared in her creamy cheeks, her teeth were very white and even between sensuous lips, and her eyes gleamed like emeralds.

'So you think it's funny, do you?' he murmured throatily as he slowly began to advance on her.

Rosie continued to smile even as she took a step backwards. 'That all of those female fans are going to have their fantasies about you dashed when they see you doing something as mundane as food-shopping? Yes, of *course* I think it's funny!' she confirmed with another chuckle.

In truth, Hawk wasn't in the least bothered by the photo. He was more interested in the amusement it was affording Rosie, and how that amusement had banished her earlier strain and replaced it with happy laughter.

He still had no answers as to why the photograph should have bothered her so much in the first place, but at that moment he didn't particularly care either. His gaze was intent upon the pouting sensuality of that smiling mouth.

Rosie saw the danger just a little too late. Her eyes widened, her hands moving up in protest as Hawk's arms moved about her and he pulled her in tightly against his body, his lips descending to claim hers.

Too late to protest, she realised, even as her lips parted

beneath his, her hands moved up his chest and over his shoulders, and her fingers become entangled in the dark thickness of his hair as she pulled him close to her.

Hawk needed no further encouragement. His lips were plundering now, taking her response and giving one back, his tongue slowly circling her lips before claiming the moistness within.

Rosie's pleasure rose swiftly, wildly. The hours since they had last been together like this seemed never to have passed—their kisses were fierce, demanding, and they couldn't seem to get enough of each other.

Her arms clung about his shoulders as she felt herself lifted up and then placed on the long sofa. Hawk briefly raised his head to hold her gaze with his as he moved to lie down beside her, then his mouth claimed hers once more.

He felt so good, tasted so good, she discovered as she ran her tongue fleetingly against his lips. She was almost afraid of her own response, but not wanting him to stop. Never wanting him to stop!

His hands caressed her restlessly from breast to thigh, igniting, setting fire wherever they touched, so that the whole of her body, it seemed, burned and quivered at his slightest touch.

Her neck arched as his lips moved from hers to the creamy column of her throat, to taste and gently bite, sending shivers of pleasure down her spine, creating a throbbing warmth between her thighs.

'And what are *your* fantasies, Rosie…?' he encouraged.

'Touch me, Hawk!' she groaned huskily. 'I want you to touch me!' Her plea turned to an aching sigh of pleasure as his hands pushed her jumper aside and he bared her breasts to his questing hands and lips.

Rosie stopped breathing altogether as she felt the moisture of his tongue encircling the throb of her nipple, slowly licking that hardened nub before drawing it into the moist heat of his mouth, suckling first gently, and then more deeply, as she arched instinctively against him.

The warmth between her thighs turned to heat, hot and molten, and she moved against him in rhythm, spiralling out of control, taking her with it, until she thought she would totally disintegrate with the force of the pleasure Hawk was giving to her.

She pushed his own jumper aside, skin against skin now, and the friction of the dark hair on his chest was arousing against her bared breasts. Hawk groaned low in his throat as her hands travelled down the length of his spine to cup him to her, to feel the hard throb of his own need against her.

He raised his head to once more capture her mouth with his, his kiss hard and demanding even as he moved a hand between them and dispensed with the fastenings and zips on both pairs of denims. He pushed the material impatiently aside, his hardness against her as his hand once again captured her breast, to caress its fiery tip with the soft pad of his thumb.

Rosie's hand moved to touch him. Steel encased in velvet, throbbing, pulsing. So good to touch. So powerful, and yet so velvety smooth.

She wanted him inside her. To fill her. Wanted him to assuage the need inside her as she wanted to assuage the need she could feel pulsing inside him. They—

Hawk suddenly wrenched his mouth from hers. 'We have to stop, Rosie!' he groaned regretfully, moving to rest his forehead against hers as he breathed raggedly in an effort to regain control. 'We can't make love here,' he went on softly, his expression regretful, his eyes dark as he pulled her jumper down to cover the temptation of her breasts, still full and roused from the caress of his hands and mouth.

He hadn't wanted to stop. Never wanted to stop kissing and touching this woman. He wanted nothing more than to bury himself in her softness, to move against and inside her, taking them both over the edge of that pleasure as they found release.

But a part of him had remained aware, even if Rosie wasn't, that they weren't completely alone in the house—that Donald, as unwell as he was, could quite easily walk in on them at any time. And he doubted Rosie wanted that to happen any more than he did.

'Rosie—'

'Don't!' she choked, no longer looking at him, her face once again pale. 'Please let me up,' she pleaded tautly as she pushed ineffectually against his chest.

Hawk reached out to grasp the tops of her arms. 'Rosie, you have to listen to me—'

'Why do I?' she demanded, all her earlier laughter having gone now as she glared up at him. 'Isn't it enough that you've obviously made yet another conquest without having a post-mortem about it?'

Hawk was shocked. 'Is that what you imagine this is?'

'Well, isn't it?' she challenged. Not waiting for him to move, she scrambled to the bottom of the sofa and stood up to turn away from him as she refastened her denims and straightened her jumper. 'Obviously that photograph dented your ego a little more than I had appreciated!' she turned to add scathingly.

Hawk stared up at her incredulously. One minute so hot and aroused in his arms, and now she had all the softness of a spitting tigress!

He shook her head. 'It wasn't like that—'

'Wasn't it?' Rosie scorned, absolutely devastated by her uninhibited response to him seconds ago—a response that still made her body ache! 'Let's face it, Hawk, I'm the only available female around for miles for you to seduce!' she exclaimed, sure she was hurting herself more with her scorn than she was hurting him.

Hawk sat up, his gaze dark on hers. 'And are you?' he said softly. 'Available?' he added pointedly at her surprised look.

She blushed slightly. 'Of course I'm available! What sort of woman do you think I am?' she cried.

'I wish I knew...'

'What's that supposed to mean?' Rosie demanded.

Hawk looked at her levelly. 'You've told me so little about yourself. How can I be expected to know what sort of woman you are...?'

She had walked right into that one, Rosie realised belatedly. Well, if he thought he was going to get anything out of her that way, he was mistaken!

'The point is, Hawk,' she emphasised, biting her lips, 'you don't *need* to know what sort of woman I am! I'm here to visit Donald, not you. In fact,' she continued hardly, 'I think it might be better if I keep to my father's flat for the rest of my stay here!'

Which was going to be extremely confining. But, as she intended leaving as soon as she and Donald had had their talk, it hopefully wouldn't be for too long.

'You mean because we don't seem to be able to be in the same room together without taking each other's clothes off?' Hawk taunted, and he stood up to pointedly fasten his own jeans.

Rosie gave him a frustrated glare before turning abruptly on her heel and marching determinedly from the room.

And she didn't stop walking until she had reached the sanctuary of her father's flat, closing the door behind her as she desperately tried not to think about Hawk, or the things he had said.

But Hawk was right. She knew he was right. They *didn't* seem to be able to be together without wanting to take each other's clothes off!

In fact, she accepted shakily, Hawk, and the undeniable attraction she felt towards him, had become much more of a danger to the peace of mind she was seeking than anything or anyone else had ever been…!

CHAPTER ELEVEN

'YES?' Rosie stood squarely in the bedroom doorway of her father's flat the following morning after opening the door to Hawk's knock—looking bright and alert, Hawk noted impatiently, after probably sleeping for almost sixteen hours.

The same number of hours *he* had spent trying to make some sense of his feelings towards her—and coming to absolutely no conclusion. The hot desire he felt for her was at complete odds with his usual caution towards romantic involvement.

He willed himself not to react to her challenge now, knowing that was exactly what he had done last night. As he had been *meant* to do, he had realised, once she had walked away from him.

But Hawk wasn't feeling in a good humour himself this morning. For good reason! 'I came to check on how Donald is this morning,' he replied tersely.

Rosie seemed to relax the tension in her shoulders slightly. 'A little better, thank you,' she answered with cool politeness. 'In fact, he's taking a shower right now.'

Hawk had so many questions he wanted to ask this woman. Questions that had only increased after he'd read the newspaper this morning…!

'I guess he's out of the shower now,' Hawk observed, as he heard the sound of music playing in the bedroom—one of the classical CDs Donald often liked to play in the car when he drove Hawk. Although *that* was no longer the reason Hawk recognised it!

'I guess he is,' Rosie acknowledged, appearing distracted. 'Look, I'll tell him you enquired after him—'

'Oh, no, you don't!' Hawk managed to put his foot inside the door just as Rosie was about to shut it in his face. 'I would rather come in and speak to Donald myself, if you don't mind,' he asserted, as he pushed the door back open.

'And if I *do* mind?' Rosie faced him challengingly, eyes sparkling, deeply green.

He shrugged. 'As you pointed out yesterday—it's my house.' His gaze narrowed on her warningly.

When he was filming his work schedule was such that he often went short of sleep—so it wasn't last night's insomnia that was making him so irritable this morning but his rapidly increasing anger towards this woman. A woman who, if the way he couldn't stop thinking about her was anything to go by, had got to him more deeply than any other. A woman who had totally deceived him…!

Rosie's mouth thinned. 'So it is,' she acknowledged mockingly, and she stepped back to allow him to come into the flat.

The music her father had on the CD-player in the bedroom could be heard more clearly. It was a piece that Rosie recognised all too easily. She should do—*she* was the violin soloist, and she was playing the concerto that she had written herself…!

'Here—I went out and got this earlier.' Hawk held out the newspaper that Rosie hadn't noticed he had been carrying under his arm. 'Page three,' he added hardly, as Rosie slowly took the newspaper from him.

She gave him another brief glance before opening the paper and turning the pages, her curiosity such—despite the melancholy strains of music that now filled the flat—that she couldn't *not* have opened it.

It was the same photograph that Hawk's agent had e-mailed to him yesterday. Perhaps not quite as blurred as the downloaded copy had been, but there was still too little of her face visible for her to be recognisable.

Nevertheless, her hands shook slightly as she shut the newspaper abruptly and put it down on the coffee table. 'I—It seems harmless enough,' she dismissed stiffly, still slightly thrown by the fact that it was *her* CD her father was playing in his bedroom.

Her latest album—a compilation of her music that had only been released the previous month…

'Don't you have something to tell me, Rosie?' Hawk queried, his impatience growing by the second.

She looked surprised. 'Something to tell you…?' she repeated slowly. 'I don't think so.'

Hawk was pretty sure he was going to put this woman over his knee and spank her delicious little bottom in a minute! A shapely bottom, encased in blue denim this morning, and a green sweater the same vivid emerald as her eyes…

Better. Much better, Hawk decided, glad that she hadn't chosen black today.

Although that didn't alter the fact that he had received just about all the evasion he intended taking from this woman. He wanted answers—answers that only Rosie could give him. Something she didn't seem inclined to do…

He reached out to grasp her arm as she would have turned away. 'Maybe you should read a little more of the paper this morning, Rosie,' he warned. 'The second photograph of you—of Rosemary Harris!—is much more flattering!' he added grimly.

Her face became haunted as she glanced at the paper she had thrown down so dismissively only seconds ago, her wariness increasing. 'What—?'

'Hawk!' Her father greeted him warmly as he came through from the bedroom. 'I was just coming through to see you,' Donald croaked, having pulled on faded denims and a navy blue sweater after his shower.

He looked much better than he had an hour ago, when Rosie had taken him a cup of coffee in bed, and although it was clear that he was nowhere near well yet, he was obviously feeling brighter this morning. He had resisted all Rosie's efforts to keep him in bed, insisting he had to go and talk to Hawk this morning.

The probability that their talk was going to be about her wasn't in the least reassuring!

She easily pulled away from Hawk's hand as he relaxed his grip on her wrist, turning to face her father. 'I'm sure you shouldn't be out of bed yet—'

'Don't fuss, Rosie.' Donald smiled, taking any sting out of his words, moving slowly across the room to place his arm lightly about her shoulders. He turned away to cough, then prompted, 'So, what do you think of my daughter, Hawk?' He looked down at her proudly.

Rosie winced. Her dad probably didn't want to know what Hawk really thought of his daughter at this moment!

Hawk studied father and daughter, realising that Donald's

prematurely white hair had probably once been as red as his daughter's. He could see a similarity in their facial structure too, now that he knew of their relationship, although Donald's eyes were hazel where Rosie's were that vivid green.

But he also knew this similarity to Donald was *not* the reason she had seemed so familiar to him yesterday!

He turned to the older man. 'She's very beautiful.' He stated the obvious.

'I didn't mean the way she looks!' Donald grinned. 'Although you're right—she is very beautiful,' he agreed, with a proud beam. 'But I was actually referring to—'

'I'm sure Hawk is far too busy to be bothered with all of this just now, Fa—Dad,' Rosie cut in hastily.

'I'm not busy at all,' Hawk assured her tightly.

Donald gave him a merry smile. 'Don't you recognise the music, Hawk?'

Hawk had never particularly been into classical music, although he did recognise certain pieces when he heard them being played. The piece he could hear at the moment wasn't familiar to him, though. Only the player…

'It's very—evocative,' he acknowledged, looking challengingly at Rosie as the violin rose to a crescendo of aching loneliness that was almost painful to listen to.

Rosie, he could easily see, looked distinctively uncomfortable. And so she damn well ought to after the way she had deceived him!

Rosie turned abruptly away from Hawk's piercing gaze. She had wanted to talk to her father alone this morning. Before she left.

Because she *was* leaving. She had realised that as she lay awake last night thinking of Hawk, of the emotions that were

never far below the surface whenever they were together—
even when they *weren't* together, she had pondered, as she'd
fought the need she still felt for him!

Now she realised that she couldn't run away any more.

Her days of running were over. And all the evasion and prevarication between herself and Hawk had to be over too.

And then she had to go back to England and face whatever
needed to be faced...

But first it seemed she had to face Hawk.

And if his guarded remarks about the newspaper article she
hadn't yet seen were anything to go by, then she needed to
get reading.

If his sarcasm was anything to go by, something had alerted
Hawk to more than who she really was...

CHAPTER TWELVE

'DAD, Hawk doesn't—didn't know about any of that,' she amended. Warily, she shot Hawk a nervous glance.

Donald gave him a beaming smile. 'Nevertheless, I'm sure that he's heard of the violinist La Bella Rosa…'

'Dad—'

'The beautiful rose?' Hawk translated dryly.

A teenage protégée. A musical phenomenon who had performed all over the world for seven, eight years to sell-out audiences, her beauty as renowned as her incredible talent.

The violinist on the CD Donald was playing.

A woman who, it was well-known, always wore black.

For Rosie Harrison read Rosemary Harris.

Because Rosie was definitely La Bella Rosa!

Making a complete nonsense of Hawk's suspicions that she might be here to wheedle money out of Donald. Hawk might not know a lot about classical music, but he did know that Rosemary Harris was one of the highest-paid classical musicians in the world!

Hawk was still waiting for the friend he had called in England to get back to him with any information he could find on Rosie Harrison. But after seeing her photograph in the newspaper this morning, and the article that went with it, Hawk had realised that he didn't need his friend—because he already knew exactly who and what she was!

If he had expected to see Rosemary Harris, world-famous violinist, in his Canadian home... But all he had seen yesterday morning was a hauntingly beautiful woman who had claimed—eventually!—to be Donald's long-lost daughter, Rosie.

Damn it, Hawk had been determined to know the truth about her—he just hadn't expected to find it out by reading in a newspaper!

He looked at her coldly. 'You certainly had me fooled, Rosie—or should I call you Rosemary?' he enquired harshly.

'Rosie will do,' she assured him quietly, inwardly wincing at the anger she could hear in his voice. She wanted to explain, to tell him everything now, but she knew from the coldness of his gaze as he looked at her so scathingly that he no longer wanted to hear it. That whatever he had read in the newspaper this morning about Rosemary Harris made it too late for explanations.

He stood up, appearing very tall and powerful in the confines of Donald's flat. And even more remote. 'I think I should leave the two of you to talk—'

'Hawk, please—' The coldness of his gaze silenced her as she would have protested. She swallowed hard. 'I really would like you to stay,' she told him, almost pleadingly.

He had to listen—had to understand—

No, she realised heavily. Hawk didn't have to listen or understand anything if he chose not to.

And why should he choose to?

Because he had kissed her? Because she had kissed him?

Because they had shared a time of such exquisite passion that she hadn't been able to think of anything else all night?

Because she believed she was falling in love with him? If she hadn't already done so!

But that was only how *she* felt, not Hawk. What had happened between them yesterday might have been nothing out of the ordinary to him…

That didn't alter the fact that she owed him an explanation.

'Did I miss something…?' Her father looked confused by the obvious tension between Rosie and Hawk.

Only ten years of her life, Rosie choked inwardly to herself as she moved away from the warmth of her father's arm. Ten years that stretched between them like a yawning chasm.

'Nothing at all,' Hawk assured the older man tautly, his blue eyes glacial as he gave Rosie a hard glance. 'Rosie, why don't you start by telling us the reason for your unexpected visit?' he prompted hardly. 'I presume there has to *be* a reason you've just turned up like this…?'

Rosie looked at him searchingly, seeing only the implacability in his gaze and his set and unsmiling mouth.

'What…what did you read in the newspaper, Hawk?' she questioned slowly.

'What do you think?'

She didn't know. But she could guess. Oh, yes—knowing her mother as well as she did, Rosie could certainly guess.

Yes. It would be better if Hawk stayed and heard her explanations now, with her father present. Because it was obvious from Hawk's accusing expression that he had no interest in hearing anything she would like to say to him in private!

She straightened, tensing her shoulders even as she drew in a controlling breath, not looking at either man now, just wanting to have her say before leaving. 'Firstly, I think you should both know I'm already booked on a flight back to England later today—'

'No!' her father groaned protestingly, even as he sank down weakly into an armchair, his face pale as he stared up at her.

'Why?' Hawk probed abruptly. 'What's back in England that you have to leave before you and Donald have spent any time together?'

Rosie turned to give him a smile. Not that mischievous smile with the infectious laughter of yesterday, but a smile tinged with sadness.

That same haunting sadness he had heard in her music minutes ago...

'Or should I have asked *who*...?' he amended pointedly.

Rosie shook her head, her smile rueful now. 'Don't believe everything you read, Hawk!'

What the hell did *that* mean?

That he shouldn't believe the announcement he had seen in the newspaper? That it wasn't true that 'La Bella Rosa' Rosemary Harris—Rosie!—was to be married on Christmas Eve?

'Gloria!' Donald spoke with flat disgust. 'That's who you came here to get away from, Rosie, isn't it?' He looked up at his daughter searchingly.

Gloria. Donald's ex-partner. Rosie's mother...

Rosie gave her father a weary smile as she nodded. 'I should have made a complete break years ago.'

'Easier said than done,' Donald acknowledged. 'It took me almost fourteen years—until you were twelve years old, Rosie!—to realise I couldn't live with my own wife any more!'

Hawk tried to hide his surprise. Gloria had been Donald's

wife? Donald had lived with Rosie and her mother for the first twelve years of Rosie's life?

And then what?

Donald had left, obviously. But what of Rosie? What had Donald done about his twelve-year-old daughter?

Hawk had a hollow feeling in the pit of his stomach—just as he had a feeling he already knew the answer to that question!

Rosie had told Hawk she hadn't seen her father for years. Ten years…?

Donald's next words confirmed that. 'I should have taken you with me when I left, shouldn't I, Rosie?' he said emotionally. 'You haven't been as happy and successful as I always imagined you were, have you?' he realised gruffly.

Hawk looked searchingly at Rosie, seeing the unhappiness in her face for what it was now. Those shadows in her eyes. Her unsmiling mouth. The music she played—still audible in the background—with such aching loneliness.

Rosie frowned across at her father. 'As you always imagined…?' she repeated slowly.

Hawk looked from daughter to father, remembering all those classical concerts that Donald had disappeared to so often over the years. The fact that he was playing one of Rosie's CDs now. The fact that he always played Rosemary Harris on the stereo in the car…

Donald might have left his wife and daughter ten years ago, but that didn't mean he hadn't kept in touch with Rosie's life in all that time—that he hadn't gone to one theatre venue or another all over the planet just to see and hear her play.

'I used to watch you, Rosie.' Donald softly confirmed Hawk's suspicions. 'I would just sit back in my seat, close my eyes and listen to the sweet music you produced so easily. And

I would think *That's my daughter down there on that stage—my Rosie,*' he added proudly.

Hawk watched Rosie as she took in the full import of what Donald was saying.

She hadn't known!

She had never known of Donald's presence at any of her concerts over the years—hadn't realised that he'd sat in the darkness with hundreds of other people and watched his own daughter perform on the stage.

Until now…

CHAPTER THIRTEEN

ROSIE stared at her father disbelievingly. All those years... All that time when she had imagined... All that time when she had believed her father had forgotten her very existence...!

'You came to my concerts?' she finally managed to say.

'Five, six times a year,' Donald confirmed. 'As often as I could get away.'

She gave a dazed shake of her head. 'But why—? You never let me know you were there! You never came backstage and spoke to me...!' she cried emotionally. 'All these years I've thought—believed—'

'What did you believe, Rosie?' Hawk was the one to prompt softly.

Her eyes were so full of tears when she looked at him that she couldn't even see him. 'I thought he had left me. That he had abandoned me. Sometimes I used to lie awake at night—' She broke off as her voice failed her.

'It's okay, Rosie,' her father encouraged gruffly. 'Everything is going to be okay.'

She nodded. 'Sometimes I would lie awake at night,' she repeated firmly, once she had herself under control. 'I would imagine that you would somehow be at one of my concerts—

that you would realise I was Rosemary Harris. Gloria decided on that shortened version of our name very early in my career!' she explained. 'I hoped and prayed that you would be there, that you would come and see me, that you would tell me it had all been a mistake, that—that you still loved me,' she ended shakily.

'I've never stopped loving you, Rosie!' her father protested, and he stood up, his face very pale.

She had wished for those things so much, so often, but they had never happened. And with time she had learnt to accept that her father had cut her out of his life as completely as he had her mother.

She had accepted it—but never understood it.

'Then why did you never come for me?' she cried. 'Why did you just leave me with—leave me like that?'

Leave her with her mother. Hawk knew what she had been going to say and then hadn't.

He had never thought—never guessed at the heartbreak behind this visit to her father. He had only looked at Rosie, unaware she was Rosemary Harris, and questioned why she had never been to see Donald before now, wondered why she was here now.

A part of Hawk so wanted to go to her, to put his arms around her and tell her it was going to be okay, that he would allow no one and nothing to ever hurt her again. But it wasn't his place to do that. Rosie had a fiancé back in England—the man she was due to marry in a matter of days...!

If anyone comforted her now then it had to be Donald.

'Gloria said— Your mother told me you didn't want to see me.' Donald spoke flatly now. 'For eighteen months after we separated I telephoned, I came to the house, but each time I did she told me you didn't want to speak to me. I finally gave up beating my head against that brick wall and took off for America.' He looked incredibly sad. 'Gloria was lying when she said you didn't want anything to do with me, wasn't she…?'

'Yes,' Rosie confirmed huskily, her hands clenched so tightly together her knuckles showed white. 'Is that why you never came backstage at any of my concerts? Because you thought I didn't want to see you?'

Donald closed his eyes. 'I've been such a fool, haven't I?' He shook his head self-disgustedly.

'We both have,' Rosie said huskily. 'I should have known— should have guessed when I found your current telephone number a couple of days ago, in the same box as she keeps our passports, that all of this was Gloria's doing…' She gave a shake of her head, her expression pained. 'She's known where you were all along, hasn't she?'

'I always made sure she knew where to contact me if—if you should ever change your mind and want to see me again,' her father confirmed grimly. 'I sent birthday and Christmas presents every year too.' He looked at her questioningly.

Rosie swallowed hard. 'I never received them.'

'I can't believe— All these years…!' Donald groaned, his eyes glittering angrily now at his ex-wife's machinations.

Hawk could well understand the older man's anger. He felt slightly murderous towards Gloria Harrison himself.

He could see the hurt and bewildered child inside Rosie now, the loneliness that was so apparent in her playing of the violin. Could understand the reason she had talked of Donald these last couple of days as if he were a stranger to her. He understood her reserve towards Donald, for that was what it was—a barrier against being hurt again, against being rejected by her father again, as she had thought she had been rejected as a child.

His own anger towards Rosie for her deception wasn't important right now—at that moment he just wanted to strangle Gloria Harrison for the pain she had caused her ex-husband and her daughter!

Rosie gave a shaky smile. 'But we know the truth now...' She spoke almost questioningly.

'We certainly do,' her father responded tautly, his expression softening as he saw the way she looked at him so uncertainly. 'Is it too late, Rosie?' he questioned uncertainly. 'Do you—? Can we start again, do you think?' He looked at her anxiously.

She had believed it was too late, that too many years had passed for her and her father ever to have a real relationship again. But as she looked at her dad he was once again the strong and loving man of her childhood—the man she had always looked up to and adored. The man who, despite believing she didn't want any more to do with him, had travelled the world just to see her perform...!

She gave a tremulous smile. 'No, it's not too late,' she assured him.

'Rosie...!' her father groaned emotionally, and he enfolded her into the strength of his arms.

Hawk felt decidedly out of place now. He knew he shouldn't be here—that this moment belonged to Rosie and Donald.

Neither Rosie nor Donald seemed to notice as he quietly let himself out of the apartment and went back downstairs, a perplexed expression on his face as he tried to work out how he really felt about Rosie's wedding on Christmas Eve...

'I came to say goodbye.' Rosie spoke gruffly when she found Hawk in the farmhouse kitchen, sitting at the breakfast bar, an hour or so later, drinking coffee.

It had been a very emotional hour. She and her father had talked and talked as they'd learnt how each of them had spent the last decade, coming to an acceptance that they had been kept apart by the selfish ambitions of a woman who had deliberately done so, using Rosie's talent to make a life for herself regardless of who else she was hurting.

They had a long way to go yet before they relaxed in their relationship as father and daughter, but Rosie had no doubts that they would get there.

In the meantime, she intended going through with her decision to return to the UK later today. She knew she had the emotional strength she had been searching for to confront her mother once and for all.

But first she had to say goodbye to Hawk...

And she didn't want to!

Twenty-four hours. A single day. That was how long she had known Hawk. But already she knew that she loved him. That saying goodbye to him was going to be harder than all those years of believing her father didn't care about her.

Because there would be no happy-ever-after between herself and Hawk. Rosie knew that the most she could ever be to him was the daughter of his employee and friend Donald Harrison.

Yes, saying goodbye to Hawk would be the hardest thing she had ever done in her life.

'I'll be leaving for the airport soon,' she told Hawk brightly as he looked up at her guardedly. 'I'm afraid I never did get around to helping you decorate the Christmas trees,' she added ruefully. 'But my father insists he's well enough to drive me to the airport, so perhaps he'll help you when he gets back.' She shrugged, Hawk's continued silence making her uncomfortable.

His eyes widened. 'Donald isn't coming to England with you?'

'No,' Rosie replied softly.

'Why the hell not?' Hawk rasped, not at all happy with the idea of her confronting her mother alone—he didn't like the sound of Gloria Harrison at all!

She grimaced. 'He wanted to—but I have to do this for myself, Hawk.'

He could understand that. He knew that there were things Rosie wanted to say to her mother that perhaps no one else should hear. He just didn't like the idea of her facing it alone.

Rosie raised her chin determinedly. 'As you already know—read in the newspaper—my returning to England is also a little more—complicated than just talking to my mother,' she explained awkwardly.

Hawk's gaze narrowed on the delicate beauty of her face. A face he knew was going to haunt his nights as well as his days!

'Because you're supposed to be getting married on Christmas Eve?' he grated harshly, knowing she must have finally got around to reading the article in the newspaper he had given her, that claimed 'La Bella Rosa'—violinist Rosemary Harris—wasn't available for comment at the moment, but that her wedding to the conductor Edmund Price would be taking place on Christmas Eve as expected!

Rosie turned away, unable to meet the condemnation in Hawk's gaze. 'I told you it was complicated,' she said.

'You also told me not to believe everything I read,' he reminded her directly.

She drew in a deep breath. 'Because I'm *not* getting married—on Christmas Eve or at any other time!'

'You just forgot to tell your fiancé that?'

'No, I—Look, I really do have to go now.' Rosie sighed wearily. 'I have to pack. I only came to say goodbye, and to—to thank you for your hospitality—'

'What hospitality would that be?' Hawk cut in. 'Unless you're referring to the fact that I almost took you to bed yesterday?' he continued angrily. 'What was I, Rosie? A last fling before you accepted the bonds of matrimony?'

Her cheeks flamed fiery-red. 'Of course not—'

'Of course, *yes*!' Hawk contradicted furiously, standing up to move sharply away from her.

'I just told you I'm *not* getting married on Christmas Eve—'

'That isn't what the newspaper says—'

'The newspaper is wrong!' she insisted fiercely. 'Hawk—'

'Why all the fuss, Rosie?' Hawk cut in tauntingly. 'Do I really look as if I'm interested one way or the other?' he scorned.

Rosie stared at the uncompromising rigidness of Hawk's expression for several long, painful seconds before turning on her heel and hurrying back up to her father's flat.

Hawk was right. The two of them had nothing left to say to each other…

CHAPTER FOURTEEN

Three days later...

'YOUR flight should be ready for boarding in half an hour or so, Miss Harris,' the hostess in the executive lounge at Heathrow Airport told Rosie as she cleared away Rosie's used cup. 'Could I get you another drink while you're waiting?'

Rosie looked up to return the other woman's smile. 'A coffee would be lovely, thank you,' she accepted, not too bothered by the slight delay in her flight.

The last few days had been hectic, to say the least, and it was nice just to sit down in the airport lounge and relax, away from the barrage of reporters who seemed to have been dogging her every move since she'd arrived back in England. At least they couldn't follow her in here!

Rosie couldn't help smiling as she looked across the room at two small children standing gazing at the enormous Christmas tree that dominated one corner of the room, their faces glowing as they looked up at the multitude of coloured lights and the star shining at the top of the tree. The light snow falling outside on the airport runways was a perfect backdrop for their obvious excitement at the rapidly approaching time for Father Christmas to arrive.

The snow reminded her of Canada. Of Hawk…

'Could you make that two coffees, please?' a familiar voice drawled huskily from just behind Rosie.

She spun sharply round in her chair to look up at Hawk with dazed eyes. It was almost as if just thinking about him had brought him here!

But he really *was* here!

Not just in England, but *here*, in the executive lounge at Heathrow Airport, of all places!

'Of course, Mr Hawkley.' The hostess gave him a beaming smile, before disappearing back to her workstation.

Rosie barely noticed the other woman leaving, having eyes only for Hawk.

She had thought of him so often since they had parted three days ago—of how his dark overlong hair felt so silky to touch, of his eyes that deep, warm blue in his ruggedly handsome face, a face she loved so much!—that for a moment she remained speechless and just continued to stare at him.

Hawk tilted his head slightly sideways, smiling ruefully as he looked down at her. 'Can I sit down?' he prompted softly.

'I—of course,' she replied awkwardly. 'Please do.' She indicated the chair opposite hers—a gesture he ignored as he lowered his long length into the chair next to her. 'I didn't even know you were in Britain…?' She had spoken to her father several times over the last few days, and again only a few hours ago, and he hadn't mentioned that Hawk was in the UK…

Hawk gave a half-smile. 'I'm not. Well, I am—obviously—but only just.' He grimaced. 'Rosie, I got off the plane that just arrived from Calgary…'

The same flight she would be getting on to return to Canada...

Now she was thoroughly confused. If Hawk had only just *arrived*, what was he doing in the executive lounge...?

Where to begin? That was Hawk's problem. It had all seemed so much easier after he had seen the announcement of the cancellation of Rosie's wedding in the newspaper. He would fly over, see her, talk to her—see if he couldn't persuade her that there was now no reason why she couldn't come back to Canada to spend Christmas with her father. And him, of course...

Only it hadn't worked out that way!

'You telephoned Donald *when*, to tell him you were flying over for Christmas after all?' he asked.

'Just a couple of hours ago, when I managed to get booked on the flight,' Rosie said slowly.

Hawk nodded. 'And I was already on the incoming flight, coming to see you. Luckily Donald had the foresight to book me on the same flight back as you. Thanks.' He gave the hostess a warm smile as she brought them their coffee.

Only one thing in Hawk's statement really registered with Rosie. 'You flew over to see *me*...?'

Why had he flown over to see her? The two of them hadn't parted very well in Canada, or so much as spoken to each other on the telephone since she had arrived back in England, so why had Hawk flown over to see her now?

'Shouldn't you be at home with your family?' She knew from her father that Hawk's parents, sister and her family had already arrived to spend Christmas with him.

'Shouldn't you be somewhere else today too?' he came back pointedly.

Christmas Eve. Her wedding day. Except that both of them knew it wasn't.

Rosie shook her head. 'The only place I want to be for Christmas is Canada, with Donald.' *With you*, she added inwardly, still not sure what Hawk was doing here.

Hawk looked at her long and hard for several long seconds before answering. 'And the only person I want to be with for Christmas is sitting right here, next to me.' He spoke gruffly, that dark blue gaze never leaving her face.

'Hawk…?' she breathed raggedly, hardly daring to breathe at all, in case all of this was a dream and she woke up.

He shrugged powerful shoulders beneath the brown suede jacket he wore over a black silk shirt and black denims. 'I was an idiot three days ago. I should never have let you leave like that. At the very least I should have insisted on coming with you. But I thought you had only come to Canada because you'd had some sort of falling-out with the guy you were due to marry—that you would come back here and everything would be smoothed out again. Hell, Rosie,' he cried, 'you could have at least *told* me that Edmund Price is almost old enough to be your grandfather!'

'He isn't that old!' she exclaimed protestingly.

'Okay—your father, then.' Hawk scowled. 'I thought he was some young guy that— Never mind,' he dismissed impatiently, reaching out to take one of her hands in both of his. 'That relationship is definitely over?'

'As far as I was concerned it never began, really,' she admitted ruefully. 'My mother thought it would be a good idea for me to marry a prestigious conductor like Edmund—that it could only further my career. Having no backbone at the time, I went along with it.' She grimaced self-disgustedly.

'You have backbone, Rosie—'

'Now I do.' She nodded firmly. 'But no matter what you

may have thought, what that newspaper article said, I had already broken my engagement before I went to Canada to see Donald,' she added determinedly, her hand feeling very warm inside Hawk's. 'My mother was the source of the article you read in that newspaper three days ago.' She sighed. 'She refused to accept that the wedding was off—simply couldn't bear to have anyone thwart her. But I've broken all my business ties with my mother since I returned. In future I intend managing my own career and my own life,' she told him decisively.

The scene with her mother wasn't very pleasant to recall, but Rosie had no regrets. She hoped that one day—in the distant future!—she and her mother might be able to find some sort of relationship again. Just not the unforgiving business partnership they'd had for the last ten years.

'So I heard,' Hawk drawled. 'The Canadian newspapers have been full of the story these last few days too. How you sacked your mother as your manager and cancelled all your wedding plans,' he finished admiringly.

Rosie really didn't want to talk about that. She wanted to move on with her life, not look back. 'Why did you want to see me, Hawk…?' she enquired guardedly.

If anything, these last three days away from Hawk had only confirmed what she had already known in Canada: she was in love with him. Deeply, madly, completely. She just had no idea how he felt about her.

But he was here, wasn't he? He had flown to Britain especially to see her. That had to mean something.

Hawk's gaze roamed over the beauty of her face. Her hair was loose today, flowing like flame over her shoulders and down her back. And she wasn't wearing black either, but a soft cashmere dress in the same shade of green as her eyes, her legs long and silky beneath its knee-length, her high-heeled boots the same colour as her dress.

'I see you've been out shopping,' he told her approvingly.

'For Christmas presents? Yes.' She held up the large bag beside her that was full of gaily wrapped parcels. 'My credit card wasn't maxed out after all.' She grinned.

Hawk shook his head. 'I meant the dress and boots. You look—wonderful,' he assured her huskily.

A delicate blush coloured her freckle-covered cheeks. 'The black clothing was another idea of my mother's—I've given it all away to a charity shop.' She smiled ruefully. 'Hawk, you didn't answer my question: why did you want to see me?'

She had grown in confidence the last three days, Hawk acknowledged. She seemed in control of her own life now, and obviously enjoying it.

Did he have the right to ask her to give up even a little of that freedom she had only just fought for, and won so determinedly?

He looked down at her hand as it rested in both of his, his thumb moving caressingly over her creamy skin. Just touching her like this, being with her again, made him feel weak at the knees, and he knew if they weren't in such a public place that he would have taken her in his arms and kissed her by now.

His gaze returned to her face, to find her looking at him anxiously. He reached up to smooth the frown from between her brows before moving his hand to cradle her cheek. 'You are so beautiful, Rosie,' he murmured tenderly. 'So absolutely, perfectly beautiful.' He gave a shake of his head. 'I came to England to ask you, beg you if necessary, to give me a chance—to marry me. But—'

'Yes!' Rosie spoke quickly, before he could complete his

sentence. She didn't want to hear any buts. From now on there would be no second-bests in her life—no wishing, no dreaming, no negatives at all if she could prevent it.

Which was one of the reasons she was returning to Canada so soon. She wanted to spend Christmas with her father, of course, but she had wanted to see Hawk too—to see if they had any chance of a relationship together.

Though she had never thought that Hawk would come to her like this…!

Hawk became very still, his gaze moving searchingly over her face, lingering on the deep glow of her eyes and her softly parted lips. 'Yes…?' he repeated uncertainly.

She nodded. 'If that was a proposal of marriage, then I accept!'

He shook his head, his gaze unwavering. 'That wasn't a proposal of marriage, Rosie,' he breathed huskily.

Oh, God, had she just made a complete idiot—?

'*This* is a proposal of marriage!' Hawk assured her firmly, even as he moved out of the chair and got down on one knee in front of her, her hand still held tightly in his as he looked up at her. 'Rosie Harrison, will you marry me?'

She hadn't made a fool of herself! Hawk really *was* asking her to marry him!

They were surrounded by happy travellers on their way to spend Christmas with their loved ones, those two children still played happily beside the glowing Christmas tree, the snow was still falling softly outside, and Hawk had just asked her to marry him!

It was almost too magical to be true…!

'Do you think you could give me an answer soon, Rosie?' Hawk murmured ruefully when she hadn't spoken for some time. 'We're attracting quite a lot of attention,' he added self-derisively.

She glanced around them. Sure enough, the other travellers waiting in the lounge were all indulgently watching the drama taking place across the room, and the hostess was openly staring at the two of them too.

Rosie turned back to Hawk. 'Yes, yes, yes—I'll marry you!' she assured him ecstatically.

Hawk grinned triumphantly at the softly called congratulations from the crowd gathering around them, and he moved to take Rosie in his arms and kiss her with all the longing he had felt since she'd left him three days ago.

'I love you, Rosie Harrison,' he groaned when he finally came up for air. 'I had no idea it was possible to miss someone so much until you left Canada and came back to England. Since you left me!' He rested his forehead on hers, his arms still tightly wrapped about her.

'I love you too, Hawk,' Rosie breathed shakily. 'So very, very much.'

'Then that's all that matters,' he murmured. 'Loving each other, wanting to be together, is all that will ever matter.'

It was too, Rosie realised. No matter what happened in future, no matter where their individual careers took them— because she *was* going to play again, *wanted* to play again!— as long as they loved each other nothing else mattered.

'As Christmas presents go, this is quite something, Rosie,' Hawk told her gruffly exactly a year later, their baby daughter, born only a few minutes before, held carefully in his arms.

'She's our gift to each other.' Rosie smiled, gently touching the baby's hand, hardly able to believe this miracle herself.

It had been a year of smiles and laughter, of loving, of being loved, of juggling two careers and her pregnancy so that their partings weren't too often. And the birth of their daughter Sophie had only made their happiness all the richer.

'Donald and Mom and Dad will be along later this morning,' Hawk assured her as he tenderly placed their red-haired daughter into her arms, before sitting down on the hospital bed beside her. 'I telephoned Gloria and told her the good news,' he added with a grin. 'She sent her congratulations and hopes to see us all the next time we're in New York.'

Rosie's relationship with her mother was still fragile, to say the least. Her mother was now working for a PR company in Manhattan and the two women had only met twice in the last year—tense meetings, when they'd found they really had nothing to say to each other.

It didn't matter. Nothing else mattered but the happiness Rosie and Hawk had found together—a happiness that had spread to her father and to Hawk's family.

'Shall we try for a son next Christmas?' Rosie looked up at Hawk glowingly, more in love with her handsome husband than ever, as she knew he was deeply in love with her.

Hawk bent down to kiss her lingeringly on the lips. 'Glad to oblige, Mrs Hawkley,' he murmured lovingly.

Mrs Hawkley.

Not Rosemary Harris.

Not Rosie Harrison.

But Rosie Hawkley.

Hawk's wife.

That was all she ever wanted to be…

* * * * *

SNOWBOUND BRIDE

Shirley Jump

To Janet and Sue, the best women ever to be
stuck with waiting for a flight out of O'Hare. And
to my husband, who bought us the margaritas
that made the delay a whole lot more fun.

New York Times bestselling author **Shirley Jump** didn't have the willpower to diet, nor the talent to master under-eye concealer, so she bowed out of a career in television and opted instead for a career where she could be paid to eat at her desk—writing. At first, seeking revenge on her children for their grocery-store tantrums, she sold embarrassing essays about them to anthologies. However, it wasn't enough to feed her growing addiction to writing funny. So she turned to the world of romance novels, where messes are (usually) cleaned up before The End. In the worlds Shirley gets to create and control, the children listen to their parents, the husbands always remember holidays, and the housework is magically done by elves. Though she's thrilled to see her books in stores around the world, Shirley mostly writes because it gives her an excuse to avoid cleaning the toilets and helps feed her shoe habit. To learn more, visit her Web site at www.shirleyjump.com.

CHAPTER ONE

MARIETTA WESTMORE was up to her eyeballs in silk and lace. Literally.

Behind her, an impatient rumble of voices had started up in the middle of Terminal 1 in Chicago's O'Hare International Airport. One enterprising soul even snapped a cell phone picture. Marietta scowled, then quickly tucked the wedding dress back into the vinyl bag, being careful not to trample the train or slice the sheer sleeves, then worked the bag's zipper back into place. It jammed three inches from the top. Caught—Marietta shuddered to think on what.

God, please let it be a stray thread. Anything but a crucial part of the several-thousand-dollar gown she'd spent the better part of the last six months working on. "Am I okay to go now?"

The security guard grinned. Below her collar, a twinkling Rudolph pin blinked his red nose in a steady beat. "Sure. I was only kidding about the security check. I just wanted to see what the dress looked like. Wait till I tell the girls I got the first peek at *Penelope Blackburn's* wedding gown! A real celebrity's dress right here in my line, along with the designer herself. The girls are going to be so jealous." The guard chortled, then handed back Marietta's boarding pass and ID. "You have a Merry Christmas now!"

Marietta blew a lock of hair out of her face, gave the guard a smile that cracked her face, then hurried the rest of the way past the X-ray machines, mumbling about abuse of homeland security power. Now she was late and it wasn't a flight she could afford to miss.

Marietta hurried as fast as she could—for the fortieth time that day cursing the decision to wear high-heeled boots—at the same time turning the white bag around to hide the "Made by Marietta" logo and its elegant picture of a bride formed in the loop of the "y". If she'd had more time to think, she'd have grabbed a less conspicuous bag so she wouldn't garner any other curious onlookers hoping to sneak a preview peek of her celebrity client's wedding gown.

But she'd been in too much of a hurry to disguise the garment bag—and honestly, she hadn't even thought most people would make the connection. But clearly, word, and the *People* magazine gossip column got around. Probably thanks to Penelope's highly efficient publicist, who'd made sure every detail of the wedding was leaked to the press, thereby ensuring extra coverage just before Penelope's latest romantic comedy was released to theaters on Christmas Day.

Two days ago, the publicist had had the brilliant idea of moving up Penelope's wedding from December 27th to Christmas Eve. Penelope had called Marietta in Milan, where she'd been meeting with vendors, telling her to rush the dress right on over, as if it were as easy as making a peanut butter sandwich.

But Penelope was paying—well—and so here Marietta was, back from a transcontinental flight to pick the gown up at her shop in Chicago, where she'd last met with Penelope for a fitting when the actress had been in town on her publicity tour. Marietta had had a half a day to make the final touches to the dress, and now, with a thankfully completed gown in hand, she was personally escorting it on December 23rd to the West Coast. This one client had taken her from nothing more, really, than a glorified seamstress with a side business in wedding gowns to a wedding specialist with a celebrity waiting list.

It was as if Santa himself had dropped Penelope Blackburn down Marietta's company chimney. It was exactly the break Marietta had hoped for—even if it came attached to a demanding double-edged sword.

Marietta dashed across Terminal B, down the escalator, through the multi-colored lighted tunnel, back up the escalators and finally into Terminal C, the world going by in a blur of red and green, Christmas packages and holiday decorations. Just as she was catching her breath, her cell phone rang. Marietta wrangled it out of her back pocket, trying to hurry down the concourse toward her gate. "Hello?"

"Marietta? Where *are* you? I swear I'm going to have a heart attack. Can you hear me? I'm hyperventilating. I have a paper bag in my hands, Marietta. *A paper bag.* I've been up all night, and I had to wake the maids to make me a cucumber mask because now my face is all puffy. I can't get married like this! I'm a wreck. A complete wreck. Do you know what this will do to my reputation? I'll be doing infomercials for the rest of my life and I'll never get another movie deal! *Never!* I'll be like one of those 'where are they now' people!"

"I'm on my way, Penny. I should be there by two-thirty West Coast time." One thing Marietta had learned was that dealing with Penelope required not just fine needlework, but a little pop psychology on the side. "Now, close your eyes. Remember how beautiful you looked in your gown at the last fitting? You were like Princess Grace, remember?"

Penelope inhaled, exhaled. "You're right. I see it now. Beautiful, elegant. Just like the wedding. It'll go off without a hitch, right?"

In Penelope's voice, Marietta heard a hint of herself, her own worries about getting the details right. "Of course. Because you're Penelope Blackburn and you're paying for perfection."

"I am, aren't I?" She laughed. "Then I'm going to order someone in this castle of mine to bring me a sugar-free, fat-free something and tell myself it's a chocolate cake. Then I'll feel better." And then Penelope was gone.

Marietta shoved her phone back into her pocket and shifted the bulk of the dress to her other shoulder. It weighed more than your average eight-year-old. Why had she let Penelope talk her into all these diamond-encrusted flowers?

Because Penelope had wanted to sparkle more than the four dozen Christmas trees ordered for the church. Because she wanted to be the star, as befitted her status in Hollywood. And because the customer was always right. And in this case, she had been. One thing Penelope Blackburn had in abundance was great taste.

The dress was exquisite, undeniably beautiful. A full skirt, sheer sleeves, a bodice of poinsettia-shaped flowers that caught the light and seemed to dance, come alive. Every hemline was trimmed with diamonds, the train dusted with tiny sparkling gems.

For weeks Marietta had seen the dress hanging on the

muslin dressmaker form and envied Penelope, just a little. More than once she'd thought of trying it on. They were the same size, she and Penelope. But…trying it on would be wrong. No matter how stunning the dress was, or what romantic notions it inspired in Marietta.

That dress might not have turned Marietta's life into a storybook, but it had done wonders for her business. Her dreams had come true. The only problem was, she hadn't had five seconds to enjoy them.

Her PDA beeped a reminder. Eleven-forty, fifteen minutes until the flight took off. "Damn!" Marietta broke into a run, the dress banging against her back as she wove in and out among the crowds, negotiating her way through the milling passengers and down the long, long concourse toward gate C-31.

She narrowly missed a collision with an elderly man in a Santa hat pushing a wheelchair carrying a woman wearing a matching hat. A man taking a picture of the decorations at a fast food restaurant—why, Marietta didn't pause to think. A janitor cleaning up a spilled coffee, humming a Christmas song as he mopped.

And then, finally, she spied the signs for Gate C-29, Gate C-30—

Reed Hartstone.

It took a second for her brain to process his image, her mind cartwheeling through the flurry of activity around her, trying to fit this anomaly in, as if playing "What doesn't belong?"—

A father lecturing a son about running too far ahead. A weary pregnant woman collapsing into the nearest seat. An overstuffed carry-on bag exploding, revealing an embarrassment of red and white lingerie—

And still, Reed Hartstone.

Reed? Here? Now?

Why?

Her attention on him, not on where she was going, Marietta stumbled, her foot caught on the corner of a suitcase left in the aisle. She felt her weight twist on one ankle, while the rest of her was still trying to move in the opposite direction.

Her leg crumpled, a quick, sharp pain shooting up from one high-heeled boot all the way to her thigh and she winced, gasped, then straightened, still half-sure she was seeing things. "Reed?"

"Marietta?"

In the space of a breath, her mind processed every inch of him. Six feet two, short brown hair, deep blue eyes so dark they were almost black, a lean figure with broad shoulders, the kind a woman could lean on when she needed to, but also the kind that stayed in her line of sight long after the rest of him walked away. Her gut tightened—damn, still she reacted to him, all these years later—and she reminded herself there was a very good reason they were no longer together. "What are you doing here?"

A grin as familiar as the beat of her own heart curved across his face. "I could say the same as you. But let me guess. Still globe-trotting. Making your fortune or—"

And then his gaze caught the garment bag over her shoulder, the bride pictured on the front, the bit of white embroidered satin still sticking out of the open zipper. She glanced at it, about to explain, when Reed beat her to the punch and added two and two. "—or getting married."

The end of the sentence sat there between them. An assumption, one she could easily undo and explain. But then, when he found out she was still single, Reed would ask her for a cup of coffee, a drink. A few minutes to chat over old times, and before she knew it, they were returning to those times. Picking up where they had left off.

Because that was what they had always done. And every time, it had been a mistake.

"Attention passengers," said a monotone, barely recognizable as female voice on the terminal's loudspeaker system. Conversations dimmed, heads swiveled toward the sound. "Due to poor weather conditions, all flights have been grounded until further notice. As soon as the weather clears, we hope to have you on the way to your destinations. We apologize for the inconvenience." A collective irritated groan rippled through the airport.

Great. Just what Marietta needed. A delay. Maybe she'd get lucky and catch a tailwind, if tailwinds even blew east to west. Otherwise, she'd be dealing with one crazy, highly tranquilized celebrity in a few hours.

"Are you?" Reed asked. "Getting married?"

Her cell phone rang, serendipity or bad timing—she didn't question it, just answered the call. Thank God. For the first time since agreeing to design Penelope's dress, Marietta was glad for the interruption.

"The caterer just called and the Cornish game hens didn't arrive. I think they flew the coop and at this rate, with the stress this wedding is causing, I'm about ready to do the same. God, it's like a pressure cooker." Penelope drew in a breath. "Anyway, Chef Paul says we're going to have to serve *regular* chicken to two thousand guests. Do you know what people will think, Marietta? That I'm *poor*. Bankrupt. Being audited or something. Appearances are everything out here and if one more thing goes wrong with this wedding… Please tell me you'll be here soon. If I can just put on my dress, like you said, I'll feel better."

"Umm...my plane is going to be a little delayed," Marietta began. "There's a snowstorm in Chicago. So I might be a *wee* bit late."

"Late?" Penelope's voice reached decibels only dogs and astronauts could hear. "Oh, this isn't a good sign. Too much is going wrong already and I just have this feeling—"

"What?" Marietta prompted when Penelope didn't finish.

"Like this is a train that's about to go off a bridge. In my career, when I get that feeling, it's usually right. It's that flop feeling, that 'don't take this movie offer' feeling. I should never have agreed to this whole idea."

"You mean moving the wedding up?"

Penelope paused for a beat. "Yeah, that."

"Don't worry. There's still plenty of time until the wedding tomorrow."

"I don't know. My psychic said my dress is a symbol of the future. If the dress is stuck in Chicago, *what kind of symbol is that?"* Penelope's voice broke. "I have to go. I need to meditate and talk to my therapist. I'll call you later." She hung up.

Marietta sighed, put the phone back in her pocket and turned to face Reed again. Two major problems at once—just when everything in her life seemed to be going so well.

"Late for your own wedding. Now that can't be good."

"Bad weather. I'm sure plenty of people here are late for something important," she said, rather than answering the implied question. "What about you?"

"Believe it or not, I'm late for a meeting." He glanced at his watch. "Very late. My plane's been delayed twice already."

Surprise hit her hard. The Reed she remembered hadn't done meetings, business brunches or anything remotely smacking of corporate America. He'd been small-town, rural life all the way. She'd been the one hell-bent on the jet set way of life, making them the proverbial bird and the fish. Anything to get her out of Whistle Creek, the town that had never felt like home, not really. "A meeting? Really? Where?"

"Boston. I'm a financial advisor."

"You? A suit and tie and the whole nine yards?" Then she noticed his business casual attire. The dark green polo shirt and khaki pants, the tailored wool coat, shiny dress shoes. Handsome, sharp. An impressive Reed, quite the contrast to the laid-back, jeans and T-shirt man she remembered.

Then why did she feel a flicker of disappointment?

"I guess you could say I grew up," he said, a hint of bitterness tinting his voice. "Got a real job."

The words stung. She'd thrown those at him years ago, just before she'd thrown his engagement ring back—and walked away for the last time. Never expecting to see him again.

Apparently never was exactly seven years long.

"I'm happy for you. Really I am." She hefted the dress onto her shoulder, then began looking for a seat. The airport was jammed, frustrated passengers camping out in every available seat, many already setting up temporary lodging on the floor, using their suitcases for cushions, coats for pillows and blankets. She didn't see a single open chair anywhere. One couple sat down on the floor and began exchanging presents, their happy grins saying they were taking the whole thing in stride, creating a Christmas right there in the airport. Marietta turned away, for some reason unable to watch them.

Outside, the snow continued to fall, a white sheet steadily dropping from the sky, covering the airport and everything in it, already several inches deep. Marietta sighed. From the looks of the sky, she had little hope of making it to L.A. before the end of the day.

Her ankle throbbed, though the pain had begun to dim. Her arm hurt. All she wanted was to get to Los Angeles, get this dress delivered and get home to—

To what?

"Let me take that for you," Reed said, reaching for the garment bag before she could protest. "It looks like it weighs a ton."

"I'm fine, really."

"You twisted your ankle, and don't tell me it doesn't hurt because I can tell. Your face is still as readable as the *Chicago Times*, Marietta." Reed draped the bag over his arm. "Do you want to get a drink? Something to eat?"

"I really shouldn't."

"Why? You have somewhere you need to be right now?"

Again that grin. Just as irresistible as always—and just as right. "They could call the flight or—"

"The snow is coming down like crazy, no one's going anywhere for hours. You have time for something to eat."

Sitting down with Reed…probably not the best idea. But then again, it had been seven years since they'd last seen each other. They'd both grown up, moved on. Dated other people. For all she knew, he could be married now.

Her heart skipping a beat whenever their gazes connected, her pulse ratcheting up a notch—didn't mean a thing.

Surely, she could have a drink, a sandwich, with the man

and not have it go anywhere further than a couple of old lovers catching up in an airport, caught up in a holiday mood.

Yeah, that was all it was. A little curiosity. A way to pass the time.

Then why was she wondering if his left hand—the one hidden by her garment bag—had a gold band on it or not?

"Where are we going to find a seat? This place is as crowded as Bookers' Got to Hook 'Em Bait Shop on the first day of fishing season."

He shook his head. "I forgot all about that place."

"*You?* Forget about anything in Whistle Creek?"

"I've been gone from there a long time, Marietta."

Again, that hint of a different Reed, not the one she remembered.

"I remember the men in Whistle Creek lining up outside of Bookers', determined to be the first to catch that bass they'd been going on about all winter long over their beers. And then every one of them would come back to Ernie's Bar empty handed, talking about the one that got away."

"There's always one of those, isn't there? One that got away?" Reed said, and she got the feeling he didn't mean large-mouthed bass. But before she could question him, he changed the subject. "Anyway, I know a place in the airport where we can go to eat. Trust me." The familiar tightening in Marietta's gut as she met his gaze told her this wasn't going to be just a drink. A sandwich. A catching up.

It'd be a revisiting of old times. Old feelings.

Marietta shook off the thought. She was a grown-up. A confident, successful woman. A woman who'd simply been momentarily sidetracked by the Christmas carols playing on the sound system of the shops and the lovers cozying up on the uncomfortable vinyl seats. That was all. "Lunch sounds good," she said.

"I travel through here pretty often," Reed said, taking her elbow and leading the way through the crowd. Just as quickly, he released her, as if he realized he'd been touching her. "A friend of mine owns a little restaurant in the airport. He'll get us a table and make something great."

"If you can pull that off, you're truly a miracle worker." The restaurants were even more packed than the seats at the gates. Apparently they weren't the only ones with the idea of passing the time with a meal.

Marietta's stomach rumbled. The last thing she'd eaten had been a muffin she'd grabbed on the run, with a bad cup of coffee to wash it down. Not exactly a nutritional power-house for the trying day ahead.

They wove in and out among the people, down the end of the terminal and around the corner to a small restaurant. It was, like all the others, packed to the brim.

Reed sidled up to the bar that flanked the right side. "Hey, Joe!"

A robust man filling a pitcher of beer looked up, his face breaking into a wide smile. "Reed! Nice to see you in town again! Thanks for that advice on the mutual fund. My girl may get that Harvard education after all."

"Glad to hear it. If anyone's Harvard material, your Ginny is."

Joe beamed. "Brilliant, that girl. I 'bout bust a gut talking about her to the customers."

"And rightly so." Reed leaned forward. "You got a table?"

"For you, I always do." Joe slid out from behind the counter, telling the other bartender to take over for a minute, then gestured to Reed and Marietta to follow him. He took them behind the register, into a tiny little nook tucked in the back. It was so small, it was almost not a table at all, more a space, Marietta suspected, for the wait staff to take a break. "Your table, sir," Joe said, gesturing toward it with a flourish.

"Thank you." Reed pulled out Marietta's seat, then waited for her to sit.

"Uh, I have to hang up the dress. Is there somewhere…?"

"I can put it in one of the employee lockers," Joe offered. "Would that work?"

"No," Marietta said, trying to keep from shouting. If either of them knew what this dress was worth or who it was intended for, they'd never suggest a locker. "I'll, ah, just keep it with me." She draped it over her lap, but the pouf of white plastic spilled over the table.

"You can't eat like that," Reed said. "Here." He took the garment bag from her, pulled the table out a few inches, then slipped the hook over the wood partition, letting the dress hang in the space between the partition and the table. "Nice and close, and out of the way."

"You're almost as smart as my Harvard girl," Joe said, then walked off, chuckling.

"So," Marietta began, lacing her fingers together and placing her palms on the table, "how did you end up a specialist in mutual funds?"

"You mean how did the country mouse get to the big city?"

"You were never a mouse, Reed."

Their gazes met and a thread tightened between them—a thread that had never really been broken, as if the fabric of their relationship had unraveled to all but this, this one little ribbon of connection.

"And neither were you, Marietta."

His voice drew her back in, pulled her as easily as a sled across the snow, and for a second, something whispered inside her that all she had to do was pick up that thread and knit a new connection.

But then a waitress brought two glasses of ice water, greeting Reed by name, and interrupting the spell. Drawing Marietta back to the reality that nothing was that simple, and never had been. That she lived in a different world from Reed and always had.

"I assume you want two of the usual?" the waitress said.

"You know me well, Dora," Reed replied. "Joe's specialty would be great. Thanks."

"You got it. Might take a while, because we're swamped, but I suspect you both have quite a bit of time."

"With this storm, we have plenty of time. In fact." Reed's gaze met Marietta's again. "How about a drink? A real drink."

"Oh, I shouldn't…"

"To celebrate. We should celebrate, shouldn't we?" He gestured toward the garment bag. Before she could correct his assumption, he was ordering a bottle of white wine. "Thanks, Dora."

When the waitress was gone, Marietta looked at Reed. "You ordered for me. Without even asking what I wanted."

"I already knew. A Reuben sandwich. With fries and a pickle. It's your favorite. I remembered."

Two words. Simple, everyday words, but when put together, they struck a chord in Marietta, a deep chord, one she'd thought she'd buried when she left Indiana.

When she left Reed.

"Do you remember?" Reed asked.

"Yes," Marietta said, and realized as the word left her that she wasn't just talking about sandwiches, and that meant trouble, in so many ways. The very kind of trouble she'd left behind that last Christmas in Whistle Creek.

Or so she thought.

CHAPTER TWO

REED should know better.

And he did. But he sat across from Marietta Westmore all the same, and told himself he didn't still love her, wasn't attracted to her anymore, and didn't give a damn that she was about to marry another man.

As far as liars went, he was becoming a pro this Christmas.

Damn, she was still as beautiful as he remembered. More so, now that she was older. Her looks had grown more refined with age, as if a sculptor had looked at her and decided to shave a little here, a little there, perfecting what had already been absolutely exquisite. The same aquiline nose, high cheekbones, dancing green eyes, long, dark brown hair that curled around her face, lying against her shoulders lush and vibrant, begging for him to touch.

And oh, how he wanted to, wanted to run his fingers through it, haul her to him and kiss that mouth, hungry for her in ways he couldn't even begin to describe.

Instead, he curled his hand around his water glass, the icy surface doing nothing to cool the heat inside his body. "I didn't answer your question earlier about why I went into finance."

Talk about dollars and cents, Reed. Focus on anything but

Marietta. And the way that red sweater and those dark jeans hug her curves. Not to mention those high-heeled boots. Damn, those boots—

"You do have me intrigued, I have to admit. And surprised." She smiled.

He always had loved the way she smiled, how her lips curved up just a little higher on one side than the other. "That's something I haven't done in a long time."

"Well, surprise me now."

He cleared his throat. Back to business. To other topics. "My father died."

Immediately, her smile disappeared and true sympathy flooded her emerald gaze. "Oh, Reed. I'm so sorry. He was a wonderful man."

"He was. My mother misses him terribly still, and so do I." It was the kind of marriage Reed had always thought he'd have someday. Thought maybe he and Marietta—

His gaze went to the garment bag and something cold and hard hit his gut. Well, clearly that wasn't to be.

Then he glanced at her left hand. No diamond sparkled on her finger. Either she was marrying an exceedingly cheap man or Reed had made the wrong assumption.

"How did you end up in finance?" she asked. "I thought you were going to run the farm with your father. When I left, that's where you were, working the land."

The words struck a note in Reed, harkening back to who he used to be, before life had thrown a detour in his path. Seven years ago, he'd never have imagined he'd be where he was today, never have thought he'd have ever left Whistle Creek.

"That was my plan, but when my dad died, the farm turned out to be in a lot of debt. You know how hard the agricultural industry is in the Midwest." She nodded. "All of a sudden, my mother was in a financial mess. There was a small life insurance policy and I had to find a way to stretch that for her future. I found myself getting a fast education in dollars and sensible investing." He shrugged. "I liked working with money. Seemed to have a knack for investing it, turning a little into a lot. So I went to school, got a degree. Before I knew it, I had a job offer and a career."

"Wow." She sat back against the wooden chair, clearly taken aback. "I'd always thought you were going to follow in your father's footsteps."

"So did I. But things don't always work out the way you plan. Do they?" He gestured toward Marietta. "Except for you. Since the day I met you in kindergarten, you've always known what you wanted and you've gone after it. Heck, you've been drawing pictures of dresses and fashions from the first day you picked up a crayon. Now look at you. Successful. Happy."

The last ended on a slight question mark, but Marietta either didn't hear the implied question or chose to ignore it.

"Things have worked out well with my career, yes. I own a design studio in Chicago and it's taken off phenomenally in the last year." Marietta shook her head. "More than I expected. I just got back from Milan last night, and here I am, hopping on a plane to Los Angeles. After that, it'll be a trip to Paris to meet with a new client."

"And where in that hectic schedule does Christmas fall?"

She let out a laugh, one that Reed thought held a tint of bitterness. "There's no Christmas for me, not this year. I'll probably celebrate it at fifty thousand feet, with a package of stale peanuts and an overpriced teeny bottle of rum."

"That's no holiday, Marietta."

"Says the man who is also in an airport two days before Christmas."

"I'm just flying into Boston for a quick meeting and then I'm going home to see my mother."

"And where is home these days, Reed?"

"I have an apartment near the offices in South Bend, but home, this Christmas, is still where it used to be. Whistle Creek."

As soon as he said the words, he realized how true they were. It must have been seeing Marietta that had resurrected the memories of that town, coupled with the holiday, that had taken his mind—focused before today on work, on numbers, on meetings—down a whole other path.

Whistle Creek. The town popped into his head, clear as day, as if he'd never left. The old mill that had stood at the north entrance for two hundred years, still churning water through the river and greeting everyone who came to town. The feed and grain store that sat across from the mill, operated now by the great-grandsons of the original owner. The drug-store on the corner of Main and Oak, run by Gooch—no one knew his first name or his last—but everyone knew if they needed a prescription filled, or a cure for athlete's foot, old Gooch would take care of them.

"Do you go back there a lot?" she asked.

"No."

What he didn't say was why. Because it hadn't seemed the same. Not since Marietta had left. How that one spark seemed to have gone out, after that particular daisy had been plucked from the meadow.

Or how he too had changed since those days. And how it had become easier to forget Whistle Creek than to go home and not see her there.

She nodded, as if she was reading his mind. "I haven't been there either in what…?"

"Seven years."

"Yeah," she said. Silence rolled between them like a blanket, heavy, thick. "It's been a long time."

He wanted to ask why she hadn't been back. Wanted to know why she had left everything—and everyone—behind. But the days when Marietta told him why she did anything were long over.

"Here you go, Reed," Dora said, depositing two wine glasses and a bottle of wine on their table. She filled their glasses, then gave him a grin. "You'll be turning me into a regular sommelier next. I haven't had to get this fancy in weeks."

"Just keeping you on your toes, Dora. Thanks."

"Anytime. Your food should be out in a sec." She gave him a wave, then headed toward the kitchen.

Reed raised his glass toward Marietta's. "To you and your new husband." The words clogged his throat, nearly cutting off his air supply. Seven years ago, it had been *their* friends toasting him and Marietta. *His* ring had been on Marietta's hand. And now, it was clear there would never be a shot at winning her back—not that he'd ever had her in the first place. "May you have all the happiness in the world."

Marietta toyed with the stem of her glass. "Reed, that's not my wedding dress. Well, it is, but it's not." She laughed. "That doesn't make any sense, does it?"

He lowered the glass back to the table. "No, it doesn't."

"I design wedding dresses as part of my business. That's a client's dress. A very famous client, whose dress I am personally escorting to L.A."

The relief that flooded him was nearly palpable. "You're not getting married?"

She laughed. "No. Heck, I don't even have enough time to post an ad on an online match service, never mind go out on a date."

"You'd never need any help in that area. I'm sure the guys are still lining up outside your door."

Her face reddened and she turned away, directing her attention to her wine instead of him. "Not anymore, Reed."

He wanted to press her for more, but knew it wasn't his place. Knew even more that he shouldn't care. She'd made it clear years ago that she didn't want him and he should be smart and steer clear of a second heartache.

The hubbub of the restaurant and the Christmas music playing on the sound system provided a soft undertow of noise behind them, but in this little alcove, it seemed as if the world only consisted of him and Marietta.

Hadn't it always, though? Whenever they'd been alone together, that was all he'd ever seen. Heard. Thought about— Marietta Westmore.

"Why didn't you come back?" The question was out before he could stop it, his curiosity overriding any kind of politeness barriers.

"There was nothing left for me after—"

She didn't finish the sentence. She didn't have to. Reed could fill in that blank. After the accident that had turned Marietta's life inside out and erased what little family she had.

But there was me, he wanted to say. *I was still in Whistle Creek.*

But they were over, had been, for a long time. She'd made that clear.

Seven years ago, she'd told him in no uncertain terms that she didn't belong in Whistle Creek and she wanted the city life. He'd made it equally clear that his home was on the farm, with his father. They'd stood at an impasse, and rather than find a way around the wall, Marietta had turned and walked away, leaving Reed behind.

"Don't you miss Whistle Creek?" he asked.

"Miss not being able to get a pizza at two in the morning? Miss being cut off from civilization for two days when there's a blizzard? Miss having my mail misdelivered because Jamison is on the sauce again?" Marietta shook her head. "Not at all."

"Jamison's retiring this year, I hear. There'll be a new mail carrier in town."

"Whistle Creek hasn't changed at all in two hundred years, Reed. Sure, we could get a stoplight downtown and new seats in Cindy's Diner, but that's not progress. And it's not the kind of life I want." Her gaze met his. "It never was."

So they were back to square one. The same square she'd used as a leaping off point seven years ago. "Don't you get tired of it, though? The rush and fury of the city? The constant race of a career?"

"That adrenaline rush is part of what I look forward to. It's what gets me out of bed in the morning. I love the city. I love the noise, the people, the crowds. I hate all that solitude and quiet of the country. The way people there shut you off if you don't fit into their little perfect mold of how they think life should be." She shook her head. "No, Reed, I don't belong in Whistle Creek. I never did."

"Not always," he said. "There was a time when you loved that place."

When you loved me.

She took a sip of wine. "That was a long time ago, Reed. I was different then. You were different."

"Yeah, I was, wasn't I?" He'd been more gullible, more ready to believe in happily ever after. In the impossible.

Dora arrived with their food. The waitress chatted with them for a few minutes as she dropped off the plates of sandwiches, catching up on Reed's life, getting an introduction to Marietta.

By the time she was gone, Marietta was diving into her sandwich and the conversation had gone back into small talk territory. She made quick work of her meal, as if she couldn't wait to get out of there, and finished off her glass of wine, refusing a second. Clearly, there would be no tipsy mistakes, no wine-induced reunions or kisses.

And would he want her in his arms because of an alcoholic blur? No. If Marietta ever came back, Reed wanted it to be because she wanted him, not because a bottle of wine had distorted her judgment.

Marietta insisted on paying half the bill. "This isn't a date, Reed."

"Of course not," he said. "Two old friends catching up, right?"

"Yeah. That's all." But she turned away as she said it.

And he knew he should be glad, should leave it at that, but something inside him rebelled and wanted more. Wanted to push the issue, to see if maybe…

Maybe the tension he read between them wasn't from the years apart but from unfinished business. Doors that had never quite shut.

What would happen if he nudged that door open?

They called goodbye to Joe and left the restaurant.

Marietta frowned when she glanced out the wide windows and saw the storm still gusting. "It's still snowing."

"Mother Nature seems determined to give us a white Christmas." He grinned. "Or she's conspiring to keep you and me together."

"My client is going to freak. In fact—" she dug her cell phone out of her back pocket and sighed "—she's called me four times in the last hour. I bet reception was poor in that back corner and that's why I missed the calls." She started to dial, but Reed covered her hand.

"Let it go. Take a break. You look like you could use one."

She did, indeed, look tired. Faint shadows colored the pale skin beneath her eyes. Her smile seemed to sink, her shoulders sag. He wanted to take her home—not to his apartment in South Bend, but to Whistle Creek, to the one place where he'd last seen Marietta laugh—heck, the last place *he* could remember laughing.

Why was it whenever Reed thought of home, he still thought of Whistle Creek? And yet he'd so rarely gone back there? Had pushed it from his mind, focused on his career, let Whistle Creek become a stamp in his past.

Until now.

He looked at the woman whose hand he still held and knew why. Because it wasn't home without Marietta. Right now, all he wanted to do was scoop her up, take her back home, wrap one of his grandma's afghans around her, light a roaring fire and keep her with him until she had caught at least three good nights' sleep. Take care of her, because right now, Marietta looked very much like she needed someone to care.

She always had. But if there was one thing Marietta

excelled at, it was pretending everything was just fine, even as it fell apart around her.

"This is my job, Reed. I have to call her back." Marietta pulled away and dialed. An instant later, she was connected with someone on the other end, someone whose high-pitched voice carried all the way through the cell, enough that Reed could make out part of the conversation. "It's okay, Penny. I'm sure the storm will stop any time now. What do those weather people know anyway? Listen, take some deep breaths, calm down, and I'll call you the minute the storm lifts." She hung up, then let out a deep breath. "Penelope can be—"

"Exhausting?" Reed chuckled. "I got tired just listening to you deal with her. How did you end up working for a woman like that?"

"Penelope was the speaker at a bridal show in Chicago, part of a promotional tour for a romantic comedy she had a bit part in. This was before she was a star and before my business was much of a business. She stopped by my booth on her way to the restroom, fell in love with one of my designs, and we got to talking. Her next movie became a hit, *People* magazine did a spread on her wedding to Brock Wayne, who had been bachelor of the year or something, and they featured my dress." Marietta shrugged. "The rest was history. And one hell of a roller coaster ride."

"Is she always this demanding?"

Marietta laughed. "Most days she only calls me forty-five times. I've flown out to her house in L.A. for fifteen fittings, met her in ten different cities for other fittings and countless alterations. She's changed her mind fifty-two times, and just this week, moved up the wedding date by three days as a publicity stunt. But it's been worth it. She's paying a fortune for her dress, and the exposure for my company alone has made sales increase a hundred-fold. I'm so busy, I can barely breathe."

"And that's exactly what you wanted, right?"

"Of course."

But she said it too quick, too fast. He looked at her, wondering how happy she could be jetting all over the world instead of celebrating Christmas.

His gaze took in every inch of her, a face imprinted on his memory, as if Marietta had become a part of him—of his heart—a long time ago. Was it any wonder he'd never married, never even come close to loving another woman the way he'd loved her?

What if…she wasn't as happy as she claimed?

What if…there was still a chance for them?

What if…Reed took this opportunity, this serendipitous meeting—a sign from fate, to be sure—and played Clarence, pulled a little *It's a Wonderful Life*? Because if he didn't, and this storm lifted, he would always wonder exactly that—*what if?*

And Reed had already done enough second-guessing since she'd left to last a lifetime. "Come with me, Marietta. I have an idea."

"What are you talking about?"

"You said you're not going to get to celebrate Christmas because you have to travel. Then I say you do it here. Now. With me."

"Are you crazy? We can't celebrate Christmas in an airport. I mean, look at this place. It's depressing as heck." She gestured around the airport, crowded, filled with grumbling, grumpy passengers tired of the delay, the walls of gray and seats of blue, reflecting the mood in the room. None of it, as Marietta pointed out, seemed especially festive. "Reed, really, let me just grab a book, sit down and wait for the storm to stop."

"That's exactly why we should do this. Because this is no way to spend a holiday." He caught her wrist. It was the first time he'd really touched her—touched her skin, her warm, sweet, peach skin—since they'd run into each other again—grabbing her elbow for five seconds hadn't counted—and the connection seared his veins, raced heat from his fingertips to his heart. And then, it all rocketed back, every minute of their past together, rushing at him in one tidal force.

Reed inhaled, sharp, then steadied his gaze on hers. "Do you remember the cabin?"

Because he sure as hell did. If there was one thing that starred in Reed's dreams, it was the cabin. And the two Christmases he and Marietta had spent there.

The one when he gave his heart to her forever.

And the one when she broke it.

CHAPTER THREE

DID she remember the cabin?

Oh, yes, she did.

Late at night, when all was still in her apartment and her mind stopped churning through the millions of details awaiting her in the morning, and sought instead something to comfort, to calm her, the cabin appeared, like a homemade blanket. The image of the little building in the woods, part of Reed's family property, wrapped around her, bringing her back to the days when she didn't worry about the bottom lines on wedding dresses and balance sheets.

But it wasn't the logs forming the cabin walls, the fireplace that crackled and warmed the rooms, that she remembered the most. It was Reed. The nights they had spent there, curled up in the double bed, under a thick quilt, planning a future that had disappeared like a wisp of smoke when reality came crashing back to Marietta.

"I remember," she whispered, and her heart lurched.

"Do you remember the Christmas Day when we got stuck in the cabin? We'd trekked out there to—"

"Feed that orphaned fawn."

He smiled. "You remember."

"I don't run across helpless Bambis every day." But it wasn't the fawn that had stayed in her memory, or its mother, crushed by an overweight tree limb that had fallen after a storm. She'd never forget Reed rescuing the tiny animal from beneath its dying mother, then bundling it in his coat and carrying the skinny deer back to the cabin, warming it by the fire, hand-feeding it with a bottle. The two of them had journeyed out there every day for a week to tend to it, fretting over it like a baby.

"It started snowing early that morning, and we lost track of time, and before we knew it—"

"We were stuck," she finished. Stuck inside the cabin, though neither of them had minded. They'd been too busy talking to notice the storm blowing in, or the inches of snow stacking up outside the door. Marietta's mother and Reed's parents hadn't worried, figuring if the two of them were gone, it meant they were together.

So they'd built a fire in the fireplace. Heated up a can of soup, watched the fawn frolic outside before he'd finally taken his first steps into the woods and disappeared, apparently deciding he was going to be fine on his own. And then, left alone, Reed and Marietta—

"We should get going," Marietta said, the memory of the first time she and Reed had made love hitting her hard, stirring up emotions and a heat as powerful as that Christmas Day. Her hand flexed by her side, aching to touch him, to again know how his skin would feel beneath her palm. "Maybe, ah, check with the gate and see if anything has changed."

"Nothing has changed," Reed said, and Marietta read in his eyes a whole other conversation than one about flights.

"You've changed. You're a high-powered executive now."

"The kind of man you said you wanted."

The kind of man she'd thought she wanted, yes. And over the years since she'd left Whistle Creek, she'd met a hundred such men. But none of them had been Reed.

And now, for some crazy reason, she hated that Reed had become one of them—even if it had been exactly what she'd told him she'd wanted. The very reason she'd given for leaving him seven years ago.

But had it been a reason…or an excuse? A way out of that town? Away from a place that had been both a bane and a balm to her soul?

And now, seeing Reed, hearing the cynicism in his voice, seeing a side of him that she didn't recognize, she wondered—

Had she become like that too?

"We're going in two different directions now." She gestured out the window, toward the planes sitting on the tarmac, their wide-bellied bodies disappearing under the blanket of falling snow. "Literally."

"What if we'd gone in the same direction? What if you had stayed in Whistle Creek?"

"Oh, Reed. We've been through this."

He took her hand, ignoring the crowds around them, the people busy with their lives, their conversations about presents and Santa, Christmas plans and holiday wishes. Tucked in among the bursts of merriness were other rumblings of irritation and frustration, cries of bored children, people pacing and losing their temper with airline staff. Clearly, the storm was getting to everyone.

"I want you to pretend with me," Reed said, "just for today."

"I—"

"Don't tell me no. We're stuck here, for at least a few hours. What will it hurt to play the 'what if?' game?"

Her gaze met his and in that moment, Reed knew he had a chance. A shot at connecting again with her. The spark was still there, and he saw it, like a survivalist in the woods who had worked two sticks together and finally been rewarded with a puff of smoke. For today, he didn't want to think about how he was no longer the same man she had left behind. Or how much he wished he could go back to that cabin, to the days before that last Christmas, and take a different path.

For today, he wanted only to fan that last ember between them and see where the flame might lead. Take the *what if?*…and turn it into a *what could be.*

Because Reed knew if he let the spark go out now, it would disappear forever, caught in the wind of their busy lives.

And so, before she could say another word, Reed leaned down and kissed Marietta.

When Reed's lips met hers, the world spiraled wildly out of control, as if she'd hopped on in the middle of a carnival ride. Everything within her leapt to attention, memory snapping back, seven years dissolving in the space of a second.

Taking her back to that cabin, back in that bed, back in his arms.

He kissed her with the knowledge of a man who had savored her body before, who knew what made her tick. Who remembered that if he cupped her jaw and tipped her chin, he could make her melt. Who knew that when his tongue dipped inside to meet hers, they'd dance a tango of want, and her arms would snake up his back, drawing him closer, asking for more.

His fingers tangled in her hair and nerve endings she'd forgotten even existed sprang awake and ignited fire in her veins. Reed didn't just kiss her—

He made her feel like a precious gift.

And then he drew back, his lips leaving her long before his touch did. "I've missed you," he whispered. "I've never stopped thinking about you, Marietta."

"Reed, I've missed—" she began, caught up in the kiss, the long-buried emotions it had awakened.

Her cell phone rang, the tinny sound so jarring, she leapt back. Reed's hand dropped away, the spell broken. Marietta fumbled the phone out of her pocket. Saved by the Penelope bell.

"Marietta, I can't find Brock anywhere."

"I'm sure he's picking up his tux or something." Marietta turned away from Reed, from his searing blue eyes, eyes that seemed to see right through her. She focused instead on the airport, the crowds, the unhappy faces, the rising tide of grumbling that had replaced any lingering Christmas spirit. Reality, instead of fantasy.

"His mother called and said he never came home. I know it sounds awful for someone my age to be marrying a man who still lives with his mother but it's only until he gets back on his feet. He had a call-back on a pilot last week. And he's got royalties from a guest appearance on a sitcom when he was a kid." Penelope drew in a breath. "Marrying him will be a good thing, I'm sure. For both of us. He's fine with me being the more successful one. I think."

Marietta rubbed her temples. Penelope getting off track occurred with the frequency of stripes on candy canes. And yet, in Penelope's words, Marietta wondered if she heard a bit of her own life. Penelope, a woman in her thirties, who had put her career ahead of her love life for years. Was all this neediness, this continual reaching out to Marietta, a sign of regret on Penelope's part? And a few years down the road, would this be Marietta? Marietta shrugged off the thoughts. "Thanks for the résumé, but let's focus on the wedding, okay?"

"I'm trying to. But it's hard, Marietta. I'm not used to having all these doubts. In my career, everything has always been black and white but with this marriage…I'm not so sure."

Did Marietta hear cold feet? Or something more in Penelope's voice? Maybe it was just Brock being gone that had her celebrity bride so upset.

"Penny, he could have been out…" Marietta searched for a gentle way to put it "…celebrating."

"Do you really think that's all it is? That he hasn't changed his mind?"

"Of course not. Brock loves you. You're Penelope Blackburn. Why wouldn't he want to marry you?"

"Because…because…" A sniffle. "I'm high maintenance."

Penelope wasn't just high maintenance, she was the Mount Everest of maintenance, but Marietta kept that to herself. "Brock will be there, I'm sure."

"Okay. But what if…?" Penelope did a long inhale. "He changes his mind? What am I going to do? I already paid the caterer."

For the first time, Marietta wondered why Penelope Blackburn was really marrying Brock because she didn't hear love in her voice. Did Penelope feel like she'd waited so long, put her career first for so many years that she had to settle for less than everything? "Last week, didn't your psychic say Brock was—"

"Oh, that's the doorbell!" Immediately, Penelope's voice changed from doom and gloom to chipper as a magpie. "That's the manicurist. I better go. My French tips are chipped like you would not believe. Come here, Pixie, let's go get Momma's nails done."

And then Penelope was gone again, her crisis averted by a bottle of polish.

"How are things going with your bride?"

"She can't find her groom or her Cornish game hens, and her dress is stuck in Chicago, but at least she's getting her manicure."

"Ah, her priorities are in order."

Marietta laughed. "Too bad hers are on a different planet from anyone else's. Still, she's not so bad."

"Now, back to where we left off." He moved closer.

She put a hand on his chest. Still as solid as she remembered. Oh, how she wanted to touch him beneath the fabric of his shirt, to know once again what he'd feel like against her in bed, to curl up to his body, beneath that blanket, with nothing between them. But that would be a mistake. She didn't have time or room in her life for someone like Reed.

Because giving her heart to Reed, she already knew, meant giving all her heart. He didn't do things half-way, didn't take a relationship on a part-time basis. She'd been down that road with Reed before.

He was a man who put down roots, stayed in one place, believed in forever. She was a woman who had never stayed in one house, one home, long enough to hang her coat on the same hook twice or plant a garden two seasons in a row, or even bother to put her name on the mailbox.

She wasn't made for the kind of life that Reed wanted. Expected. In truth, she didn't even know how to live it.

If she got involved with him again, it would mean making space for a husband, a home, children, in a life already jammed with her business, her clients—

Just when it was all taking off, exploding around her.

"I can't, Reed. I can't go back to where we left off."

"Can't? Or won't?"

"My business is my life, Reed. I need to be there to nurture it. Don't you understand, right now I'm standing on the cusp of something amazing? With this deal—" she patted the garment bag "—my wedding gown designs have become nationally famous. I can have it all, if I play my cards right."

"Have the big office. The conglomerate. The money." His gaze met hers. "But no one to share it with. It must get awfully lonely at the top."

"I'm not lonely. I have friends. I go out."

But when had she last done that? When had she picked up the phone and called any of her friends? Gone for a girls' night out? When she got back to town, she vowed, she would do exactly that.

Reed took the garment bag from her again, draping it over his arm, then took her hand with his free one. "You really think that's the life you want?"

"Of course it is. It's what I always wanted."

"I've been living that life, Marietta, for the past few years, and I realize now it wasn't all it was cracked up to be. I think you pay a price on that climb to the top because you're too busy keeping your eyes on the highest rung of the ladder to see what you might have missed along the way."

"I'm not missing anything."

He arched a brow. "Really?"

She heard the slight sarcasm in his voice and for some reason, she thought of Penelope. "I'm not missing anything," Marietta repeated.

He just nodded. "Come on, let's pick up the *'what if's'* again."

She eyed him. "Reed…"

"There's nothing to do when you're stuck in an airport." He waved an arm toward the hundreds of passengers camped out in the seats and on the floor doing exactly that—nothing. "We may as well."

As Marietta opened her mouth to protest Reed cut her off by hauling her into a souvenir store. "We Wish You a Merry Christmas" played on the sound system, and one of the sales clerks was jauntily ringing sales wearing a bracelet made of bells, making her sound like a reindeer run amok. "What if," Reed said, bending down to whisper in Marietta's ear, "this gown was for you, and you were marrying me this Christmas?"

She started to speak, to argue, but he put a finger over her lip, silencing her.

"And what if, we were on our way home to Whistle Creek, Indiana, and we were stuck here with a little time to kill. So we stopped in this store and we decided to look around and buy something for our house."

She started to shake her head, then remembered the game. The reason she'd played it with him all those years ago. How it had helped her escape, to find a moment of peace in the chaos of her life, the jetting from house to house, back and forth between one new family after another and her mother.

Every time, it had worked. Every time, but one.

She took in a breath. Against her hip, she felt the bulge of her cell phone. The vibration of the phone ringing again. Penelope, undoubtedly, with another crisis. Marietta let it go unanswered, yet still she felt the tension of the last few days—weeks, months—in her shoulders. Her neck, her back. Everywhere.

Reed was right. Right now, she stood in the middle of a lake of chaos, an airport filled with bleakness.

What would it hurt to play along with his game? Just for a minute?

"Close your eyes, Marietta, and imagine. What if…?" His hand drifted over her face. Her eyes fluttered shut. "Now open them and tell me what you're buying for our house this Christmas. Our first Christmas as husband and wife."

Then he whispered a kiss along her neck, and for just a second, she was in that world, in his arms, and believing in Reed's magic too.

CHAPTER FOUR

REED had played with fire before. At seven, he'd found a pack of matches in the kitchen drawer. He'd taken them outside, along with some old newspapers and a few sticks of wood from the barn. He'd built himself a little fire in the firepit by the lake, even roasted a couple of marshmallows before his father found him, stomped out the flames and gave him a stern lecture about starting something when he didn't know how to finish it.

Today, Reed had just gone and done the same thing all over again. Lit a fire he wasn't sure he knew how to extinguish.

He stood behind Marietta, inhaling the soft jasmine fragrance of her perfume, wrapped as surely in her spell as he had been seven years ago, his heart hurting with want, his mind telling him he was taking a huge risk. Opening a wound it had taken him years to close.

"Those coffee mugs," she said.

He followed the direction of her finger, and saw two red mugs shaped like bulls—for the famous Chicago basketball team—and when put together, they butted heads. "Those?"

"Yep." A teasing smile lit her face. "They remind me of us."

Hope bubbled up in Reed's chest. She was playing along.

"I think only one of us is stubborn. Who refused to ask for directions when we got lost on the way to the prom?"

"Hey, you were behind the wheel."

"And contrary to stereotype, *I* wanted to stop at a gas station and ask where the hall was located." Reed picked up the mugs, handing one to Marietta. He turned it around in his palm, giving her a grin. "You really want these to be our first purchase?"

"What better way to start our day than by—" she tapped her mug to his "—knocking heads?"

"Ah, romance at its finest." He took the mug out of her hand and started weaving his way through the crowded store.

"What are you doing?"

"Buying them."

"You can't do that. We're just pretending."

"Then I'll return them next time I'm in Chicago." He turned and faced her. "But this Christmas, Marietta, let's pretend this is real. That we're going home to the house on Winterberry Lane. Not to Los Angeles or Boston. That we're together and buying these for us."

"Even though there are thousands of people here and—"

"And you're going west and I'm going east and the chances of running into each other again are nil." He put the mugs on the counter and pulled out his wallet. "Yes."

The sales clerk rang up the sale, her Santa hat bouncing with the movement, the jingle bells on her wrist singing a song. "Here you go. Merry Christmas."

"Merry Christmas." He waved off the receipt. Despite what he'd told Marietta, he had no intentions of ever returning the mugs. He'd drink his morning roast out of these for the next twenty years and remember this day. Together they exited the crowded shop. "Now, tell me what our house looks like."

"Reed, we shouldn't play this game. Besides, that house is probably long gone."

"It's still there, Marietta. Just waiting for some family to come along and fill it with memories."

"It's still there?" she repeated, so softly he almost didn't hear her. "No one ever bought it?"

"No." He didn't meet her eyes. Because then she'd see that he'd lied.

Why tell Marietta? Marietta wouldn't hop in a car, drive the three and a half hours to Whistle Creek, walk into the town clerk's office and demand to see the deed for 321 Winterberry Lane.

"Reed—"

He could hear her slipping back into reality again. "Come on, Marietta. What else are you going to do right now? Battle some elderly woman's cane for her seat? Tell me. Tell me about the house. What would you do with it?"

"You've heard that a thousand times."

"Tell me again."

A heartbeat passed. Another. Then—

"If I owned that house," Marietta said, falling into step beside Reed as they walked along the concourse, making their way among the crowds, her voice softening, slipping into the past, "I'd paint the fence white. Plant pink impatiens every spring. Hang green shutters and matching window boxes." She turned to him. "I always wanted window boxes."

"I know," Reed said. They'd talked about the house a hundred times when they'd been dating. Walked past it every day on the way home from school. And then, after he'd proposed and for that brief winter when she'd worn his ring, they'd even thought of buying it, of living there together, but then Marietta had given back the ring, and made it clear she wanted no part of Whistle Creek or him. And the idea of window boxes had disappeared like rain on a hot pavement.

Reed thought of his apartment in South Bend. Tenth floor. A great view of the city, but not a great place for a window box.

"And I'd paint the kitchen—" Her cell phone rang, breaking the spell. Marietta slipped back into work mode, the woman he'd once known erased as easily as a misspelled word. "Marietta Westmore."

Reed could hear the harried bride through the earpiece. He groaned inwardly, tempted to rip the phone away and tell Penelope Blackburn where she could put her celebrity crises.

"Penny, I'm sure Brock will turn up soon. No, I don't think it's a bad sign that one of the country club's swans died this morning. Swans die from bad…swan food. And eating bad fish." She threw her hands up and made a what-do-I-know? face at Reed. "The storm, well…" Marietta looked out the window.

Snow still fell steadily. On the TV screens hanging above the seating areas, the weather forecasters showed a grim, green monster of a storm moving across Illinois. Reed watched it inch northeast—up and away from Chicago. Soon, the snow would stop.

And Marietta would be gone.

"I'm sure the storm will lift," Marietta said, injecting a false note of hope into her voice.

And when it did, Reed would head to Boston, to a meeting that had probably already begun without him. For the first time since he'd started working at Bennett Financial, the thought of missing an important meeting, the likelihood of losing a big account, didn't bother him at all.

He'd spent three years allowing numbers to dictate his

mood—stock tickers, client investments, calendar dates. This Christmas—this day—he wasn't going to live by any numbers.

Instead, he'd act as if at the end of the day he was going to drive to Whistle Creek, put those mugs in the kitchen cabinets at 321 Winterberry Lane, and then curl up by the fire with Marietta beside him. As if they'd wake up on Christmas Eve, buy the biggest Douglas Fir they could find, and decorate it with popcorn and cranberry garlands and orange-and-clove balls. As if he'd go to bed that night and finally wake up on Christmas morning with the only present he'd ever really wanted.

Marietta.

Today, Reed Hartstone decided to pretend *what if?* had really happened. And maybe, just maybe, he could make Marietta believe it too.

It took some doing, but after a good ten minutes Marietta had Penelope under control again—or as close to under control as the high-strung actress got. She hung up the phone, let out a long sigh and crossed to one of the windows. Away from Reed.

The snow had slowed to a trickle. Finally. Crews were busy clearing the runways, deicing the planes.

Maybe Reed was right and Mother Nature had conspired to keep them together. Hadn't she done it once before? Either way, the conspiracy had come to an end.

And just in time too. She needed to get back to work. To real life, not this fantasy world conjured up in her head.

Reed came up behind her. Marietta could sense him as easily as she could a change in temperature, a shift in the wind. Beside her, a mother sat on the floor with her children, singing "Rudolph the Red-Nosed Reindeer," making her toddler laugh at his mother's spirited rendition.

Reed's arms stole around her waist. She leaned into him, into his strength, the solidity of him, even though she knew she shouldn't. She'd left Whistle Creek—and Reed—for a reason.

And that reason hadn't gone away.

"What if…those were our children?" he whispered in her ear. "And—"

She spun out of his grasp. "And what if they weren't? What if this little game of yours had gone down the road you wanted and I was desperately unhappy, Reed? Why is that never the scenario?"

"What are you talking about?"

"We were never meant to go beyond what we had in that cabin," she said, her voice low, and even still a dozen heads had swiveled in their direction, eavesdropping without shame. One woman detailing her Christmas list on a cell phone even paused in her conversation to listen to Marietta.

Reed pulled her to the side, away from the gawkers. "How can you say that? We had plans, Marietta. We were going to get married."

"That would have never worked. We were living in a fairy tale."

"You think the life you lived would have made you a terrible wife, an awful mother? Sometimes, bad things just happen, sweetheart." He took a step closer to her, his gaze tight on hers, not allowing escape. "How long are you going to make yourself pay for one night?"

One second, that was all she could hold the connection, and then she had to look away, tears burning at the back of her eyes, her throat thick. "I'm not."

"Bull. You've been lying to yourself, lying to me, for years."

Marietta sucked in a breath and faced him again. "And

maybe you're the one who's been lying to himself about how well you know me, Reed. I'm not that girl from Whistle Creek anymore. Maybe I never was."

She stalked off, the garment bag banging against her legs, her ankle beginning to throb again. She needed to sit, rest the sprain or twist, whatever it was, but there still wasn't any available seats.

What she really wanted, though, was to escape the Utopia portrait Reed kept trying to paint, the picture she used to dream of too as she was shuffled from one house to another by a well-meaning judge who believed Marietta's mother would eventually get her act together. Every time, Marietta would get her hopes up, because she'd seen that perfect life in Reed's family, seen it symbolized in the house on Winterberry Lane.

She hoped and hoped, until one night when she realized that perfect world was all an illusion, that one swipe of a wet brush would make the watercolors run, blurring them into something unrecognizable.

"Marietta, wait!"

She pivoted back. "No, Reed. I can't do this anymore."

"Why?"

"This is temporary. Tomorrow, we'll both be back to our regular lives and this storm, this whole day, will be only a memory." She gave him a smile, but it hurt her lips. "Two friends who ran into each other in an airport."

"That's all this was?" His hand came up and cupped her jaw and every ounce of Marietta wanted to lean into that touch, to close her eyes and give herself up to Reed, to the man who had loved her in a cabin in the woods, and who had once held her heart and promised her forever.

Until she'd learned forever never lasted. That she was better suited for a life away from that town.

Marietta drew in a breath, one, long, hard breath, and reached up, tugging his hand away. She held on for just a second, his large palm in hers, strong and secure, then released him. "Yes. That's all."

"Don't, Marietta." His ocean-blue eyes met hers, and in their stormy depths, she saw seven years of hurt. "I can't lose you twice."

His voice splintered and Marietta almost caved right then. "You never really had me to begin with, Reed."

Then Marietta walked away, for the second time in her life lying to Reed because she knew it was the best thing for both of them.

CHAPTER FIVE

REED watched Marietta walk away and told himself letting her leave was the best thing he could do. He couldn't exactly throw her over his shoulder cave-man style and drag her back to Whistle Creek, hold her hostage until she fell in love with him again.

Even if half of him actually considered that a good idea.

"She'll be back," said a voice beside him.

Reed turned to find an old man sitting in one of the chairs. He wore a Santa hat, green plaid shirt and even, God help him, elf shoes. "I don't think so."

The old man patted the hand of the elderly woman beside him, who wore a matching fur-trimmed hat. She'd fallen asleep in her wheelchair. The man smiled at her for a moment, then drew the knitted afghan on her lap up to her chin. "I know because my Elsie here did the same thing to me once. She turned me down flat when I proposed. Three times too. But I kept at it, and we've been married fifty-two years this January."

Reed smiled. "Congratulations."

"You know what it takes?" The man leaned forward and the white ball on his Santa hat bounced forward, dinging against his forehead. "A lot of patience. Women are…difficult. Half the time I have no idea what Elsie is thinking, but I keep on keeping on because I love her, you know what I mean?"

Reed chuckled. "Yeah, I think I do."

The man rose with the slow movements of someone who now lived with caution, taking only a step away from his wife, leaving his bulky winter coat in his chair. "Suppose I should introduce myself if I'm going to tell you my life story." He put out his hand and the two of them shook. "Jeremiah Wilson. Elsie and I are flying to Topeka to spend Christmas with the kids and grandkids." He glanced at his wife, his face softening. "Our last trip, though I haven't told her that."

"Reed Hartstone," Reed replied, wondering about the man's comment, but not intruding to ask. "I'm supposed to be on a flight to Boston for a meeting but—" He glanced at his watch. Half past four. "They probably wrapped it up without me."

Jeremiah gestured toward Reed's cell phone. "You gonna call them? See what you missed?"

"In a minute." Reed watched the sea of people in the direction Marietta had gone, but the crowd had long since swallowed her up. "I'm not in the mood for a verbal lashing right now."

Jeremiah chuckled. "I hear you. I've been retired for twenty years. Used to be in management myself. Now I get to be home with my Elsie every day. Nothing better in the world than that." He gazed at his wife, the affection he had for her as clear as a crystal ball. "To me, love is a lot like Christmas trees."

"Christmas trees?" Reed raised a dubious brow.

"Yep. Think about it. You get one image of your tree in your mind. All pretty and glittery. Star on top, the whole nine yards. Then you go out and buy the tree, get it home and the damn needles start dropping on the floor before you even hang a single ornament. The star is lopsided. Every other light goes out on the blasted string. Am I right?"

Reed chuckled. "I've had a few of those trees."

"You start thinking that your tree is nothing like what you expected." Jeremiah turned toward his wife, who slept on, unaware of her husband's conversation. He continued, his voice a little softer now. "But when you look closer at that tree, that star, those lights, you see it's beautiful in all its imperfection. All that trouble you went to, to put it up, get it working, why it made you appreciate your Christmas. If you'd had that perfect tree, you might have looked at it once, twice, then forgot all about it. But this one, the difficult one, it needed care, attention. Watering every day. A little pruning here and there, a good eye, a loving hand." He returned to his seat, curving his arm over his wife's shoulders. "And oh, how that's worth it, down the road, Reed. Worth more than all the money in Fort Knox."

A lump clogged Reed's throat, brought on by the mistiness in Jeremiah's eyes and an envy for the love he had, the way his wife, his marriage, had so clearly brought his life full circle, filled it with a depth Reed had never known.

What if Reed had done more to make things work between him and Marietta all those years ago? Would he be watching her leave on a plane to Los Angeles right now or be taking her home with him?

"That's good advice," Reed said. "You're a smart man, Mr. Wilson."

"Eh, wisdom comes with the wrinkles."

"You said this is your last trip to Topeka. Do you mind me asking why?"

Jeremiah's gaze went to some far-off spot. He remained silent for a long while, the only sounds the soft murmur of other people's conversations, the movement of feet down the concourse, the ringing of registers in the shops near them. Reed regretted asking the question, and was about to apologize and take it back when Jeremiah drew in a long, heavy breath. "I'm dying. Cancer. That devil came back, and he ain't letting go this time. I haven't had the heart to tell Elsie. I'm taking her to Topeka and we're staying. Moving in with the kids, so she'll have somebody to watch after her, make sure she takes care of herself, when I'm gone." His hand covered his wife's, protective as a shield.

The wind sucked out of Reed's lungs. He barely knew this man, and yet, he felt a sorrow so strong, he nearly cried. "I'm…I'm sorry."

"It's okay." Jeremiah's smile crinkled around his eyes. "We've had lots of years together, me and Elsie. You know what I said about Christmas trees? Under the tree there are presents too. Every day with the woman you love is a gift. And I've had so many with Elsie." He reached forward and grasped Reed's wrist. "You find that woman, Reed. You find her before it's too late. Because in the end, like I said, it's all worth it. It's worth everything." He placed a tender kiss on his wife's forehead.

Elsie stirred, then awoke, blinking against the light. "Is it time to go?"

"Almost, my dear, almost." Then Jeremiah cradled his wife against him, as tender and secure as a knight guarding a treasure.

Reed gave him a smile of thanks, mouthed "Merry Christmas," then walked away, his vision blurred.

But his head a hell of a lot clearer.

Marietta sat down against the wall by gate C-31, draping the garment bag carefully over her lap. The monitors above her were starting to flash a few departure times, and she'd seen one flight take off a second ago. Airline staff began to move around behind the counter. It seemed as if the flight to Los Angeles might get under way soon.

Then why did she feel so miserable? Why did she keep looking out the window, hoping for another snowstorm? It was simply the day catching up with her, that was all.

"Ladies and gentlemen, we're pleased to announce that United Flight 115 to Los Angeles will begin boarding shortly. We thank you for your patience." A collective cheer went up from the crowd around Marietta.

She rose, clutching the dress. She had a first class ticket, one of the few luxuries she'd indulged in when she'd gotten the downpayment for Penelope's dress, which meant she'd be one of the first to board. Marietta fished out her boarding pass from her pocket, then made her way over to the counter, every step seeming to weigh more than the one before.

She glanced over her shoulder. What, was she thinking Reed would make some last-ditch effort to convince her to stay?

And what would she say if he did?

She'd say no. Just as she had before. She and Reed had always been moving in two different directions. He wanted the one thing she couldn't give him—commitment, permanence. A life, a home, a family. He believed in the very things she'd learned not to count on.

Her cell phone rang again. Marietta rolled her eyes, then flipped it open. At this point, it'd be a blessing when the pilot ordered all passengers to turn off electronic devices. "Hi, Penelope."

"How'd you know it was me?"

"Guess I'm getting a little psychic too. What's up now?"

"I think Brock is getting cold feet and…well, I might be too."
Penelope sighed. "I was hoping you could talk me into this."

"Penny, no one should have to talk you *into* marriage, you
know that. If it's the right thing to do, you'll know in your
heart." Or not do, Marietta thought. That was why she'd
broken it off with Reed all those years ago.

But hadn't she had a few doubts then too? A voice in her
head saying this was the wrong choice? That there was a way
to work things out?

She'd quieted that voice with the practical, sensible side.
The math that added up to Reed wanting to stay in Whistle
Creek, farm his family's land, and her wanting a fast-paced
career, one that she couldn't find in the small town. Their
paths had lain in two different directions then—

And clearly, still did.

"I don't know what my heart says," Penelope said. "My
publicist says this is a really good opportunity for me. And that
dress is so pretty. I can't wait to wear it."

Marietta pulled the phone away from her ear and stared
at it for a second. She had *not* heard Penelope say that, had
she? "Did you just say that you're getting married to Brock
because this is good for your career and because you *like
the dress?*"

"Marietta, I didn't get to where I am in Hollywood by
making stupid business decisions. When Brock proposed, I
had to look at all angles."

Marietta wanted to scream. She had spent six months of
her life slaving over this wedding dress, dealing with a client
who called her four thousand times a day, changed her mind
twice as much, and most of all, Marietta had invested her heart
into this design, and this was the reason Penelope gave for

getting married? "You're really not getting married because you love Brock?"

"He's handsome, good in bed, but do I love him? Well, I guess. Yes." But her voice kind of shook on that last syllable, and Marietta suspected Penelope would flunk a love polygraph.

"And this dress…?"

"Was all about making me the star," Penelope said. "I picked you as the designer because you had the skills to create something that would get me on a magazine cover. I couldn't just wear any dress. You don't understand Hollywood weddings, Marietta. It's all about the show."

"No, Penny, you don't understand," Marietta said, forcing herself not to shout, her frustration with Penelope bubbling over into anger. "I don't design dresses for brides who think marriage has an expiration date, Penny."

"Hey, that's not very nice."

"I'm sorry, but it's the truth. These dresses mean too much to me and I can't sell you this one."

"What? How can you do that? It's *my* dress!"

Marietta knew she should pull back, rewind the verbal tape, but she couldn't. "No, it's mine, until I hand it over to you and as far as I'm concerned, you shouldn't be wearing a wedding dress like this if you're getting married to promote a movie and get your face plastered on the supermarket stands. This is the kind of dress a woman wears to marry a man she loves."

Stunned silence on the other end.

"We'll now begin boarding our first class passengers for United Flight 115 to Los Angeles," the woman at the gate announced into a microphone. "Please have your boarding pass ready."

Marietta glanced at the ticket counter. Then at her boarding pass. Half a country away, she'd just put herself out of business.

What was she thinking? Marietta drew in a breath. Swallowed back the sour taste of regret.

She was about to apologize and get on the plane when she heard the soft sounds of Penelope crying.

Oh, damn. Shoot me now.

Why hadn't she just kept her mouth shut? Flown to L.A., dropped off the dress and gone on her merry way? What did she care about why Penelope Blackburn—or anyone else for that matter—was getting married?

"Penny? You okay?"

A sniffle. A sob. Then a loud, honking nose-blowing. "No…yeah."

"I'm sorry. I never should have said any of that. It's all this being stuck in the airport and the snow and—"

"Stop, Marietta. Just stop apologizing because—" Penelope sighed. "You're right."

"Penny, really, I was mean and I, oh, damn, I feel really bad."

"Don't, I'm serious." Penelope drew in a breath. "Listen, no one around here ever tells me the truth. I'm like a poodle. They get me what I want whenever I want it, make me look pretty and ooh and ahh all day about how amazing I am. After a while, you start to think that everything is all about you."

Marietta bit her lip so she wouldn't agree too readily. "I can see where that would happen."

"And when people started telling me marrying Brock Wayne was a smart move, well, I kind of looked at it like I was Marie Antoinette, you know? She married that Louis guy because it was good for the French or something."

"It didn't end so well for her, though," Marietta said.

"Marriages of convenience or politics or even careers, aren't always a good idea. If ever."

"How smart is getting married for love? I look around me and people out here are breaking up all the time. This way, I thought at least I'd have my career if things didn't work out with Brock."

Coming from Penelope, all that practicality sounded so…sad. So empty.

Getting married for love *was* taking a risk. Opening your heart to someone and hoping they wouldn't break it.

Marietta had done that once—and then done the breaking up before it could be done to her, because she'd seen the writing on the wall, and decided to head off the train wreck while she could still see the break in the tracks.

But would Reed have broken her heart? What if she hadn't left him? Could they have found a way to make it work? To somehow marry her city ambitions with his small-town roots?

"That's the chance you take when you get married," Marietta said, though even as she said it, she wondered what kind of wisdom she had on the topic.

"But you," Penelope said, "you must believe in happy endings. Because you make wedding dresses for a living."

Marietta glanced at the garment bag in her arms. "Me? Penny, I haven't dated anyone in the last year. Haven't fallen in love since—"

Since Reed. The thought of him sucked the air right out of her. She glanced up, half expecting—half hoping—he'd be there.

But he wasn't.

"Then why are you making wedding dresses?"

Why was she? Marietta held the heavy gown to her chest, hearing the rustle of the faux and real diamonds inside, the whisper of the satin, all of it sounding almost as if the dress were talking to her. Every one of the dresses she had crafted over the years did exactly that, with each stitch, each bead, each piece of embroidery. They told their story, whispered a tale, and she worked it into the design.

"I guess I still believe, deep inside, that it's possible," Marietta said softly. "That the fairy tale can work out. Somehow. For all of us."

Penelope sighed. "Even for me?"

"Even for you. But you have to marry for love, Penny. Not to help boost opening day sales."

Marietta glanced at the monitors and saw the flight departures flash one after another, planes leaving in a parade of numbers and letters.

And then, beside the one to Boston, Reed's flight, she watched it change from BOARDING to CLOSED, and then a moment later, the flight was gone. And with it, her heart sank.

"You know, when I was a little girl, I used to dream of a wedding with Mr. Right," Penelope said. "The white dress, the flowers, the whole fantasy. He'd look at me with stars in his eyes and I'd look at him the same way. Why does that dream go away when you grow up? Why did I let it go?"

"I don't know," Marietta said. "I wish I did."

"You're right. I know you are. I can't marry Brock. I need to find someone I love. I still want that dream and I think I should hold out for something better. Something real." Penelope let out another sigh. "But what am I going to tell everyone? I mean, I already paid for the reception and the cake and the flowers. Everything."

"Make it a movie launch party." Marietta forced cheer into her voice. "Call it a publicity stunt. You're Penelope Blackburn. I know you can pull something amazing off."

Across the continent, a not-as-high-maintenance-anymore actress laughed. "Yeah, I am, aren't I? And besides, I'm paying for it. I can call it whatever I want. And who knows? Maybe Mr. Right will be the one serving the cake. Then I can have my cake and eat it too, just like Marie Antoinette."

Then Penelope was gone, leaving Marietta with a wedding dress in her arms.

And nowhere to go.

CHAPTER SIX

IT TOOK Reed five seconds to realize he was an idiot. He watched his plane depart, not even caring, because by that time, he was running down the concourse to Gate C-31, hoping to get there before Marietta boarded her plane, all the while thinking this was some scene out of a movie and all he needed was a director to cue the music for a teary reunion.

But what he got instead was a closed door and a plane taxiing away from the gate.

And no Marietta.

"Damn!" He spun around, but didn't see her anywhere. The airport was still crowded, backed-up travelers camped out everywhere, a sea of Christmas festivity. Now that the storm had lifted, so too had people's spirits and he could hear a happy hubbub of voices chatting about travel plans, connecting with loved ones. A few people had even started singing Christmas carols, creating an impromptu choir in the corner.

He sank into one of the empty chairs at the gate and flipped open his cell phone. He'd called work as soon as it looked like his flight might be delayed, but then turned the phone off the minute he'd seen Marietta, knowing at that moment that there'd been nothing more important in his life than reconnecting with her. But now she was gone, and whether he liked it or not, he had a job that he needed to return to. A life.

Either way, he was going to track Marietta down. And by Christmas or New Year's—whatever it took, someday very soon, he'd be on her doorstep once again. Regardless of what Marietta Westmore might have said, Reed had no intentions of letting her go again.

The cell phone let out a trill as it powered on, then a series of beeps announcing voice mails. The office. Reed called in, connected with his boss and sat back against the chair, prepared for a lecture.

"Reed! Where have you been? I've been trying to reach you all day."

"Stuck in Chicago, Don. How'd the meeting in Boston go?"

"They loved your proposal. Looks like we signed another new client, thanks to you. You're a real asset to this company, even when you're not in the right state." Don chuckled. "Before you know it, you'll be a partner here. That should be happy news for your Christmas."

Ambition. Lofty goals. Those had never really gone hand in hand with Reed Hartstone. All his life, he'd wanted nothing more than to follow in his father's footsteps and work the Hartstone land in Whistle Creek. He'd fallen into a financial career because he'd had to, and found himself advancing because he had a knack for numbers.

But had he been happy?

Content. Satisfied. Yes, but happy? No.

He sat in a hard plastic chair in a busy airport, replaying the day with Marietta, his mind combing over the decisions he'd made, searching the memories of the last seven years, grasping for the last time that he'd felt true happiness.

And like a broken record, his mind kept returning to the very same destination.

"So," Don went on, "when you get back in the office after the holiday, we'll start strategizing for the Howe account. There's a big piece of the pie available there too, and I'm sure with your—"

"No," Reed said.

"What?"

"I said no. I won't be there after the holiday."

"You need some time off? Hey, I understand. You work like a dog. When was the last time you took a vacation? Got some sun? You need a week on a beach with a gorgeous girl. Go ahead—take the week, go down to Jamaica or something. The Howe account will be there after New Year's."

"I meant I'm not coming back at all."

"Have we got a faulty connection? Because I thought you just said you were quitting."

"I am," Reed said, the decision final now and feeling so right, it nearly exploded in his chest. How could it have taken this long for him to make it? "I'm going home, Don, to Whistle Creek. Going to open my own business. A small one, nothing fancy, but something more my style."

"Are you nuts?" Don's voice exploded through the phone, so loud a few of the people near Reed turned to stare. "You have a future made of gold here, Reed. Why on earth would you throw it away to go live in the middle of nowhere?"

Reed smiled. "Exactly for that reason. Because it's the middle of nowhere and because—" he held up the paper bag with the two coffee mugs in it, hearing them clink together as he did "—I need a shelf."

"You're not making sense, Reed."

"For the first time in a long time, I'm making perfect sense." He rose, his chest light and full of something he dared to call hope. "You have a Merry Christmas. And, Don, when you pick out your Christmas tree, make sure you get the one that needs the most work."

Then Reed hung up and headed out of the airport.

Finally on his way home.

Marietta was crazy.

She'd hurried out of the terminal and on her way out, paid too much for a Chicago Bulls winter coat in the airport, because she hadn't really had anything warm with her—a winter coat wouldn't have been a necessity in Los Angeles—and then paid an even more ridiculous sum for a last-minute rental car. She'd called information, gotten the number for Reed's office in South Bend, and left him a voice mail, with her cell phone number, but he was probably somewhere over New Jersey right now, on his way to Boston.

And either way, not talking to her.

So she drove. She picked up a map at the car rental desk, used it negotiate the tangled web of Chicago's roads, and then found she knew the rest of the way by heart, by instinct, navigating along the toll road, and then down the Indiana highways that brought her through farm country and finally, in the dark of night, to Whistle Creek.

The old mill still stood at the entrance to the town, a welcoming beacon into the past. She slowed the sedan, headlights winking off the water wheel, glinting on the frozen creek. The tires clacked over the wooden bridge, then went silent when she hit the paved roads of downtown.

The town was buttoned up tight. It was, after all, past ten.

The night before Christmas Eve. Even Ernie's Bar was quiet. In Whistle Creek, people spent Christmas with their families, not chugging back beers with their buddies.

Marietta reduced her speed, not because she worried about getting a ticket—chances were even Paulie, the town cop, was home with his family—but because the sight of the town hit her harder than she'd expected. Her chest tightened, her throat clogged and something burned behind her eyes. Years of memories washed over her, coming in one big tidal wave.

How normal Whistle Creek looked, when her childhood here had been the opposite of normal. She'd bounced back and forth between foster families, the anomaly in a sea of two-parent, two-car garages. But as Marietta drove, the resentment she'd felt as an outsider disappeared. Instead, an odd feeling of nostalgia settled over her, giving way to—

Fondness. As if her heart had softened with the new-fallen snow dusting Whistle Creek's friendly shop fronts and narrow streets.

"It's beautiful," Marietta whispered to herself. Garlands swung between the light posts, joined at each juncture by bright red bows. Wreaths hung over the doorways, tiny white lights twinkled in the skinny bare trees lining the sidewalks. Every shop window had a holiday greeting, a bright red "Merry Christmas" or a cheery gold "Happy Holidays!"

Only one window glowed, almost beckoning her to come and visit. Cindy's Diner. Of course. Marietta smiled, then pulled over in front of the restaurant and stopped the car. She got out, peeking in the windows. The interior was still lit, and she wondered if maybe—

And then Cindy herself came around the counter, caught sight of the face peering in through the glass. The older woman's jaw dropped in surprise and she touched a hand to her gray bun, then her mouth, before bursting into action. Before Marietta could move, Cindy had hurried across the shop, opened the door and drew Marietta in with a tight, warm hug. She held her for a long time, making up for years of absence. "You came home!"

In the welcoming embrace of a friend so close she'd nearly been a grandmother, Marietta did, indeed, feel welcomed. "I stopped in for a visit."

"Well, come on in for some coffee and pie. And lots of catching up." Cindy nearly hauled Marietta into the shop, pulled her over to a stool at the counter and had a piece of chocolate silk pie and decaf coffee in front of her in seconds. "I was just cleaning up, about to go home, and then, what do I see, but a ghost from the past? It's about time I saw you in person instead of talking to you over the phone. What brings you to town?"

Marietta considered lying. But what good had that ever done? Besides, if anyone would understand—would know Marietta—it was Cindy. "Reed. I ran into him today."

"Reed? *Hartstone?* Where did you see him?"

"In Chicago of all places. We got stuck at the airport together. And seeing him brought up lots of unfinished memories."

"That man is handsome on a stick. If I was forty years younger…" Cindy grinned. "He's still available, from what his mother says."

"He is." Marietta forked up a piece of pie. "This is awesome. You still are the best cook in Whistle Creek."

"Don't go changing the subject by trying to butter me up with compliments." Cindy chuckled. "Even if they're well deserved." She leaned forward on the counter. "Now tell me all about Reed and why seeing him has you here. Because last I heard, wild horses couldn't have dragged you back to this town."

"That's because I was too busy riding one out of here." Marietta pushed away her plate, crossed her hands in front of her. It was well past time she faced what she'd left behind if she ever hoped to move past it. "I thought after my mother died, that I'd be better off leaving this place. That I'd be happier somewhere else."

"Oh, sweetie, I know it was hard on you living here. You were always back and forth, practically living out of a suitcase." Cindy laid a hand on Marietta's. "*Were* you happier away from here?"

"I thought I was. Until I saw Reed."

"A man'll do that, if you love him." Cindy's gaze filled with concern. "Do you?"

"I don't know. I mean, it could just be Christmas melancholy or not enough sleep or—"

"Or love," Cindy finished. "Face it, sweetie, you have loved that man since the first day you met him. Even though you've had it rough, it doesn't mean you don't get to have the Cinderella ending, you know. If you want it."

Marietta sighed. "That's the problem. I don't know what I want. Twenty-four hours ago, I had my life all planned out, then I run into Reed, and I start to wonder…"

"Wonder what?"

"What might have been." Marietta pushed her empty plate aside. "I ran away from this town, Cindy. I told Reed it was about my career, but it was more than that. And I'm back because I realized that I can't move forward until I deal with what I left behind here, and why I left it."

Cindy took the empty pie plate and coffee cup away and

dumped them into the dishpan. "Well, it's about time, honey." She gave her a kind smile, one filled with support. "Speaking of old things, I have something for you. Hold on a minute. It's out back." Cindy disappeared into the back room and when she came back, she blew a bit of dust off a small package. "This was left here, a long time ago."

Marietta turned the small box over in her palm. Wrapped in dark green paper, it had only a simple card with her name, nothing more, no indication of what it was or who had given it to her. "Who left it for me?"

Cindy shrugged, busy rinsing the mug. "I, ah, don't really remember."

Marietta gave the box a second look, then tucked it into the top of her purse. Right now, she had bigger things on her mind than mysterious boxes from unknown people. It was probably nothing—over the years, kindly neighbors and teachers had left gifts with Cindy when they weren't sure what house Marietta was living in, to give the little girl a bit of a Christmas. It was probably left over from that time.

"Anyway, I've got a lot of thinking to do, some old haunts to visit. And then…" She sucked in a breath. "I don't know where Reed and I will go…if anywhere."

"I know you, sweetie, and you'd rather climb a telephone pole than deal with the hard stuff. I'm proud of you for doing this." Cindy came around the counter and drew Marietta into a hug. "Honey, you deserve happiness. And you especially deserve a good Christmas." Cindy pulled back and wagged a finger at her. "And don't you go skipping out of town before you get a proper holiday. I'm willing to bet you haven't had a good Christmas in years. Every time I invited you down here you've always had one excuse or another why you couldn't come. So no more begging off. You're here in the flesh and I expect you to show up with your jingle bells on."

Marietta's smile tasted bittersweet. Cindy always had thought of her at Christmas, even when she'd been a little girl. "You're right."

"Then be at my house bright and early Christmas morning. My husband, my kids and my grandkids will all be there. Them and their dogs, and Lord knows what else. We're going to have a ham, mashed potatoes, and a lot of craziness. And pies, of course."

Marietta laughed. "Well then, count me in."

Cindy gave her a warm smile. "You know there's always a place at my table for you."

"Thank you, Cindy." She gave her a quick hug, one that said more than Marietta could manage with her heart so full, then left the diner. One hurdle had been conquered, but the biggest one had yet to be touched.

Reed opened the door, expecting a miracle.

He didn't know why he had. Maybe because it was Christmas, only an hour until Christmas Eve, and he'd watched way too many Christmas movies when he was a kid. But when he had pulled up to the cabin and seen tire tracks in the snow, he'd thought maybe—

But the small building was dark inside. Cold. No one had been here for days. Weeks, probably. The tire tracks were likely from some hunter's truck, or someone who'd come to cut down their own Christmas tree.

Not from Marietta, transported here by magic elves, or Santa himself, from Los Angeles to the cabin in the woods.

Nope, there was no one here but him.

He shook off the cold, crossed the room to the fireplace and took a few minutes to build a fire with the supply of kindling and newspapers kept by the hearth. After a few minutes, he fed in a couple of logs, then sat back and warmed his hands.

Despite the fire, the candles he'd lit, the warmth spreading throughout the room, the cabin had lost its magic. It felt about as cozy and welcoming as a meat locker. Reed rose. What had he been thinking?

He was about to put out the fire and go back to South Bend when he heard a sound outside, a rustling that could be an animal, but Reed had a feeling wasn't. He shrugged on his coat and slipped out the cabin door, sliding around the side of the building toward the woods.

It took a second for his eyes to adjust to the darkness and then his breath caught, held. He didn't dare exhale.

Because standing under the iridescent curtain of the moonlight on the crust of new snow, was Reed's miracle.

CHAPTER SEVEN

"Did you hitch a ride on Santa's sleigh?"

Marietta turned. The stars reflected in her eyes, and Reed dared to hope. "No room. Those elves are pretty territorial."

He laughed. "I saw the tire tracks. Rental car?"

"Yeah. I parked it around the side. I didn't want to worry your mom if she looked out the kitchen window and saw a strange car parked by the cabin." She gestured toward a sedan that he now saw in the shadows of the trees. "I couldn't go inside yet."

"Why?" Reed took a step closer. His breath frosted into a cloud.

"I had some thinking to do. And I came here because…" She threw up her hands. "I don't really belong anywhere else in Whistle Creek. If I ever did."

"You belong with me. You always did, Marietta. Right here with me." He drew her against him, pulling Marietta into his warmth. She didn't resist, but still she stayed stiff. Any hope he'd had that everything had been settled, simply because she was here, disappeared. A lump dropped to the bottom of his gut. "What is it?"

Marietta pulled away and wandered off a few steps. She

trailed a hand along one of the birch saplings, its bark peeled, stripping the tree bare to winter's wrath. "Do you know why I really left Whistle Creek, Reed?"

"Because you wanted a career in the city. And there weren't many opportunities for dress designers in a little rinky-dink town like this." He nearly spat the words, sentences sitting in his memory all this time. "And I was part of that rinky-dink town too."

"It wasn't just that." She blew out a gust, then faced him, a shimmer now clouding the stars in her eyes. "Why didn't you come after me?"

The question hovered in the air, the lone untouched icicle that had hung in the seven-year winter between them.

"I didn't just leave, Reed. You *let* me go too."

Truth, Reed discovered, weighed more than lies. When spoken, it fell like bricks, with hard, painful thuds. "You're right." He sighed. "I did. Because I had to."

"Why?" Her voice broke.

Right then, Reed would have done anything to pick those bricks back up, slot them into the places where they had been. But all he'd end up doing was building a new wall and where would that leave them?

"I didn't know what else to do." He reached up and cupped Marietta's chin, warming the cold curve of her jaw. "When your mother died, your entire life turned upside down and I knew all you wanted to do was get away from here. If I'd held you here, convinced you to stay, you would have hated it. Hated me. I could see that in your eyes that Christmas."

"When I came here to give back the ring."

There'd been no fawn here that year. No warm, sweet afternoon in the double bed, no whispered promises of forever.

Just a tearful, awful rending of Reed's heart, when she'd placed that ring in his palm and walked away.

And never looked back.

He nodded and lowered his palm. He'd walk away right now if she wanted him to because in the end, he'd do whatever it took to protect Marietta, to save her. Even if it meant reliving that pain all over again. "I couldn't look in your eyes and see you hurt like that again. I loved you too much, Marietta. I couldn't tie you to a place you hated, not anymore. You'd been through enough." He drew in a breath, and the ice that came with it seared his lungs. "So I let you go. I thought you'd be happier. But it killed me to do it and…" He drew in a breath. "It was the biggest mistake of my life."

Her tears brimmed but didn't spill over, Marietta trembling to hold back the watershed. "I thought I would be happier too, but I couldn't forget this place, Reed. I couldn't leave it behind. No matter where I went, I remembered." Her voice cracked, splintering like thin ice, breaking her tenuous hold on her emotions and finally spilling out in one tear, then another, and a stutter of words. "I remembered *everything*."

He knew she didn't mean just him. This cabin. The good parts. But all the terrible things that had happened too.

Brave Marietta, the responsible one in a fractured family. Her father gone after she was born, her mother acting more like a friend than a parent. And when her mother fell off the wagon, Marietta would get yanked out of the home for a day, a week, a month, to live with strangers. Then she'd go back, always standing on shaky ground that could shift at any moment. Reed remembered the other kids in school always seeing Marietta as the odd one, who rarely had a parent in the audience for plays, a mother along on a field trip. And so he'd become her protector, her friend, from that first day in kindergarten.

It was no wonder that she'd latched on to him, to his grounded, working class family. To the quiet, simple cabin in the woods. "That's why you always wanted to come here."

Her gaze went to the cabin and a soft smile stole over her face. "Because I felt safe here," she whispered. "With you."

"And when I was here with you, it was like a vacation from the farm, from all the work my dad heaped on my shoulders. You found Nirvana and I found Jamaica." He looked at her, saw her shiver, and realized then how cold it was. "Speaking of which, it's freezing out here. Let's go inside and get warm."

He draped an arm across her shoulders and together they headed into the cabin. Inside, they hung up their coats, stomped the snow off their shoes and warmed their hands by the fire. Reed spread a quilt on the floor, threw down a few pillows, then lay down beside Marietta. If Reed closed his eyes, he could pretend they'd gone back in time. He almost wished they didn't have to speak, to deal with the real reasons she'd come back.

"Being here has always been like escaping," Marietta said, then she sighed. "And that was the problem."

Reed propped himself up on one elbow and gazed down at her. Orange and yellow light danced across her delicate features. "How is that bad?"

"It kept me from dealing with the reality. I learned to escape, and kept on doing it. I never latched on to anyone because the next day or the next week, I'd be leaving to go back to my mother."

"And she'd end up letting you down," he said softly.

Marietta nodded. "I tried, Reed, I tried so hard to keep her and I together, but I couldn't. So when the accident happened, I did what I always did. I escaped, by running from you. And when I ran into you in the airport, and all those old feelings came back, I got scared."

"And so you ran."

She nodded. "I can't play the *what if* game, Reed, because…" She sucked in a breath, opening that last fissure to him, because she knew if she didn't, if she ran now, she'd always be running. And Marietta was tired of running, of never having a place to truly call her own. "Because those were all the things I always wanted, the things I dared to have once, and every time, they'd be taken away. I couldn't bear to dream again and—"

"And what?" he prompted when she didn't finish.

"Find out it's all an illusion." She shifted her gaze away from his, not wanting to see her deepest fear. Doubt in Reed's heart.

Because that doubt still lingered in Marietta. That she wasn't meant for this life, no matter how badly she wanted it. Always, it had been like the Christmas present she'd dreamed of, and never found under the tree. "I don't belong here, Reed, I don't belong anywhere."

"I thought you were happy in Chicago."

"I *work* there," she said. "But I don't *live* there. I get on planes, I fly all over the place and then I hole up in a little sewing room and create gowns for women who believe in happily ever after and white picket fences." Tears brimmed in her eyes again, but she didn't shed them. She had to say what she'd come to say, and then let him go, let him have a woman who could give him everything he wanted. He deserved it all, a wife, a family. And if she could sever these ties once and for all, then maybe they both could move on. "I came back here to thank you."

"For what?"

"For today. For giving me a peek inside that dream."

He cupped her jaw and she leaned into his touch, one more time. So warm. So perfect. "What if it could be real, Marietta? What if it wasn't just a dream? What if Christmas really came this year, to stay?"

"Reed, if there's one thing I've learned, it's that Christmas doesn't last. December twenty-sixth always arrives and then you take down the tree and put away the ornaments and it all goes away." She shook her head. "Only a fool keeps believing in a fairy tale."

"Then meet your fool," Reed said with a grin. He got to his feet, pulling Marietta up with him. "Come on, I have something to show you."

CHAPTER EIGHT

"WHAT are we doing here?" Marietta stared at the house at 321 Winterberry Lane from the passenger's seat of her rented sedan. A white picket fence marched across the front, the gate open to reveal a snow-covered walkway. "There are lights on inside. I thought you told me it was vacant, that no one owned it."

"I, ah, lied."

She spun on the seat to face him. "Someone bought it?" The disappointment sank like a stone. She'd been gone from town for seven years, it was to be expected, but still, the weight of sorrow seemed to root her to the cushioned seat.

"Do you want to see inside? The owner is a friend of mine."

"Reed, it's one in the morning on Christmas Eve. We can't just go ring the doorbell."

"Sure we can." He got out of the car, came around to her side, opened her door, helped her out and onto the sidewalk. Then he reached inside and retrieved the garment bag. "I better get this too. I hear those Made by Marietta wedding gowns are worth a mint."

He was crazy—the whole idea was crazy—but Marietta indulged Reed. She'd pay a visit to the house, make her visit to Whistle Creek come full circle and then leave.

A light burned on the front porch, revealing the dark green shutters that hung on either side of the windows. Matching window boxes were attached to the sills, waiting to be filled with spring blooms.

Marietta's pulse quickened as they reached the door. Warning bells sounded in her head. "Reed? Whose house is this?"

He ignored her question, just kept grinning the same silly grin that had been on his face since they'd left the cabin. "Why don't you open that box Cindy gave you earlier?"

"How do you...?" Then her jaw dropped when he placed it in her palm.

"I saw it sticking out of your purse and grabbed it when I got the dress." Another, wider grin. "I know you, and I know Cindy would have been one of your first stops if you came back to town. Now, open it."

Her fingers shook, but the old wrapping paper gave way easily and fell with a flutter to the ground. She pulled off the cover. Nestled on a white cushion was a key.

She glanced up at him, and in his smile, she knew where the key fit, but still, none of it seemed to make sense. She stared at him, until he gestured toward the door. Marietta picked up the key and slid it into the lock. She turned it, heard the tumbler mechanisms give way, and then the door unlatched and opened.

She took a tentative step inside. Behind her, Reed flicked on a light, revealing not just rooms, but a *home*.

A home filled with furniture. Not too much, just enough to start. A plump cranberry sofa. Low slung coffee table. Matching end tables, topped with fabric covered lamps. And down the hall—

A yellow kitchen.

She moved forward, mute. This wasn't just any yellow, it was a butter cream, the exact color she had talked about a hundred times over the years.

"It can't be," she said. But it was, and the color hit her with a tightening of her gut, a tremble in her step. Marietta stopped in the center of the kitchen and spun in a slow circle, the pieces falling into place, one at a time, each corner, each detail slamming into her heart. She held her breath, sure she was hallucinating.

Then she noticed a cabinet door, slightly ajar. Marietta crossed to it, knowing before she opened it what she would find.

There, indeed, sitting on the shelf, was the answer to everything.

Two red bulls, butting their ceramic mug-shaped heads.

Her vision blurred and her heart constricted. "Oh, Reed. This is your house."

He came up behind her, his arms encircling her waist. She leaned into him, wrapping her touch against his. "No, Marietta, it's not. It's *yours*. It always was."

She circled to face him. "You bought this? For me? When?"

"When you left town. So no one else ever could." He trailed a finger along her jaw, his gaze softening, his smile tender. "And so that you would always have a place to come home to. A place where you belonged."

He'd given Marietta the only thing she'd ever needed, ever wanted. This man, who knew her like a well-thumbed book, had sacrificed his heart all those years ago, and now had given it to her in this house, simply to make her happy.

He'd left the key with Cindy, knowing someday, she'd return, and know exactly which door that key opened.

Christmas, he'd said, could come and stay. Marietta had

never believed that, never counted on anything coming to stay, especially not her. Until now. Her tears spilled over, a river running down her cheeks, but he whisked them away, then kissed her. "Don't cry, Marietta."

But she couldn't stop, couldn't get past the lump in her throat, the joy bursting in her heart. "You painted my kitchen, and put the mugs on the shelf," she said. "Why?"

"You have to ask? Because I love you, Marietta. I always have."

She'd made a journey, not in miles, but in her heart, and this time, hearing those words made Marietta want to stay. Put down roots. Plant a garden. And drink from those mugs with Reed every day for the rest of her life.

"I love you too," she said, and lifted her lips to meet his. She had finally come home.

EPILOGUE

MARIETTA didn't show up at Cindy's house for Christmas morning, but Cindy didn't mind. Instead, she arrived at 321 Winterberry Lane that afternoon with husband, kids and grandkids in tow to see Marietta Westmore marry Reed Hartstone. Cindy brought the ham, the potatoes and even the pies for an impromptu reception.

Marietta and Reed had gotten their license and blood test early Christmas Eve morning and convinced Reverend Evans to come to the house Christmas Day to officiate. With Reed's mother and Cindy's family there, it was the perfect small wedding Marietta had always envisioned. It didn't matter if there were ten thousand or ten people there. Once she looked in Reed's eyes and said, "I do," Marietta didn't see another soul.

"Have I told you how beautiful you look?" Reed said to his wife, after the last guest had left. They stood by the tree he'd set up that morning, with a fire crackling in the fireplace. Beside it sat the enormous gift basket Penelope had sent by overnight delivery, brimming with housewares.

"Only a thousand times."

"I'm glad Penelope Blackburn called off her wedding. This dress was meant for you, not her." Reed hadn't been able to take his eyes off Marietta ever since she'd descended the staircase. The stunning gown made her look like she'd tumbled from the night sky. From the way the floral design sparkled with gems to the train that seemed to sweep endlessly behind her, Reed would have thought he was marrying an angel.

And considering it was Christmas, maybe he was.

"I told Penelope that I weave a story into the design of every dress," Marietta said.

"And what's this one's story?"

A teasing smile lit her face. "It's a bedtime story. I'll tell you tonight."

He chuckled, then drew her against him, placing a long, searing kiss on her lips. He wasn't planning on waiting long for bedtime.

Marietta fingered the popcorn and cranberry garland ringing the fir tree. "Next year, we'll get some real ornaments."

"That tree's perfect just the way it is," Reed said.

"But look how it's leaning a little to the right. And there's a hole where it's missing some branches. That's what we get for buying a tree at the last minute."

"It's a tree that needs some TLC. And that's exactly the kind I wanted." He drew his wife closer, counting his blessings and thinking of Jeremiah and Elsie somewhere in Topeka, undoubtedly doing the same.

"You're right. Anything worth having is worth a little work." Marietta curved against him. "Still, I feel bad that I don't have a Christmas present for you."

"A wise man once told me every day with the woman you love is a gift." He brushed a kiss along her lips.

Outside, snow started to fall in big, thick flakes. "Looks like we might be stuck here for a while," Marietta said.

"Forever would be just fine with me." And when Reed kissed Marietta, neither of them noticed the storm, the dress, the Christmas tree or anything but each other.

* * * * *

THEIR CHRISTMAS VOWS

Margaret McDonagh

Margaret McDonagh tells us, "I began losing myself in the magical world of books from a very young age, and I always knew that I had to write. I pursued the dream for over twenty years, often with cussed stubbornness in the face of rejection letters! Although I had numerous romance novellas, short stories and serials published, the news that my first "proper book" had been accepted by Harlequin Mills & Boon for their Medical Romance line brought indescribable joy! Having a passion for learning makes researching an involving pleasure, and I love developing new characters, getting to know them, setting them challenges to overcome. The hardest part is saying goodbye to them, because they become so real to me. And I always fall in love with my heroes!"

www.margaretmcdonagh.com
margaret.mcdonagh@hotmail.co.uk

Dear Reader,

It was such an honor to be asked to contribute to this *Christmas Weddings* anthology. If you are new to my books, then I hope you will enjoy stepping into the fictional world of Strathlochan, around which many of my books are set. On this occasion we meet Frazer and Callie.

Callie has a difficult journey to make, not only due to her frightening brush with illness, but also because her experiences have made it hard for her to trust. In Frazer, has she found a man she can believe in? Can she trust him—and herself—and step toward a happy and loving future?

Most of us know of someone whose life has been touched by breast cancer. It makes us stop and remember the things that are most important— those in our lives who give love and support no matter what. I hope I've captured such feelings in my story.

Thank you for reading this anthology. Encouraged by my wonderful editor, I am currently working on some exciting new projects, but I hope to be back in Strathlochan telling Annie's story very soon.

I wish you all a Merry Christmas and a New Year filled with good health, good friendships and happy-ever-afters.

Margaret
www.margaretmcdonagh.com

CHAPTER ONE

TODAY was the first day of the rest of her life, and Callie Grogan was determined that nothing would go wrong.

On the cusp of dawn she left her car in the parking area and stood to stare across at the hangar looming adjacent to the building which housed the air ambulance base on the outskirts of town. Streamers of mist whispered low over the icy ground, while frost edged the fences and the bare branches of the trees and bushes around the perimeter. A line of mini-icicles hung off the gutters along the roofline of the single-storey building. Her breath misted the air and she stamped her feet, wishing she had pulled on an extra pair of socks before putting on her boots. As it was, she was wearing thermal underwear, a pair of jogging bottoms and a long-sleeved fleece under her flight suit. Yes, it was winter in Scotland, but she hadn't expected Strathlochan to be *this* cold.

A grey, wet November had given way to a December which had brought with it a blast of unexpected cold. Winter had taken a firm grip, with hard frosts, fog, ice and even the threat of early snow. Not ideal conditions for flying, but ones that increased the need for emergency care with an upsurge in accidents and weather-induced incidents.

Under a lowering sky, the hangar doors peeped open, and as she approached the building she could see the engineering crew, who had worked on routine maintenance overnight, preparing the helicopter for the day's work. When the threat of ice lifted, they would steer it out onto the forecourt, from where they could take off within a couple of minutes of an emergency call coming in.

Callie felt a renewed burst of excitement. She couldn't wait to begin her shift. After a terrible eighteen months, this was her chance for a whole new life. She was healthy. She'd thrown herself into work, determined to be the best she could possibly be. She was also alone. But that was nothing new. Aside from the brief misjudgement with Ed, she had always been alone. From now on she always would be. It had taken time, she had been at her lowest ebb, but she had put her life back together. Now she planned to make the most of the unexpected opportunity moving to Strathlochan had given her.

She had been working as a paramedic in Glasgow when she had learned of the new air ambulance base opening further south, and she had lost no time in applying for a position. Having completed her additional training and safety courses to work on the helicopter, she had imagined she would have to spend time on the road ambulances before a vacancy became available. The news that she was top of the list and headed for the flight team straight away had delighted her. Until she had arrived in town and heard all about the playboy doctor who was to be her flight partner. Frazer McInnes.

Callie had been in Strathlochan for a week now. A week that had thankfully coincided with Dr McInnes's holiday. A week which had been full of learning, orientation and finding her feet. Several times she had been out on flights as an observer. She had spent time with the land ambulance crews, whose base was combined with that of the fire rescue service and was situated a few hundred yards along the road from the air base, with easy access to the town and the motorway. After learning her way around the area with them, she'd visited the hospital, especially the A and E department, familiarising herself with the layout so she would be prepared when delivering a casualty for urgent treatment.

She had known what a long and fine tradition the Scottish ambulance service had in providing medical air cover throughout the country, both to the mainland and the islands, with helicopters and fixed wing aircraft. How the new air ambulance base in Strathlochan had come into being was something she had discovered from her new boss, Dr Archie Stewart, during their first detailed briefing.

'The publicity surrounding Sir Morrison Ackerman's funding of the new self-harm and eating disorders clinic near the town sparked local campaigns for further investment in Strathlochan's medical facilities,' Archie had explained. 'Strathlochan has grown immensely over the years, and serves a large rural population scattered over a vast area, not to mention the busy motorway, road and rail links that pass through. The region is on the edge of the existing air services, which means having a helicopter based here significantly cuts down response times. It has been running for six months now, and has paid for itself time and again, saving umpteen lives.' Archie Stewart's pride in the achievement of his staff had been evident. 'Our operation is affiliated to, yet separate and run slightly differently from, the main air service in the rest of Scotland. We have our own shift patterns and we're crewed along the lines of the successful HEMS unit in London, with a pilot and a flight trauma doctor teamed with a specially trained flight paramedic.'

Callie had learned that there were three full-time crews who worked three days on, three nights on and then had three days off—night work and bad weather seeing crews using the all-terrain road vehicle rather than the helicopter. There was a relief crew, and individual relief staff, who filled in for holidays, illness and emergencies.

'The helicopter can fly at night, but landings are dangerous if the pilot cannot see obstacles, cables and so on, so we tend to avoid it unless absolutely necessary,' Archie had explained. A smile had creased his weathered face. 'You'll find we're a good team here—like a second family... We work together, watch out for each other, socialise together. You're a part of that now, Callie.'

A second family. Except she didn't even have a *first* family. She never had done. Having always been alone, on the outside looking in, this was a chance to experience what it was like to belong. If only she could let down some of her protective barriers. That was easier said than done—especially after Ed, and all she had been through these last months—but she knew she needed to try and be more social, to make an effort to fit in to her new home in Strathlochan. So she had gone out one evening last week, enjoying a drink with her new workmates and meeting up with colleagues from the hospital and other emergency services at their favourite hangout, the Strathlochan Arms. The banter had been friendly, the welcome warm.

Despite her wariness with people, she had particularly bonded with Annie Webster, one of the A and E doctors. It gave Callie hope that she had been right to come here, putting her troubled past behind her. However, the gossip about Frazer McInnes, the doctor Archie had paired her with, worried her. One hungry-looking casualty nurse had been outspoken on her views of the alleged romeo, but her unsubtle comments about Frazer's supposed prowess and love-them-and-leave-them lifestyle had made Annie roll her eyes in distaste.

'Take no notice of Olivia and her claimed conquests, Callie. She has her eye on every man around here under sixty, but that doesn't mean they return her interest. Frazer may be one of Strathlochan's most sought-after bachelors, and he certainly enjoys a good time, but he's a lovely guy. He's also a great doctor,' Annie had reassured her.

At least, Callie assumed the words had been meant as re-assuring. They just hadn't entirely had that effect. Everything she had heard about Frazer McInnes made her nervous and brought fresh waves of doubt. But she would keep up her guard and reserve judgement until she met him. And today was the day. All her struggles and preparations had led her here, to the moment she would begin her exciting, long-dreamed-of new job as flight paramedic, when all the extra training and hard work she had done would pay off. Professionally. Personally she still had a very long way to go.

Hesitating outside the entrance, she twisted the narrow gold band on her ring finger before sliding it off and fixing it to a chain around her neck, out of the way for work. She didn't like what it said about her, the fact that she was insecure enough to wear it, using it as an emotional shield, a protective screen. She'd hoped she had come further than that these last eighteen months. Apparently not. A shiver—one that had nothing to do with the cold—rippled down her spine.

Hearing noises in the hangar, she pulled herself together

and sucked in a steadying breath, trying to calm the nerves that were rampaging inside her. Time to head inside and prepare for her first proper shift. And face her first meeting with the man who would be her work partner for the foreseeable future.

Dr Frazer McInnes jogged across the frosty car park towards the base, his Border terrier, Hamish, trotting at his heels. If the forecast was to be believed—and from the icy blast that had greeted him this morning it was—he had arrived back in Strathlochan after ten days in Perthshire, climbing Monroes with friends, just in time.

He loved this time of year—the run up to Christmas, the festive spirit, the parties, the fun—but it also brought a lot of hard work, and the extra-harsh weather this December was a warning that there could be even more problems than usual ahead of them. Not that hard work bothered him. He loved it. Loved what he did. The buzz of being a flight doctor, of never knowing what was going to happen next, always brought a burst of adrenalin. It was what everyone said about him—that he worked hard and played hard. As far as he was concerned life was for living, and he always planned to live it to the fullest.

The holiday had been great, but he had a smile on his face as he pushed through the door, anticipation at being back with the team and getting on with the job bubbling inside him. Hearing chat and laughter coming from along the corridor, he stowed his belongings in his locker and then made his way to the crew room, where the team going off-shift were preparing to hand over to his own before heading for home. He paused for a moment, soaking up the atmosphere, sketching a wave to his pilot, Craig Dalglish, who was helping himself to a mug of coffee in the refreshment area which housed food and drink supplies, a fridge-freezer and a microwave. The rest of the large but comfortable room was filled with easy chairs, sofa, tables, a work space, a small pool table, a piano, shelves of books and a TV with assorted DVDs.

As Hamish, unofficial base mascot, made himself the centre of attention and reacquainted himself with his adoring public, Frazer glanced around the room, his smile broadening as he spied his quarry. In her forties, married with two teenage boys, Mel Watson was his friend and colleague. They had a great working relationship and were always playing pranks on each other. In fact, he owed her for that last practical joke before his holiday, and with her rear end pointing straight at him as she bent over to reach something, he'd been gifted with the perfect opportunity to get his own back. It was way too much temptation to resist.

Silently, he moved up behind her and teasingly fondled her shapely curves. For a millisecond unease nudged his brain that the delectable feminine form beneath his hands wasn't as familiar as it should have been. The next moment…

Bam!

The blow caught him unprepared. Delivered with surprising force and accuracy, it drove all the air from his lungs and dropped him like a sack of potatoes. Stunned, he landed on his backside, a grunt of shock escaping as he sprawled unceremoniously on the floor. His assailant—*not* Mel, he registered now it was far too late—spun round and glared at him, fists clenched at her sides, her feet planted hip-width apart as if readying for battle. Wow! If he had managed to regain any breath at all, he would have lost it all again just looking at the unknown woman. In her late twenties, she couldn't be more than five feet four, and that was being generous, so how on earth could her legs possibly seem to go on for ever? The yellow Nomex flight suit she wore was a good two sizes too big, masking the female shape he had all too briefly felt beneath his hands and swamping her small frame. Short dark brown hair, layered and feathery, framed delicate features, a cute nose and lush, rosy lips, while the most amazing eyes he had ever seen—surely they couldn't really be *purple*?—fizzed with fire and fury.

Silence descended on the room for several drawn-out moments. Then his colleagues laughed uproariously at his plight. Their reaction, however, made the woman even more angry, and he regretted the flash of humiliation he could see in her eyes. He'd never do anything to show someone up. This had all been a ghastly mistake. His hand went to the point of pain at his midriff, where her elbow had delivered the killer blow, and he tried to suck some much-needed oxygen back into painfully starved lungs so he could speak.

But she didn't wait around to concern herself with his apology…or his recovery. Instead, she stepped around him, giving him a wide berth, then marched from the room. It was an impressive march, too, for such a tiny thing. Now he had seen the whole impressive package, he couldn't understand how he had ever mistaken the stranger for the taller, more robust Mel, who was also a decade or more older than the fire-brand who'd just decked him. As he sat there, bemused and bewildered, his friends' merriment continued at his expense. Only Hamish came to check on his well-being. Thankful for at least one display of loyalty, Frazer scratched the dog behind the ears, his fingers sinking below the harsh outer coat to the softer one below.

'Trust you to make such a great first impression, Frazer,' Craig, the pilot on his flight team, tormented him.

'Yeah, I wish I wasn't going home,' Rick Duncan, a paramedic coming off-shift, added with evident enjoyment. 'I'd love to be around for the fireworks to come. You've met your match now, buddy.'

Still winded, Frazer frowned. 'Who *was* that?'

'The new flight paramedic.'

A sick feeling of dread settled inside him at Craig's grin. 'Whose?'

'Yours!'

'Damnation.' Groaning, he levered himself up off the floor, his dignity well and truly shot to pieces.

Rick's smile was distinctly unsympathetic. 'That'll teach you. See you guys in three days—if you're all still alive!'

'Welcome back, Frazer,' Craig chuckled as Rick and the others left. He poured a second mug of coffee and handed it over. 'Here, you're going to need it. Archie wants to see you.'

Frazer gratefully accepted the caffeine fix, and wondered what their boss, a former flight doctor himself, and now base director, would have to say. 'Where's Mel? What's been going on around here? I've only been away ten days.'

'Archie will explain.'

'Terrific.'

He took a slug of hot coffee, wincing at the burn on his tongue and down his throat. He had the distinct feeling he was not going to like whatever news was to come…and that the mistake he had just made with the new paramedic was going to return to haunt him. A few moments later he walked along to the office to learn his fate and rapped on the door.

'Come on in, Frazer,' Archie called. The older man looked

up with a smile, running one hand across his receding hairline. 'How was the holiday?'

'Wonderful. But it's good to be back.'

Archie nodded. 'Good to have you back. Take a seat.'

'So what's the story with Mel?' he asked, pulling a chair up to his boss's desk.

'She's grounded, Frazer. Health reasons.'

Another dart of shock stabbed him. 'What? But she just had a touch of flu when I left.'

'That's what we all thought.' Archie shook his head. 'Turns out Mel has an inner ear problem. She was poorly for several days, and the medical advice is that she shouldn't fly again. At least not in the foreseeable future.'

'Damn. Poor Mel. How is she? What's she going to do?'

'She's philosophical about it—says she was getting a bit long in the tooth to go on.'

'Rubbish.' Frazer swore, bringing a grin to his boss's face. 'I'll talk to her.'

His smile fading, Archie watched him a moment. 'She'll be delighted to see you, of course. But her mind is made up, Frazer. This has just brought forward her decision, that's all. Be pleased for her. She's looking forward to working part-time with a land crew when she feels up to it, and spending more time with John. He's taking early retirement next year and they have plans.'

'I see.'

He didn't. This was all news to him. And it hurt that Mel had never confided in him that she was thinking of taking a back seat. They had formed a close friendship and working partnership these last six months, and Mel had given no sign that things would change.

'I know it isn't the situation you expected to come back to,' Archie said now, shuffling some papers, sympathetic understanding in his hazel eyes. 'But Callie Grogan joined us a week ago from Glasgow and you'll be partnering her from now on.'

'Great,' he muttered, with a distinct lack of enthusiasm. And not just because he had made the worst first impression on his new flight paramedic. He had a nasty feeling his working relationship with Callie was not going to be as smooth and light-hearted as the one he had enjoyed with Mel.

'She's good, Frazer. This is her first posting with a flight crew, but she is dedicated, committed and extremely qualified. And she's taken every additional course available to enhance her all-round skills. Callie topped the shortlist in every way, and her orientation week here impressed us all.'

Frazer tried to concentrate as his boss sang Callie's praises, but all he could think about were those eyes, and the anger and disdain in them when she had looked at him.

'Callie's new to Strathlochan. I want you to take her under your wing, help her settle in.'

He stifled a groan at Archie's direction, not at all sure that his new charge would welcome his input. 'I'll do my best.' The promise was reluctant and full of misgivings.

'I'll have her join us and introduce you—give you a few moments to get acquainted before any calls come in.' Having sent for Callie, Archie leaned back and continued, 'We need to keep our wits about us; I have a bad feeling December is going to be a difficult month.'

Just as the office door opened and his new team member stepped in, glancing at him as if he was something she'd scrape off her boots, the emergency alarm sounded, letting them know they had a call-out. Frazer rose to his feet, focusing on Archie, who was taking the sheet of paper that clattered out of the printer with the first basic details of the incident.

'What do we have, boss?'

'Three-car pile-up on the motorway. Northbound, ten miles south of us. Off you go. We'll have our welcome chat and briefing later on.'

Frazer caught up with Callie in the supply room, where their emergency packs and drugs were stored. He grabbed his pack, pausing to smile at her and see if she needed any assistance, only to be met with an expression of cold indifference. Gee, welcome back. Scowling, he followed as Callie turned away from him and ran for the hangar. So much for the festive season, peace and goodwill to all men. Yeah, right!

The yellow helicopter was being rolled from the hangar, the icy conditions still treacherous outside. Craig was already aboard, doing his pre-flight checks, and Frazer moved up beside Callie as they waited for the all-clear to join him.

'Everything OK?' he asked, attempting another conciliatory smile, concerned she might be nervous about her first official flight.

Callie glanced at him with an expression as chill as the wintry weather. 'Fine.'

'Look, Callie, we started off on the wrong foot. I made a mistake. I'm sorry, I thought you were someone else.'

He paused, filled with the sense that he was digging himself deeper into a hole. Not a flicker of interest or thawing showed in eyes that were the most unusual colour he had ever seen. They really *were* a true purple. He frowned, trying to reject an unexpected surge of attraction and get himself back on track. This apology apparently wasn't working. Disconcerted, he was unable to remember a time when he had not been able to talk a woman round.

'What's the matter?' she snapped at him, and he realised he had been staring.

'Nothing.' He gave himself a mental shake, drawn back to reality as the technicians cleared the aircraft and one of the guys opened the door for them. 'I've just never met anyone with such amazing eyes.'

'Oh, please. You don't really find that kind of line works, do you?'

'It wasn't a line,' he protested, cut by her scorn.

'Shall we get on, Dr McInnes?'

Out of sorts, Frazer followed as Callie moved forward. Instinctively, he went to help her, but she batted his hands away.

'I'm quite capable, thank you. I don't need you pawing me.'

'I wasn't!'

She swung to face him, cold anger evident. 'Let's get something straight. Keep your hands and your corny chat-up lines to yourself and we'll get on with our work just fine.'

Simmering at the injustice of it, Frazer tried to ignore her as they took their places. The helicopter came to life with a characteristic whine, the rotor blades picking up speed, and he had to focus on the emergency call that lay ahead. But he had a sinking feeling that being partnered with feisty, prickly and intriguingly attractive Callie Grogan was never going to work.

CHAPTER TWO

'HELI-Med Echo-Two-Seven, clear to go.'

Craig's voice, confirming take-off and their course to the map reference of the accident site, sounded through her earpiece as Callie strapped herself into her seat on board the helicopter and put on her helmet. She tested to ensure her microphone was functional. In flight it was noisy, and they needed the system to communicate with each other and the ground. The helicopter was new and state-of-the-art, complete with a comprehensive medical bulkhead with everything they would need to hand. There was also more internal space, so they could work on the patient during a flight and give them whatever treatment and monitoring was necessary. Callie forced herself to concentrate on double-checking equipment and supplies—anything but think about wretched Frazer McInnes, who had turned out to be every bit as bad as she'd expected.

'Frazer might look like a playboy, he might even act like one sometimes, but I've never met a better doctor or a more loyal friend. There is no one else I would rather have on my side if I was injured, ill or in a tight spot.'

Quite an endorsement, Callie recalled, and she didn't imagine Archie Stewart suffered fools gladly. But her own impressions of Frazer had confirmed all her worst fears about the man. Wicked. That was the first word that had come to mind when she had looked at him and been subjected to that practised, lethal smile. It was a smile that promised every kind of sensual sin and carved twin dimples in his lean cheeks. There was no doubt about it. By any standard Frazer was stunningly, impossibly gorgeous. He oozed charm and the kind of smouldering sexuality that made female knees weaken at fifty paces. His hair was cut short, the thick, lustrous strands having a silky black sheen, while the mischievous gleam in eyes the colour of melted dark chocolate was dangerous to any woman's well-being. She didn't even want to think about his mouth, or what those perfectly shaped mobile lips could do to a woman, how they would feel, how he would kiss, how... Stop it!

Callie was furious with the man. But she was even more furious with herself and her own inexplicable reaction to him. Those few heart-stopping moments when the unknown masculine hands had touched her had fired a shocking response through her body, stirring things—deep, surprising, scary things—she had not felt before. How could that be? Not only was the man a stranger, and reputed to go through women the way other people went through hot dinners, but she had assumed herself resistant, uninterested, immune. It must have been the surprise of the moment that had made her pulse race like a mad thing and caused an ache to knot low inside her, Callie reassured herself. Any other explanation was impossible—and far too frightening to consider.

'ETA one minute,' Craig informed them, drawing her from her disturbing thoughts.

An unwanted tingle raised the hairs on the back on her neck when Frazer's throaty voice responded. 'Any update on casualties?' he asked, and she sneaked a glance at him. How could he sound sexy just asking a simple work-related question?

'There are four reported, one with serious injuries.' Craig paused a moment as he flew over the scene of the crash and looked for a safe place to land, bringing the aircraft down on the area of carriageway that had been cordoned off for them as close as possible to the site. 'The fire service are cutting out a middle-aged woman now. You're needed there.'

As the helicopter landed, Callie unstrapped herself and grabbed her pack, feeling a rush of adrenalin spill through her veins as she faced her very first call. Too bad it had to be in the company of Frazer McInnes, she groused to herself, following close on his heels as he ran towards the tangled wreckage. Her new boots, protected with steel toecaps and ankle supports, still felt cumbersome, while the full pack she carried was heavy, but she kept up as they were directed by a waiting policeman towards the worst of the injured. The other, less serious casualties, were already being assessed and taken to hospital by road.

'Hello, Rory, what do we have?' Frazer enquired as they came to a halt beside the mangled remains of a car.

'Hi, Doc,' the paramedic on scene greeted him, giving basic details of the patient and her condition, while his partner, Tim, remained in the car to monitor her as the firefighters worked. 'Her name is Barbara Allen, fifty-one years old. We have a neck collar on her as a precaution and she's receiving oxygen. She's conscious, but having difficulty talking and breathing, and she's complaining of chest pains. No head injury, and as far as we can tell her legs are clear. The problem was the buckling, and the way the steering column caved in to her chest and abdomen.'

Fearing internal injuries, Callie set out their packs and readied herself, waiting for their casualty to be freed. Another few moments and the firefighters had gently and skilfully removed the woman from her car, a backboard in place as a precaution. Frazer knelt opposite her, speaking reassuringly as he carried out his preliminary assessment.

'Can you hear me, Barbara? My name's Frazer, I'm a doctor, and this is Callie, a paramedic. I know you are scared, and in pain, but we're going to do all we can to make you more comfortable and get you off to hospital,' he told her, his voice calm, instilling confidence. Callie held Barbara's hand, feeling the slight squeeze of her fingers as Frazer continued. 'Are you hurting anywhere else but your chest, Barbara? Any pain in your tummy?'

'No.' The response was weak, and plainly the woman was finding it increasingly difficult to breathe.

Callie smiled at Rory as the other paramedic took over monitoring the oxygen flow and saturation, replacing the mask over Barbara's face, leaving Callie free to carry out her own observations and do what needed to be done.

'Airway is clear, saturation ninety-two per cent on oxygen, respirations twenty-one, pulse one-twenty, blood pressure one-ten over seventy-five, pupils even and reactive to light,' she informed Frazer when he had finished listening to the patient's chest.

'Unequal air entry,' he reported with a frown. 'Her left lung sounds clear, but she has broken ribs on the right and her right lung is hyper-resonant, no breath sounds.'

'Pneumothorax?'

Frazer nodded, sparing her a glance from those rich dark eyes—one that might have been brief but still had the effect of a physical touch, sending a prickle of unwanted awareness along her spine.

'Let's get to work.'

Callie was thankful to snap herself out of her moment of madness and follow Frazer's decree.

Impressed by Callie's quiet efficiency, Frazer noted that she had already inserted one large-bore cannula and was running the colloid infusion he had requested before obtaining a second IV access. He gave the order for analgesia, confirming the correct dosage before it was administered. While he prepared to decompress the pneumothorax, giving local anaesthetic to ease the patient's distress, Callie spoke quietly to Barbara, reassuring her.

When he was ready to proceed, Callie had a sixteen-gauge cannula waiting for him, and he felt for the intercostal space between the second and third ribs in the mid-clavicular line before inserting it, satisfied when he heard the hiss of gas as he withdrew the needle. Tape was prepared for him without the need to ask, along with all he required to insert a chest drain on the affected side. He made the incision above the sixth rib and spread the tissues down to the pleural space. After puncturing the pleura with artery forceps, he felt with a gloved finger to make sure the passage was clear before inserting the drain, connecting it to the seal and securing it in place. Taking his stethoscope, he listened again to his patient's chest and nodded.

'OK, I'm done. Everything set?' At Callie's confirmation, and after another run-down of Barbara's obs, they began packing up and readied their patient for transfer. 'Let's get you off to hospital, Barbara.'

Willing hands aided them as they hurried the stretcher back to the helicopter, where Craig was waiting, and Frazer thanked paramedics Rory and Tim for their valuable help. Once on board, he was impressed with the way Callie held Barbara's hand, her gaze alert as she constantly checked the monitors for any change in observation readings or condition, while still finding time to spare some reassuring words.

Thankfully it was a short flight to Strathlochan Hospital, and within minutes they were wheeling the stretcher into A and E to be met by Will Brown, one of the duty doctors, who whisked the injured woman straight into Resus, where the waiting team set to work.

Conscious of Callie's presence beside him, the faint hint of her sexy coconut scent teasing him, he stepped away, disturbed by his awareness. Forcing himself to concentrate, Frazer gave full details of the treatment given and the state of Barbara's condition at the scene of the accident and on the journey.

'Good job, Callie.' He smiled at her as they wheeled their stretcher back to the helicopter, keeping his praise understated as he sensed her unease now the emergency situation was over. 'Thank you—you did well out there.'

A brief nod was her only response before she climbed aboard and strapped herself back in. Frazer sighed. He had been pleasantly surprised at finding Callie calm, knowledgeable and efficient, not to mention caring of their patient. She might look as if a gust of wind would knock her over, but she had shown surprising physical strength, and mentally she appeared as tough as nails. And not remotely ready to forgive him. Clearly things were not going to run smoothly with the rest of their working relationship, and he would have a job on his hands to mend fences and make up for their unfortunate start.

They had hardly arrived back at base, taking time to restock the emergency packs, check the drugs and fill in the required paperwork, before they were called out again. It set the pattern for the rest of the day. They had a rushed lunch on the run, and there wasn't even time for their chat with Archie Stewart.

The freezing weather had brought with it an upsurge in road traffic collisions, as well as other incidents, and on top of these there was a call-out to a woman suffering a heart attack, and to a teenager at an outlying farm whose GP, Conor Anderson, had diagnosed a burst appendix and who needed to get to hospital as swiftly as possible for an urgent operation.

Now they were on their way back to Strathlochan after their last job of the day: transferring a patient with a nasty head injury to the neurological unit in Glasgow. His condition had given cause for concern on the flight, and Frazer had been relieved to have Callie's expert help before they handed the patient over to the specialist team who would care for him.

Frazer glanced across at Callie, her eyes closed as she relaxed on the flight home. Throughout an inordinately busy day he had kept a surreptitious eye on his new partner, finding himself more and more intrigued by all her contradictions as time went on. He had discovered that Callie was most comfortable when she was occupied in her role as paramedic. Her unease was only apparent in personal situations. While she projected most of the chill onto him, she was reserved with everyone outside a work setting, and unwilling and awkward when asked questions about herself. Yet she was warm and friendly to patients and any colleagues working with her. Once the incident was over she closed in on herself again. Interesting. He sensed there was much beneath the surface that Callie was hiding from the world.

Given their disastrous start, Frazer had expected working with Callie to be torturous. But nothing proved further from the truth. He'd rarely had to ask for anything. Callie was an amazingly competent paramedic and seemingly unflappable. He was stunned at how quickly she seemed to anticipate everything he needed, from equipment to medications. It was as if she was inside his head, interpreting his thoughts before he'd even registered them. Whatever difficulties they had getting along on a personal level, they'd made a uniquely special team on the job—something that usually took weeks or months to build. He'd never worked with anyone so attuned to him...and certainly not in the space of a day. Which was a bit scary, too.

He was thinking far, far too much about Callie Grogan.

It was dark by the time they came to land at the base in Strathlochan, and the temperature was dropping even further, signalling another icy night to come. While Craig did his own checks of the aircraft, and talked to the technicians who would work on it overnight, Frazer accompanied Callie to the supply room, restocking the packs and checking the drugs, making sure all was in order for the crew who would be taking over from them.

'Tired?' Frazer asked, looking up with an understanding smile as she stifled a yawn.

'A bit.' She'd gone all stiff and awkward with him again, he noted. 'I enjoy the work, though.'

Frazer nodded, filling in an incident report form, watching her out of the corner of his eye. 'I can see that. You were excellent today.'

'Thanks.' Was that a faint tinge of colour staining her cheeks at his approval?

'Fancy coming out for a drink?' he asked casually, hoping to end the day on a lighter and more friendly note after the unfortunate way it had begun. 'We're going to be working closely together, and it's been so busy today we haven't had a chance to get to know each other.'

The minuscule hint of warmth she had shown was replaced with wariness, her whole body tensing, dark shadows forming in those incredible purple eyes. 'No, thanks.'

'Callie, I really want to make amends for earlier.' He tried another smile, but she moved towards the door, putting distance between them.

'I have other things to do.'

He watched as she took a ring off the chain around her neck and slipped it on her finger. Frazer stared at the simple gold band, confused at the feelings churning inside him. 'You're married?' The question popped out, and he cursed the tell-tale shock in his voice.

'Mmm.'

'I didn't realise.' That wasn't a sickening sense of disappointment chilling him. No way. He didn't even know her—didn't like her. She was prickly and difficult. No, he wasn't interested in Callie Grogan in any way other than establishing a comfortable working relationship.

'What's the matter? Afraid my husband will be upset when he hears about the way you "introduced" yourself this morning?'

His jaw tightened at the mocking sarcasm in her voice. 'No.'

'I don't imagine disgruntled husbands are entirely new to you.'

'What the hell does that mean?' he gritted, banking down a flare of anger.

She gave a dismissive shrug. 'In the short time I've been

here, everyone has seemed intent on filling me in on your legendary reputation... Apparently they can't see how uninteresting that is. Excuse me. I have a home to go to.'

And a husband waiting for her to get there. Frazer wanted to growl out loud. That or throw something. Bloody woman. She'd got under his skin. Not in a good way, but like an annoying, persistent grass seed, worming its way into his flesh, irritating him and resisting all efforts to remove it. He'd always laughed off his exaggerated reputation, but the scathing way Callie had looked at him had stung. He wasn't the kind of man she thought he was. Damned if he knew why it should matter what she thought of him, but it did. And that made him madder than ever.

Hamish nuzzled against him, and Frazer scratched the loyal little dog behind the ears. At least he could count on somebody. To hell with Callie Grogan. She was nothing to him. It was a bonus that they worked well together, but it was clear that any friendship or understanding beyond that was never going to happen. So be it. If that was the way she wanted things, it was fine with him. He wouldn't give the infuriating woman another thought.

A low woof drew him from his reverie.

'You're right, Hamish. Life is too short. Let's get out of here and have some fun.'

The dog trotting at his heels, he went to complete the handover to the shift coming on for the night, left a pile of paperwork on Archie's desk and, after phoning the hospital to check on the condition of the casualties they had seen that day, feeling pleased all were stable, went to collect his things before heading for home. He'd pick up some flowers and pay a visit to the one woman who always gave him a warm welcome. His grandmother, Lily. The decision made, he slipped out his cellphone and pressed the key for one of the few numbers he had on speed dial.

'Hi, sweetheart, it's me,' he greeted, smiling at the sound of the familiar voice.

'How's my favourite woman? No, I'm leaving now. I thought I'd pick something up and spend the evening with you. Of course! You know I'd do anything for you! See you soon.'

Frazer's sexy voice and intimate words rang in Callie's ears. She ducked back into the female locker room, cursing herself for eavesdropping, even if it had been accidental. And to think she had considered apologising for turning down Frazer's invitation. It hadn't taken him long to line up another date for the evening with one of his many women, had it? How foolish of her to ever think he had been sincere, genuine. Collecting her things, thankful to avoid seeing him again, she made her escape, fretting all the way home to the small house she had rented in town.

She'd baited Frazer on purpose, and even though she was annoyed at the way he had reacted, turning swiftly to one of his women, she now felt bad about her own actions. Mostly because her reasoning was so skewed. She'd been scared of weakening, so she had deliberately created more of a barrier between them—just as she had used her wedding ring as an emotional shield, slipping it back on her finger in front of Frazer as a statement. It certainly wasn't because she wanted any reminder of feckless, uncaring Ed, the man who had done a runner after a few months of marriage, rejecting her the moment things had become remotely tough. A cynical smile twisted her lips as she thought of the vows they had made at the register office. For better or worse, in sickness and in health. Yeah, right. Bastard.

Once home, she felt the tension of the day drain out of her. She was exhausted—they had been manically busy—and yet the exhilaration of the job was everything she had imagined it would be. The buzz, the adrenalin rush, never knowing what was going to happen next. If only it was all like that, with none of the difficult moments with Frazer in between, or Craig and the others asking questions about her that she didn't want to answer.

Eyes watched her as she flopped down on the sofa.

'You want to know about my day?' she asked of her silent audience, thankful to have someone with whom she could let off steam. 'I made an idiot of myself. The work part was good, though. More than good. I loved it. But meeting Frazer McInnes was an experience I'll never forget.'

Frazer. Just thinking about him brought a mix of unsettling sensations. She could still remember the feel of his hands on her for those brief moments, the awareness that had rippled through her, the needy response of her body. It had shocked her. The last thing she had expected was to be attracted to him. And however much she wished to deny it—and she would never admit it to another living soul—Frazer was the most deliciously sexy man she had ever met. No wonder he had women falling over themselves to catch his attention. That brought a return of her scowl as she wondered who he was with that night, who had filled the gap after she had turned down a drink with him. Not that she was interested.

On the professional side, Frazer was an amazing doctor—not just skilled, but calm and empathetic with patients, too. She admired that. She didn't want to, didn't want to like anything about him, but he'd slipped under her skin in just one day. In future she would have to be careful to make sure she maintained her distance, because she very much feared she could be as foolish as the next woman and lose her head if she allowed that stealthy charm and blatant sexuality to affect her.

'Thank you. I could use a cuddle right about now.' She smiled as her audience of two rescue cats sidled closer and vied for prime position in her lap, purring with contentment as she stroked their soft fur. 'And he has a dog.' The purring briefly ceased, and she could almost see both cats narrow their green eyes at the mention of the 'd' word. 'Exactly. You wouldn't like Hamish, would you? Shows just how polar opposite Frazer and I are. We're as different as…well, cats and dogs. Anyway, nothing could ever come of any unlikely attraction.' Not if Frazer—or any man—found out the truth about her, she added silently, her jaw stiffening with stubborn pride as she fought back any hint of self pity. 'Much the best thing to focus on work and work only. Who needs a man, anyway?'

Paws gently kneaded her thigh and Callie sighed, disgruntled with her thoughts, turning her attention back to her companions. Both cats had been stuck in a shelter in Glasgow for a long time, unwanted because they weren't perfect. Pecan had lost part of her tail, and Maple had needed one front leg amputated after being hit by a car. Callie knew all about not being perfect, and about rejection, so she had immediately been drawn to the two middle-aged sisters. There had never been any doubt that the pair were coming home with her. They were both an unusual dark tortoiseshell, their coats streaked and mottled with shades of gold, buff, copper and brown. She had chosen their names partly due to their colour and partly due to her favourite flavours in Danish pastries and ice cream, for which she had a sinful passion.

She was disconcerted that thoughts of sinful passion brought Frazer back to mind. No way was she going there. But she had been amazed at how well they had worked together—as if they had been doing it for years and were already an established team. Whatever else she thought of him—and she really didn't want to spend too long assessing her disturbing personal reaction to the man—Frazer was an exceptional doctor. That impression had only been enhanced as her first day whizzed by, leaving her little time to worry about Frazer the man as she worked alongside him with increasing admiration for his medical skills.

Her new life in Strathlochan was filled with hope and promise. She thought of Annie Webster and realised she had the opportunity to make her first real friend. Maybe more than one. Perhaps she could even come to feel as if she belonged somewhere for the first time in her life. And maybe, just maybe, this Christmas wouldn't be a lonely one. All she had to do was find the courage to reach out and take what she sensed was possible here. It almost sounded easy, but she knew it wouldn't be.

As for work, the job itself was everything she had imagined. The only problem was Frazer. But she couldn't allow the playboy doctor and her unwanted reaction to him to spoil the best chance she had for a fresh start. In the days and weeks ahead she just hoped she could keep up her guard and ensure that any dealings with Frazer remained strictly professional.

CHAPTER THREE

'LIE still, Paul.'

Frazer heard the edge of exasperation in Callie's voice as she struggled to insert the first of two large-bore cannulae while coping with their fractious patient. 'He's in hypovolaemic shock,' he commented, knowing that accounted for some of the young man's confusion and aggression.

The emergency call had come in at four in the morning, waking them from a light doze after what had been the quietest shift so far—the final one in their first six-day rotation together. Now they were kneeling on the hard wet tarmac. It was dark, raining and freezing cold, and the only available light came from the headlights of their vehicle and that of the police car on scene. They had arrived at the site of the accident to find twenty-two-year-old Paul in pain and uncooperative to say the least. His pulse-rate was high, he was tachycardic, his blood pressure showed normal systolic but raised diastolic levels, he was cold and clammy and his skin had an unnatural pallor.

'Get off me,' the man complained, not for the first time.

Callie's voice remained admirably calm. 'Let us help you.'

Paul had suffered a serious leg injury when he had been

knocked off his bike, trying to cycle back to an outlying village from one of the nightclubs in Strathlochan. A hit and run, according to the local policeman who had been first on the scene, and who remained now to assist them, with his partner taking evidence. Paul had a badly broken left leg, with open fractures of both fibula and tibia apparent. Considerable blood loss, combined with possible internal injuries and bleeding, had resulted in him going into hypovolaemic shock. As Callie concentrated on getting fluids into him, along with the analgesia he'd prescribed, Frazer was working to stem the haemorrhage in the leg…bringing the bones back into line to restore circulation to the foot, maintaining pressure and raising the limb to control the bleeding.

'How's he doing?' Frazer asked, waiting as Callie re-checked the vital signs, calling them off to him.

'Capillary refill is slow, pulse one-twenty, no change in blood pressure, respiration twenty per minute, saturation ninety-two per cent on oxygen.'

'Thanks. Run a second pack of Hartmann's in, please, Callie.'

As she moved to do as requested Paul lashed out, thrashing on the ground. His powerful arm caught her with a heavy blow on the shoulder, sending her sprawling, and she cried out as she impacted with the crash-bars on the front of their all-terrain vehicle, smashing the ribs high up on her right side.

'Callie!'

His heart thudding with concern, frustrated because he was unable to leave his post and reduce pressure on Paul's leg, Frazer could only watch as one of the two policemen ran across to help her. Gingerly she steadied herself, but he saw her wince, her hand briefly straying to a place high on her right side. Cursing under his breath, he accepted the policeman's assistance to control the patient's movements.

'Callie, are you all right?' he demanded, his gaze raking over her as she returned to her place and set up the extra IV fluid infusion he had asked for.

'I'm fine.' He was sure she was lying. She tried to mask it, but he could hear the shakiness in her voice. 'I'm running the Hartmann's now.'

Frazer beckoned to the policeman. 'Can you pull some gloves on and put pressure on this leg? That's it—just there. Thanks. Callie, I'm going to sedate and tube him. Any word on the other paramedic team arriving?' he queried, moving up to the other side of the patient.

'ETA five minutes,' the second policeman confirmed.

Again the patient pulled off the oxygen mask, and Frazer moved to replace it while Callie prepared the items he needed.

'He's not responding as quickly as I would expect after the fluid replacement.' Frazer frowned, trying to do another check of the vital signs while catching hold of Paul's flailing arm. 'OK, buddy, calm down. We're trying to help you here. I'm worried he might have an exsanguinating haemorrhage from a pelvic injury. Ready, Callie?'

'Ready.'

As she handed him the required doses of etomide and suxamethonium, he swiftly anaesthetised and intubated Paul, regaining some control of the situation. At least they could now work without further risk to the patient or themselves.

'Maintain fluid resuscitation, please, and we'll top up the sedation with some propofol as necessary.'

'Do you want the pelvic splint as well as the leg one?' Callie asked, and he frowned as he noted the way she unconsciously pressed a hand to her injured side, near the curve of her breast.

'I'll get them.'

Frazer's gaze lingered on her for a moment before he moved off to their vehicle, returning after a couple of moments with the items he needed. As he fitted the pelvic splint, to stabilise any damage and reduce possible bleeding, he reflected again on how well he and Callie worked together—and yet she was as much of a mystery to him now as when they had first met. She had been particularly uncomfortable once their night shifts had started. At first he had wondered if her nervousness was due to her husband. Was he difficult? Did he dislike her having to stay overnight at the base? Yet to his knowledge she had never telephoned anyone, and no phone calls had arrived from her husband, checking she was all right. Not that Callie was ever anything less than efficient and independent. She was just edgy, difficult to get to know, reserved. Despite all his efforts over the last six days he had been unable to draw her out, and she remained disinclined to talk. About anything. Only on the job was she relaxed, vocal and at ease.

'The ambulance is here.'

He looked up, thankful to have the back-up to transfer the patient to hospital. 'I'm going to splint the leg now, then I want Paul out of here asap.' After completing the task, securing the leg, he moved back to face Callie. 'Are you all right to drive back if I go in the ambulance?'

'Of course. I'll clear up here and meet you at the hospital.'

The false cheeriness in her tone didn't fool him for a second. Frazer hesitated, wanting to argue, but she kept her gaze averted, her hands busy, and he knew he couldn't delay any longer. Their patient needed urgent surgical intervention. Pulling off his bloodied gloves, he reached out and caught her chin, holding her gaze to his. For a moment he was side-tracked by the feel of impossibly soft skin, and his fingers lingered, caressing her cheek, betraying him. He saw those stunning eyes widen with shock and an unexpected vulnerability. Just for a moment, so brief he was sure he must have imagined it, she pressed her face to his palm, and he tried to ignore the sudden and inappropriate flare of heat that coursed through his body in response.

'Be careful,' he instructed her, his voice huskier than he'd intended, knowing the words could equally apply to himself and how he was feeling about this enigmatic woman.

This enigmatic, *married* woman.

The unsettling thought made him retreat. Dropping his hand, feeling burned and aroused from that all-too-short physical contact with her, confused by his jumbled emotions, he rose to his feet and put distance between them. Pulling on fresh gloves, he helped the two paramedics transfer Paul to the ambulance, then climbed inside. For a moment, before the door closed, he glanced back at Callie, seeing the careful way she held herself while trying to pretend nothing was wrong. He didn't like leaving her. Not at all. And he wasn't buying her act. The minute he had her safely back at the base he was going to satisfy himself about the extent of her injury—whether she liked it or not.

Callie had no idea how she made it to Strathlochan. After accepting help from the young policeman to pack the kit back into the four-by-four, she left him and his partner to their investigations of the hit and run accident and drove slowly to the hospital, mindful of the appalling road conditions. Her side burned with pain, but thankfully it wasn't the side she had to use to change gears. It was, however, the side of her body that had been the site of the problems which had started eighteen months ago.

The only thing that stopped the discomfort from swamping her was the unnerving memory of the feel of Frazer's touch. Her skin tingled even now from the feel of his fingers, the gentle yet masculine brush of them, which had sent a bolt of electric current through her body, centring on a throbbing ache deep within her. And she was mortified that she had sought his touch, had lingered, had pressed her face to him. Why had she done that? She couldn't feel any attraction for Frazer. She just couldn't. And she had to hide how much she hurt or he would get suspicious—and no way was she ever letting him see. It was too terrible to contemplate that he should find out about her, know she wasn't whole, wasn't normal.

She remembered his teasing with some of the guys over a famous singer's 'assets' in the crew room a couple of days ago.

'Don't you just love a woman's breasts?' one of the techs had sighed, clearly smitten with the busty blonde in the magazine.

'I'm a leg man myself,' Craig, their pilot, had drawled, before commenting lovingly on his wife. 'A fact Eve uses un-mercifully to torment me.'

Frazer had laughed. 'I love all of a woman.'

Callie felt cold remembering. He loved all of a woman...if she was perfect, undamaged. She could imagine how disgusted he would be if he knew about her, if he saw her. Which was never going to happen. She couldn't explain the way she reacted to Frazer. She was scared because he made her feel things that were alien to her, made her desire things she knew she would never be able to have. He was way too gorgeous and sexy for her peace of mind, and because she wasn't immune to him she had to do all she could to put barriers between them and keep him at bay.

She had always found it difficult to trust, to open herself to another person. The one time in her life she had tried it, taking a chance on Ed at his most charming and marrying him, she had been betrayed soon afterwards. He had shown her what a mistake it was to trust anyone but herself. It wouldn't happen again. She planned never to let anyone else get close to her again. It hurt too much.

She would never forget the things Ed had said to her at the end. The whole marriage experience had been a disappointment as his charm had been only surface-deep. Unlike his lies and deception. But those had only been revealed once the problems had begun. She never should have married him—she had no idea now why she had done so. Only that she had felt an overwhelming need to belong, to have a family. It hadn't happened. Now it never would.

'It's not working between us, Callie. It never has. Sex with you is boring. You were always plain and ordinary, and you never let go, but now you're not a complete woman any more any desire I once had has died. I've met someone else—someone sexy and feminine. I'm leaving you to be with her.'

Callie had been furious, and so hurt. Ed had caught her at her lowest ebb, still recovering from surgery, still scared of the outcome and long-term prognosis. The one time she'd really needed someone, the first time she had ever allowed herself to trust anyone, and she had been let down in the most cruel and savage way. But she had learned the lesson. Never again would she depend on anyone but herself. Never again would she grant her trust and risk her body or her heart.

Frazer would be no different from Ed. No man would. She blocked her mind to the rest of Ed's deception, the other major, unforgivable thing she had only found out as he had left her. Soon the divorce would come through and she would be finished with that painful, horrible episode for good. Here in Strathlochan she hoped to make a new life…but one without a man.

The passenger door of the vehicle swung open and she gasped in surprise, having been so lost in her thoughts she hadn't seen Frazer walking towards her from the direction of A and E.

'Callie, how are you?' he demanded, the interior light revealing the concern on his face.

'I'm fine.' She pulled herself together, hiding both her mental anguish and her physical discomfort. 'What's the news on Paul?'

Frazer ran the fingers of one hand through the springy thickness of his hair, looking disconcerted at her change of subject. 'They've stabilised him and he's going up to the operating theatre now.'

'I hope he'll be OK.'

'Me, too. I'll call later for an update. Want me to drive back?' he asked, hesitating at the passenger side.

'Not at all.' Ignoring the ache across her ribs, she started the engine. 'Shut the door. You're letting in the cold.'

The short journey was completed in an uncomfortable silence, and, feeling Frazer's intense gaze upon her, Callie was glad of the protection the darkness gave her. Back at base she was quick to escape, thankful when Frazer was waylaid by one of the technicians. She planned to complete her tasks and make her way home as quickly as possible. She would have a hot bath and take some painkillers. Hopefully her side wouldn't stiffen up and she would be all right to work her next shift in three days' time. No way was she going to show any weakness.

Paperwork complete, the shift nearing its end, Frazer went in search of Callie, well aware she had been avoiding him. With Hamish at his heels, he tried the crew room, the supply room, the two small dorms and the office without success. Knowing she wouldn't be in the gym, that just left the locker room, and the fact it was ladies only wasn't going to stop him.

The door was ajar. He peeped inside, his concern increasing as he saw Callie sitting on the bench, bent forward and clutching her side. Emotion welled inside him at her determination to keep herself apart, to pretend she was tough and didn't need anyone. Stepping inside with Hamish, he quietly closed the door and walked across, squatting down in front of her.

'Callie?'

He watched as she jerked upright, wincing at the pain, a startled moan escaping her, a thread of fear in her eyes before she masked it. 'What are you doing in here?'

'Checking on you.' He remained calm, realising her first instinct was to attack, as if it was some kind of defence mechanism. 'You're more hurt than you are letting on.'

'I'm fine.'

'You're lying, Callie. But for some reason you'd rather keep people at a distance than ever accept any help or friendship.'

He could tell his words hit home. A dark shadow clouded her eyes, turning them a deep purple, before she shrugged and turned her face away, making him even more certain she was hiding much more than the injury she had received that night. And he was even more determined that he was going to uncover her mysteries. He shouldn't be thinking about a married woman. It wasn't his style. He'd never poached on another man's territory, had never wanted to. What was it about Callie that gave him no peace and drew him in against his will? But he couldn't think about his disturbing reaction to her now. He had more important matters to attend to, and had to treat her like a friend and colleague.

She stiffened as he took one of her hands in his, her breathing short and raspy as she tried to avoid the pain. 'Callie, you need to let me take a look at you.'

'Absolutely not!'

'Don't be silly. I'm a doctor, and you—'

She batted his hands away and rose unsteadily to her feet, putting distance between them before repeating her mantra. 'I'm fine.'

'We both know that isn't true.' A frown creased his brow as she continued to retreat from him. He sat back on his heels, watching her, puzzled at the intensity of her response, the real fear she couldn't hide. 'What's going on?'

'Nothing. I just don't need your help.'

'You can't ignore this, Callie. Either you let me examine you or…'

Panic danced across her face like a living thing. 'Or what?'

'Or I take you to the hospital to be checked out there.'

'Fine. I'll go to the hospital.' She glared at him, a stubborn set to her chin, making him want to smile despite his worry and annoyance. 'But I can go by myself. I don't need you.'

Unexpected hurt twisted inside him at her determined rejection. 'Tough. That's the deal, Callie. Take it or leave it,' he insisted, hardening his heart and doing what he knew was best for her.

Clearly furious, she collected her things from her locker, banging the door shut, refusing his offer of help. Sighing, he followed as she stalked outside, deftly snagging her car keys from her and steering her across to his own four-by-four. No way was he letting her drive again today.

'We'll take my car.'

Conscious of the slippery ground, not wanting any more accidents, he kept a careful hold on her left arm, watching with impatience as she shrugged off his help and awkwardly levered herself into the vehicle, clearly uncomfortable. Not that she would admit that to him or anyone else, he was sure. Exasperating woman. With Hamish safely installed in the back, Frazer slipped behind the wheel and headed away from the base. He could literally feel her tension, feel her nervousness growing the closer they came to the hospital. Why? Was she worried she had done more damage than she wanted to admit? Or was there some other reason for her anxiety? He regretted the lateness of the December dawn, the current darkness preventing him from reading her expression. But one way or another, with or without her co-operation, he was going to ensure she was safe and taken care of.

By the time Frazer pulled into a parking space near the casualty department Callie was literally shaking. It was stupid. She came here every day for work and it never bothered her, but the underlying fear that had haunted her when *she* was a patient was back with a vengeance. She really didn't want to be examined. The only reason she would go through with it was because it was preferable to having Frazer see her, touch her, even in a professional capacity. She could imagine his reaction. Uncharacteristic tears pricked her eyes but she fought them away. Aware Frazer was looking at her with concern, she slipped out of the vehicle unaided and headed towards the entrance, frowning at him as he followed.

'You don't have to stay.'

'Of course I'm staying,' he refuted with infuriating calm, taking control of the situation, his hand resting at the small of her back as he steered her towards the reception desk.

'I can manage.'

'Today you don't have to. Get used to it.'

She couldn't get used to it. All her life she had been alone, fending for herself. No way was Dr High-and-Mighty going to ride roughshod over her wants and needs. Thankfully, while he was talking to a nurse, Callie spotted Annie Webster coming out of a cubicle nearby. She slipped away from Frazer and went to meet her friend.

'Callie! Hi, I—' Blue eyes darkened with concern as Annie's smile faded. 'What's happened?'

'I hurt myself at work. Frazer insists I get checked out, but it's nothing.'

Annie drew her into a vacant cubicle and closed the curtain. 'If Frazer thinks it should be looked at, I'm with him.'

'Great.'

'Cut the sarcasm, Tough Girl. I see right through it.' Annie's smile was back, kind and concerned. 'I'll go and get Frazer.'

'No!' Panicked, Callie grabbed her arm.

Annie hesitated, scanning her face. 'OK. Want to tell me what's going on?'

'Nothing.' Callie sucked in a ragged breath, wincing at the pain. 'Annie, please. If I have to do this at all, I don't want to see anyone but you.' She paused, hating her weakness. 'If you don't mind.'

'Of course I don't mind, Callie... Look, let me get the chart, and then we'll have a chat and a look-see—all right?'

Anxious, scared, Callie nodded. 'Don't let Frazer come in, Annie. Promise me.'

'Sure.' Her friend sent her a curious and worried smile. 'If that's what you want.'

Hearing Frazer's voice as Annie ducked out of the curtain, Callie froze.

'Annie. I'm looking for Callie. One minute she was by my side, the next—'

'She's fine,' her friend interrupted. 'I'm with her now, Frazer. You go and wait in Reception.'

'I need to see her. I didn't know the details to put down for next of kin.'

Callie smothered a groan of despair.

'She doesn't have any next of kin,' Annie responded.

'Of course she does! What about her husband, for goodness' sake?'

'No, that isn't right. He's not—'

Thankfully Annie's voice snapped off, and Callie held her breath, waiting to hear what happened next.

'He's not what?' Frazer demanded, sounding thwarted and frustrated.

'Nothing. I'll see to everything. Leave it with me,' Annie reassured him, and Callie released her breath in a painful rush.

It seemed Frazer wasn't about to let it go. 'But—'

'This way,' Annie urged, and Callie had to smile, wishing she could see the expression on Frazer's face. 'You can talk to Callie when I've finished and not before.'

'But—'

The renewed protest died and Callie heard their footsteps

retreating. Thank goodness. She had a few moments' reprieve before Annie was back again.

'Frazer's really worried about you,' she commented, closing the curtain.

'It's his job.'

Annie shook her head. 'He cares about you, Callie.'

'Nonsense.' It was something she didn't want to consider. She had enough trouble trying to ignore her own confused and growing feelings for him, knowing they could never come to anything. She really didn't want him interested in her. 'I'm just a work colleague.'

'Is that why you haven't told him about your marriage being over?'

'It's no one's business,' she muttered, warmth heating her cheeks.

Annie paused a moment, her gaze considering. Whether or not she read something of her desperation, Callie was relieved when she let the subject drop. For now. 'All right, let's see what we can do for you, shall we? Take a look at that side? Can we lose the clothes?'

Sitting on the bed, Callie undid her flight suit and peeled it down to her waist. Her fingers shook as she then took off the jumper and T-shirt she wore beneath, hesitating further as she came to her adapted bra. She couldn't do it.

Annie glanced across and smiled. 'Need some help?'

Callie shook her head, stupid tears threatening again. She closed her eyes against them.

'Callie?'

Biting her lip, ignoring the pain in her side, she reached to unhook her bra and slowly slid the straps off her shoulders, unable to look at Annie as the garment dropped away. She heard her friend's sharp intake of breath and waited for the inevitable rejection, the revulsion when Annie saw what remained of her right breast.

CHAPTER FOUR

CALLIE was amazed when Annie stepped forward and enveloped her in a hug. 'Oh, God! Callie.'

She'd never been hugged before, had never had a friend or someone who cared about her. Not even Ed. A sob escaped. She tried to choke it back but she couldn't. Tears squeezed between her lashes and trickled down her cheeks. She *never* cried. Annie's arms tightened as she held her, and when she finally stepped back a pace to look at her, Callie was stunned to see answering tears on her friend's face.

'How long?' Annie asked, her voice wavering as she reached for a tissue.

'Eighteen months.'

'And are you all right? What's the news?'

Callie wiped away the salty wetness from her face. 'I'm OK,' she reassured her and filled her in on what had happened—the medical details, at least. 'The oncologist is optimistic. There's no sign of any further pre-cancerous cells, and there was no spread to any tissue or nodes under my arm. They caught things early and I've been clear since. Another six months and it will be two years—the all-important milestone. I didn't need chemotherapy or radiotherapy. The DCIS—ductal carcinoma in situ—pre-cancer was of a low grade, so the risk is small,' she explained, her smile wavering again.

'Many women never have another episode—never go on to develop cancer,' Annie commented, offering her another tissue. 'Are you on medication?'

Callie nodded. 'I have to take it for another few months. They're going to assess it at my next check-up.'

'What about reconstruction?'

'I know…it looks horrible.' Her voice wobbled and she looked away from the sympathy in her friend's blue eyes.

Annie caught her hand. 'That's not what I meant, Callie. I just wondered how you felt, but it's clear it affects you deeply.'

'The wide local incision wasn't meant to be like this. They had to cut away more than expected. They tried some reconstruction, but things went wrong. I reacted badly to it and got an infection.' She sucked in a steadying breath, trying not to react to the memories of that time. 'At the moment I can't face trying again—even if it would help this time. I just want to live my life and do my work.'

'Oh, Callie, it must have been so awful for you. What about your husband? Wasn't he there to support you?'

'Hardly.' She tried to damp down the pain. 'It's why he left me. He said I was no longer a complete woman.'

'Bastard!' Annie paced the small floor, her fury evident.

'He did me a favour. I'm better off without him. I don't need anyone.'

Annie's expression was sad as she turned back to her. 'I suppose Frazer doesn't know about this, either?'

'Of course not!' She stared at her friend in horror. 'No one knows. And they are not to know. Annie, promise me.'

'I promise. But if this is why you are keeping your distance from Frazer, I think you are doing him a disservice. And yourself. You'd be good together.' A speculative gleam appeared in Annie's blue eyes.

'Hardly—you know what Frazer is like, playing the field.'

'That's rumour and gossip,' Annie protested. 'He's so much more than you think, Callie.'

'Well, I'm not finally divorced yet. I've been through a lot, Annie, and I'm not ready for anything else.' She might never be, she admitted to herself. But if and when she was, it wouldn't be with someone like Frazer, who went for model-types with perfect bodies.

Annie kept silent, concentrating on examining her damaged side, where bruises were already marking her skin. 'I'd like you to have an X-ray, just to ensure nothing is broken, but I think you've just badly banged yourself. Don't worry,' she added, seeing the panic Callie couldn't contain. 'I'll ring radiology and speak to Francesca Scott. She's lovely, Callie—truly. I'll explain and she'll be fine—not to mention one hundred per cent discreet.'

'OK.'

'Slip your flight suit back on for now while I call. If Francesca isn't in yet, I know she'll be happy to help us and come straight here. Leave it with me.'

Callie did as suggested, feeling less vulnerable as she covered herself again, listening as Annie made the call. It seemed Francesca was already on her way to the hospital, and would come to Casualty first and be happy to help. Before they could speak again, nurse Gina McNaught popped her head round the curtain.

'Sorry to bother you, Annie, but Dr McInnes is getting very impatient.' The young woman grinned knowingly, casting an interested eye over Callie.

'Thanks, I'll be out in a minute.' When Gina had gone, Annie squeezed her hand. 'I'll go and speak to him, stop him worrying, and then I'll meet up with Francesca and we'll get those X-rays sorted out.'

'You won't say anything…'

'I'm your doctor as well as your friend, Callie. My advice in both capacities is that you give Frazer a chance, but I'll respect your wishes,' she reassured her.

'Thanks.'

As Annie disappeared again, Callie could do no more than sit and fret and pray that Frazer would never find out.

Increasingly frustrated, Frazer paced the waiting area. Whatever was taking so long? He'd suspected Callie was hurt, but the wretched woman had toughed it out, refusing to give in until she couldn't hide the pain any longer. Idiot. She made him so mad sometimes. He didn't know which desire to give in to first—to spank her or kiss her senseless. Either would likely get his face slapped. Or his eye blackened. By Callie herself if not her husband.

At last he saw Annie pop out from behind the curtain. She glanced towards him and took a step forward, only to hesitate and turn round, setting off in the opposite direction to meet up with someone. Francesca Scott, he noted, one of the hospital's radiographers, and he frowned as both women closeted themselves in a small glass-partitioned office.

Annie closed the door, but he could see them through the window, deep in discussion, although he couldn't hear what they were saying. Something was definitely not right about this situation, and his instinct was prodding him, hounding him. What was wrong with Callie? Determined, he set off towards the closed curtain of the cubicle, growling in frustration as the office door opened and he was cut off at the pass. Again.

'Francesca, how are you?'

'Fine thanks, Frazer. And you?'

He made a non-committal reply as the tall, athletic radiographer, who had amazing dark red hair that fell in long corkscrew curls down her back, smiled at him. A rare smile. The Ice Maiden, as the hospital grapevine unfairly dubbed her, didn't count many people as friends, but they had a platonic history and he liked her. He knew she and Annie were friends, too, which gave weight to his suspicions that something was going on.

Before he could ask questions, Annie linked her arm through his. 'Frazer, you come with me. Thanks, Francesca.'

As the redhead disappeared behind the curtain to see Callie, Frazer reluctantly allowed Annie to tug him towards the office. He studied her closely, frowning, because her eyes seemed over-bright, as if she had been crying recently.

'OK—talk.' He paced the small room. 'What the hell is going on?'

'Nothing.' She smiled, but evaded his gaze.

'I want to know about Callie. How is she?'

Annie sat down, closing a file and leaning her arms on it. Callie's file. 'She's doing fine, Frazer. I've asked for a precautionary X-ray, just to be on the safe side, but I'm sure there's nothing broken. Her side is badly bruised and very sore, though. Providing the X-rays are clear, as I am sure they will be, I'll be sending her home with some anti-inflammatories and painkillers and she'll be back at work in a few days.'

'And that's it?'

'That's it.'

He didn't believe her. His jaw clenched. 'Annie…'

'Frazer, Callie is fine. There are just a few bruises from what happened today. That's all.'

The phone rang, curtailing his next barrage of queries, and Annie looked relieved to pick it up. He realised straight away that the call was from Francesca and that the X-rays were over.

'I'll be back in a few minutes,' Annie told him, rising to her feet. 'I'm just going to check the pictures and then Callie can go.'

'I'd like to see them.'

Annie looked shocked. 'No way! You are not Callie's doctor and you know as much about patient confidentiality as I do.'

He did, and he had no sway here to impose his will, but he didn't like it. There was something Annie wasn't telling him. He just knew it. Something important about Callie. Annie was being evasive, careful in what she said. But why? What was going on in Callie's life that he was not supposed to know? As he waited for Annie to return, he thought back over what had happened since Callie had been hurt.

She had been adamant that she didn't want to be examined. At first he had thought she just had an aversion to *him*, but she had been scared of coming to hospital in a way she never was in a work capacity. OK, so many people were nervous in medical situations. Yet this seemed more. Callie had been relieved to find Annie, a friend she trusted—as much as he thought Callie trusted anyone—and they had been in that cubicle talking for a ridiculously long time…far longer than a few simple bruises warranted. Then there was the look in Annie's eyes now, the signs she'd been crying not long before. About something Callie had told her? There had also been a strange moment about next of kin, and Annie's initial rebuttal regarding Callie's husband.

A nasty thought occurred to him. Was this about the husband? Was Callie scared of him? Did he hurt her in some way? Was that why Callie didn't want anyone to see her? He didn't want to believe it—couldn't believe it, not given how feisty Callie was, how tough and capable of sticking up for herself. Look how she'd floored him at their first meeting. She was no shrinking violet who would allow anyone to walk all over her. But the feeling that something was wrong with Callie's life persisted, took root, refused to diminish. He didn't know what that something was, but he intended to find out.

Before he could get his wits together, and even consider the temptation of peeking at Callie's file, Annie came back into the office.

'The X-rays are clear, Frazer. I've given Callie a shot to make her more comfortable, now I'm just waiting for the prescribed medication to come up from the pharmacy and then you can take her home.' Tossing her dark ponytail over her shoulder, she leaned against the desk, arms folded, a knowing look in her blue eyes. 'You care about her, don't you?'

'She's my flight partner.'

A chuckle escaped, and there was a mischievous smile on her elfin face. 'Right.'

'It doesn't matter if I *do* feel anything, Annie,' he conceded with a deep sigh. 'Callie's married. I don't go there. Ever.'

'I can agree with that view—if there's a husband, it's the right thing to keep away.'

'If?' The young doctor looked as if she wanted to say something more, and Frazer's eyes narrowed as she blushed and withdrew her gaze. 'What is it? I know something else is going on here. I just want to help. Is it him? Her husband. Has he hurt her or something? Is that why she was scared to be examined? Is that why you said "today's injury"?'

'Frazer, I can't break a confidence, but I can assure you that you that there is no way Ed could have laid a hand on her.'

He let out a huff of relief, then Annie's choice of words began to sink in. Callie's husband *couldn't* have laid a hand on her. Why not? 'Annie…'

'I'm going to see if Callie is ready to go home.' She straightened, her gaze serious as she looked at him, as if trying to impart some message. 'The medication may make Callie sleepy and disorientated. I'd be glad if she wasn't left on her own.'

'I'll take care of it.'

She nodded, a small smile playing at her mouth. 'I get off at two, so if you need to go home, or to your gran's, ring me and I'll come by and stay with Callie.'

'What time does her husband get in?' His question was met with a telling silence. Frazer's attention sharpened. 'Or doesn't he get in? Isn't he living with her? Aren't they together?'

Annie simply raised an eyebrow before turning away to pick up the file. He watched as she went off to fetch Callie, his mind a whirl of thought as he puzzled over what had and hadn't been said. There was more going on here than he knew. She obviously couldn't tell him, but Annie was clearly wanting him to read between the lines and see that all was not as it seemed in Callie's life.

There was so much more to his new flight partner than her prickly exterior. The more time he spent with her, the more he came to know her, and the more he wanted to understand, to win her trust. Callie could be distant and difficult, but damn if she didn't capture his interest. He had thought her married and out of bounds. If she wasn't... He had to know for sure. Had to know whether to stay well away—or give his desire for her free rein.

He'd been with his fair share of women. He enjoyed them. He sure as hell enjoyed sex. But he was tired of the dating merry-go-round. Although he had done little to refute his reputation, he wished people would see the man inside, not the happy-go-lucky supposed romeo. He had never lived with a woman, had never been in love. But ever since he'd visited his sister and her family in Australia nine months ago, and played with his nieces and nephews, he'd begun to wonder if he was missing out—if maybe it was time to settle down and start thinking about a pack of kids of his own. For which he needed the right woman. He'd never really had a type. He'd been attracted to all kinds of women over the years. But what he felt for Callie just seemed *more*. More of everything... More intense, more intriguing, more urgent.

There was something different about Callie, and he'd never wanted anyone the way he wanted her. She fascinated him. Even in a baggy flight suit, with no make-up and spitting icy darts at him, she was the most gorgeous woman he'd ever seen. He wanted to learn all about her, to discover the real Callie hidden behind that defensive wall and know what had happened to hurt her so badly and make her so distrustful, so alone...and so determined to stay that way.

Frazer enjoyed a good mystery—sorting out the clues and the secrets from the red herrings and putting pieces of the picture together until it made sense. He had a feeling that the puzzle that was Callie Grogan was going to be one of his biggest challenges to solve—and potentially the most rewarding.

'Are you all set to go?'

Callie nodded in response to Annie's question, feeling increasingly groggy and lethargic. 'Thanks for everything, Annie.'

'No problem. That's what friends are for.' Taking a piece of paper, Annie slipped it into one of Callie's pockets. 'My home and mobile numbers. Ring me if there's anything you need. Any time.'

'OK.'

'When you're feeling up to it, we'll get together—have lunch and do some Christmas shopping.'

Callie found herself returning Annie's infectious smile. 'I'd like that.'

'Good.' She linked her arm with hers. 'Come on, then. There's a very impatient, very gorgeous flight doctor waiting for you.'

'Annie…'

Her friend ignored the warning. 'He's a good man, Callie. One of a kind.'

'And one who has his pick of available women.'

'You *are* available.' Annie smiled. 'And it's clear he's taken with you.'

Callie sucked in a painful breath. Heaven knew why—she had done everything to discourage him. 'He wouldn't be if he knew.'

'You're wrong, Callie. Not everyone is like your ex. Don't be scared to give Frazer a chance.'

But she was scared. 'I'm not interested.' The words burned in her throat and she cringed inwardly, knowing they were a lie.

When Annie whisked back the curtain, Callie's gaze immediately settled on Frazer. Melted chocolate eyes contained worry, frustration and the kind of slow-burn heat that made her stomach turn over. Annie handed him the bag from the pharmacy containing her pills, then stepped aside. Callie was disconcerted to discover that she swayed alarmingly once her friend's support was removed, but Frazer stepped forward, his arm sliding far too possessively around her waist.

'Thanks, Annie. I'll take care of her.'

Callie wanted to protest, but somehow the words wouldn't come. A pale sun was rising above the eastern hills behind the loch when they went outside, and a light dusting of snow had fallen in the last couple of hours. Uncharacteristically docile, she allowed Frazer to help her into the passenger seat and gently strap her in. He was so close she could smell his earthy sandalwood fragrance. Dismayed at the ache of desire inside her, she was grateful when he moved away and closed the door. Hamish pushed his head between the front seats and nuzzled her shoulder, distracting her, and she smiled, giving the dog a hug. Then Frazer was behind the wheel, and before she knew it they were at her house. He came around to open the passenger door, before unclipping the seatbelt.

'Keys?' he asked, his voice seeming huskier than usual.

Frowning, she fumbled in her pockets, wondering why her brain felt so fuzzy. 'Keys,' she murmured, handing them over.

'Wait a minute and let me help you.' Frazer stepped back from the door, but she ignored him, sliding out in ungainly fashion. 'Callie…'

'I can walk.'

The full-voltage dimpled smile he sent her increased the shaky feeling in her legs. 'Of course you can.' Folding his arms, he stood back and watched her.

Hamish sat on the pavement and gave a single, sharp bark—whether of encouragement or disapproval she didn't know. Licking her lips, and finding it took far more concentration than usual to put one foot in front of the other, Callie headed towards the house. Or tried to. She weaved a bit, a cry of surprise escaping as she slipped on ground that was icy under its recent dusting of powdery snow. She was even more surprised when Frazer caught her before she could fall, drawing her up against the solid length of his body. A very masculine body. It was far too tempting to rest there, to cuddle even closer, but she had just enough sense left to know that was a very bad and very dangerous idea.

Pushing against him, she struggled for space. 'Frazer, I can manage.'

'Sure. I see that.' She felt a chuckle rumble from inside him as he all but carried her up the path. 'Let's get you indoors.'

'Cats.'

'Excuse me?'

Against her better judgement, she leaned on him while he dealt with opening her front door. 'I have cats.'

'Good for you,' Frazer murmured, guiding them inside the narrow hallway.

'I meant because of Hamish.'

'Don't worry, I have cats at home, too.' One strong arm held her up while he closed and locked the door. 'Hamish is used to them. He won't hurt yours.'

She swayed again, feeling groggier by the minute. 'Pecan and Maple don't like dogs. *They* might hurt *him.*'

Frazer didn't appear concerned. Extracting herself from his hold, she weaved her way into her small, impersonal living room and flopped onto the sofa, curling up in a ball. Why did she feel so spaced-out? What was Frazer doing in her house? This wasn't good. Not good at all.

'You can go now,' she mumbled, finding it hard to focus on him as he walked towards her.

'I'm not leaving you alone. I promised Annie.'

Callie's frown deepened. 'Go away,' she instructed, when he knelt down on the floor in front of her, one warm palm brushing aside her wispy fringe and resting on her forehead.

'Is there someone I can call for you?' She shook her head at such a stupid suggestion. 'No one? What about family?'

'Never had one. Never had anyone. All alone. Except Ed. Briefly.'

The hand moved from her forehead, fingertips brushing her cheek, making her skin tingle with sensation. 'Your husband?'

'Soon to be *ex*-husband. Thankfully. Bastard left me when I needed him.' She struggled to focus, sure she shouldn't be saying these things, but her words spilled out, even if they were slurred. It was impossible to stay awake. 'I'm not desirable.'

Frazer sat back on his heels and struggled to absorb all he had learned—things he knew Callie would be mortified at having confessed had she had her wits about her. Her husband had told her she wasn't desirable? He had left her? The man had to be a fool. He'd like a few moments alone with him to take him to task for hurting Callie, for abandoning her. What had she said? That he'd left when she had needed him? What had happened? He was sure there was much more to this story, but her soft, endearing little snores told him he wasn't going to discover any more now. Or anything at all when she woke up and the effects of the medication had worn off. She'd be mad as hell if she remembered just how indiscreet she had been and what she had revealed to him.

He really ought to put her to bed, but she looked so comfortable. The flight suit was loose enough that it wasn't constricting her, and she was peaceful and clearly not in pain. Moving her might disturb that and what she needed most right now was rest. There were things he needed to do, but for a moment he just stayed motionless, watching her. She looked fragile, but aside from her unexpected physical strength she had a tenacious spirit, and if it was true that she had never had a family, had always been alone, who knew what she had coped with? It explained her independence. And made him impossibly sad.

Reaching out, he brushed a few strands of short, feathery hair back from her face. Her skin was flawless, almost translucent. Under the light, her dark brown hair gleamed with unexpected tints of darkest copper and russet. She wore little, if any make-up—and, given the number of women he had known who spent inordinate amounts of time fussing with their appearance, he knew that Callie's natural, understated beauty and complete lack of artifice was unusual. Special. Long, sooty lashes fringed those exceptional eyes, closed now in sleep. He couldn't get over their colour. They captivated him. And for all her outward prickles and her front of hardness, he sensed a very different woman was locked inside.

Callie, with her hidden secrets, the hurt and aloneness she tried so hard to hide and yet which seemed such a part of her being. He planned to find the key that would unlock the real Callie Grogan and allow her to flourish and fly free.

With a sigh he rose to his feet, halting when he looked towards an armchair and saw two intriguingly coloured cats staring at him through mistrustful green eyes. Pecan and Maple, he presumed. Equally suspicious, Hamish sat across the other side of the room, regarding the felines warily. There seemed to be an uncomfortable stand-off. Smiling, Frazer crossed to the fireplace and spent a few moments lighting a new fire, putting the guard round it once the kindling had caught and flames were licking at the seasoned logs he had set on top. He looked around the room, seeing no photos, no homely touches. It felt lonely...like Callie.

In the kitchen, he found cat food, and something that would suit Hamish. He fed the animals, seeing to fresh water and setting the bowls far apart to avoid any fur flying. He noted that one of the cats had three legs and the other was missing part of its tail. So, Callie shared his penchant of caring for the underdog. Or undercat in this case. Smiling to himself, he made some toast, then put a pot of coffee on, sure Callie would appreciate some when she woke. While it brewed, he went up to the bathroom, lingering to smell her coconut soap and shampoo, closing his eyes as he recalled how the fragrance clung sensuously to her hair and skin. He found a blanket and a pillow to make Callie more comfortable, reflecting on the way back downstairs on the absence of any male presence in the house.

Just how long ago had her creep of a husband walked out? A while, if the divorce was imminent. Annie had some insight, had tried to tip him off without breaking a confidence. So why was Callie hiding behind her wedding ring? Did she use it to keep a distance between them because she felt the same pull he did and was scared by it? Threatened? The idea intrigued him. Just what else was Callie hiding?

Back in the living room, he gently slid the pillow under her head, then tucked the blanket around her, dropping a kiss on her forehead before collecting his toast and coffee from the kitchen. Selecting an adventure novel from the well-stocked bookshelves in an alcove beside the fireplace, he sat in a chair near her to plan his campaign to gain her trust and win her heart. Now he knew there was no husband in the picture he had no intention of backing away from the attraction he felt for Callie. But she needed careful handling. If she was still asleep after lunch he'd phone Annie to take over for a while. He had things to do, ideas to set in motion.

Callie might not think she had anyone in her life who cared about her, but she was wrong. With the spirit of Christmas growing every day, and the warmth of the Strathlochan community all around them, he'd make sure to spend time with this mysterious, intriguing woman, and prove to her that she didn't have to be alone any more. If he had his way, she'd never be alone again.

CHAPTER FIVE

THERE was blood everywhere.

The tension in the helicopter was tangible as they sped back to Strathlochan Hospital, where an emergency team was on standby, awaiting their arrival.

'How long, Craig?' Frazer demanded, swallowing a curse as the bumpy flight in appalling weather jostled them, and his gloved, bloodied hand lost its grip on Desmond Pollock's mangled, partially severed right arm.

'ETA seven minutes,' Craig responded, his voice betraying his own stress. 'Six if we're lucky.'

'We sure as hell need some luck if this guy is going to make it.'

At first Frazer had worried about Desmond losing his arm... Now the concern was whether the man would even live. Looking up, he met Callie's anxious gaze. Like him, she was covered in blood and dirt, monitoring Desmond's condition while squeezing yet another bag of fluids as fast as possible through the IV in his uninjured arm.

'BP's dropping,' Callie announced quietly, leaning over the unconscious man as she called out the levels for pulse and respiration. 'Saturation on oxygen ninety per cent and falling.'

'Thanks.'

Cursing under his breath, Frazer adjusted the tourniquet again, working hard to control the haemorrhaging. In the worst December weather in living memory, Desmond had been outside, trying to cut more logs for the fire, when his chainsaw had slipped and nearly taken off his arm above the elbow. His distraught wife had managed to keep her head sufficiently to call for help, and had then done her best to stem the blood loss until the air ambulance arrived.

An immediate assessment had told Frazer there was no time for delay or heroics at the scene. They had just scooped Desmond up and made a dash for the hospital. Aside from the significant vascular damage and haemorrhage, there was considerable injury to tendons, nerves, muscle and bone. Desmond would face at least one major operation to repair the damage. Vein and tendon implantation, pins to fix the broken humerus, skin grafting and a long rehabilitation to regain what use he could of arm and hand function. If he lived. Frazer didn't want to think about having to tell Desmond's wife and children that the man they loved hadn't survived.

Finally, the hospital loomed into view, and it was a bumpy landing in the lashing rain and gusting Arctic winds. The casualty team were ready for them, and the hand-over was swift as Desmond was transferred to Resus for emergency work before being whisked up to the operating theatre.

'I hope he makes it.' Callie sounded tired as she began to gather up their things.

'We did everything we could.' He took off his gloves and tossed them in the bin, glancing down at his soiled flight suit and jacket. 'Time to get back and clean up before the next emergency.'

'A hot shower sounds like heaven right now.'

Her comment brought a rush of erotic images to his mind. He closed his eyes, seeing Callie's compact, curvy body under the spray of water, soapy rivulets running down her skin, and his hands— He snapped off his inappropriate thoughts and opened his eyes, his gaze clashing with hers. He could drown in those purple depths. The longing to be alone with her, to touch her, to kiss her, threatened to overwhelm him, but, sensing her nervousness, he reined in his need and stepped back a pace.

He'd been as patient as he could this last week, careful not to crowd her while at the same time making sure she felt more involved and part of things, gently getting closer to her. It was difficult—not only because it was taking longer than he'd hoped to win her trust, but also because with every passing day he just wanted to take her in his arms and love her. He had never had such an intense attraction to a woman as he did to Callie. He wanted to protect her, care for her, share all of himself with her.

Keeping things light—for now—he tapped the tip of her nose with one finger before ushering her ahead of him out of the hospital and back to the helicopter, where Craig was waiting for them. Resisting the urge to sweep her up in his arms, his let his gaze stray over her shapely form, clad in the too-baggy clothes, as she climbed aboard for the short flight back to base.

The rest of their shift was hectic, and he had little time to worry about the apparent slowness of his campaign to win Callie round. They attended a middle-aged man with diabetes who was hypoglycemic…confused and shaky from low blood sugar. A fast-acting oral carbohydrate, an injection of glucagon and an intravenous dextrose solution followed by a saline flush helped to stabilise him, but given that he had no one at home to care for him, and he was unsure how he had allowed his blood sugar levels to dip, they took him to the hospital for further monitoring.

Next they saw a toddler who had pulled a kettle off the kitchen worktop, resulting in partial thickness burns to her arm and leg, and a woman suffering an asthma attack whose oxygen saturation was worryingly low at eighty per cent, and who needed salbutamol via nebuliser and pure oxygen. Both patients required hospitalisation. Their final call was to yet another motorway collision, involving several vehicles, where they met Rigtownbrae GP and BASICS doctor Kyle Sinclair at the scene. Kyle had called for them to transfer a teenage boy with a nasty penetrating wound to his abdomen and suspected damage to his liver, who needed urgent surgical intervention.

Away from the base, Frazer wished he could spend more time with Callie, especially in the run-up to Christmas, but she was still wary, and he knew he needed to take things slowly, however frustrating it felt. His chance came a couple of days later. Having involved her in some activities, he couldn't wait until lunch time, when he was picking her up for the next stage in his plan.

Smiling, wrapped up against the cold, he left his hillside cottage and walked Hamish through the woods and part of the sprawling grounds of Strathlochan Castle—the laird and his family having opened paths for local people to enjoy the countryside and the loch.

Frazer glanced at his watch, his impatience growing, his surroundings giving him less satisfaction than usual. All he wanted was to see Callie.

* * *

Something very strange had been happening since the morning Frazer had made her go to the hospital. Callie's recollection of what had taken place after he'd driven her back to her rented house was hazy, to say the least, and all she really remembered was waking up in the afternoon, groggy and confused, to find Annie *in situ*. But everything had subtly shifted, and she hadn't been able to get things back in balance since.

She wished she could recall exactly what had happened with Frazer. She had a nasty feeling that, under the influence of the medication, she had told him things she shouldn't have, but of course she couldn't mention it now, or ask him about it—not without the horrifying possibility of opening a can of worms.

Since that day Frazer had been increasingly warm and friendly, frequently touching her, draping an arm around her shoulders or resting a hand at the small of her back, ensuring she was all right. He had somehow cajoled her into taking part in things around the base and beyond—so much so that she had even started to feel that she did, indeed, belong in Strathlochan. In the week following her injury she had been sweet-talked into going with him to give a talk about their work to a group of children at a local school. Then he and Annie had dragged her out one evening to go ten-pin bowling, which had proved to be massive fun, involving various departments and medical disciplines forming teams and resorting to outrageous tactics to try and win. Annie, Will Brown and two of the nurses from A and E, Gina McNaught and Holly Tait, had been vocally victorious.

Next had come a Christmas pizza night at the Strathlochan Arms, with the large but cosy pub decked out in festive finery, log fires burning. Again she'd had fun—far more so than she had expected—finding herself drawn in to the welcoming, friendly warmth. People seemed to be accepting her and Frazer as a couple beyond their work partnership, and it was most disconcerting. But, whilst attentive and caring, Frazer himself had been a model of propriety. Yet she was more and more aware of him with every day that passed. It was scary.

Yesterday had been spent with Annie, having lunch and doing some Christmas shopping. Strathlochan had been full of colour and cheer. Bursting with excitement, children had lined up to visit Santa's grotto, while tinny carols rang out of nearly every shop doorway and a local band played in the town centre, the stand lavishly decorated and strung with flickering lights. Sellers nearby had plied shoppers with roasted chestnuts and hot chocolate. It had been the best day ever, a completely new experience: and Callie had soon been laden down with gifts for her new colleagues, for Annie, Craig and Francesca…and for Frazer. She had never had people to buy presents for before. Had never had a friend to giggle and gossip with, either. But Annie was incorrigible, singing Frazer's praises and pushing her at him despite her protests, and despite knowing the truth about her.

Today, she had been suckered into joining in with some Christmas decoration party. Whatever the hell that was. Frazer was picking her up at any moment, which was why she was a nervous wreck and ridiculously flustered. She kept telling herself that this was just another work-related event—so why had she spent for ever fretting over what to wear? And why were a whole troop of butterflies conducting acrobatic manoeuvres in her stomach?

Having fed Pecan and Maple, she crossed to the window and looked out at the wintry scene. The wind had dropped and a pale sun struggled through patches of grey cloud. A new fall of snow overnight had coated the small garden, the pristine white blanket disturbed only by a few spiky footprints made by wild birds seeking scraps from the table and nut-holders she kept well stocked for them.

She tried to reassure herself that Frazer was only being nice to her because they were colleagues and, despite her initial chilly stance, he had stuck it out and helped her settle in. Unfortunately, she feared she was fooling herself. She couldn't understand why he was remotely interested in her, but there was definite desire in his chocolate eyes when he looked at her. And with the unspoken acceptance that her marriage was over, her defences had been stripped away, the shield which she had been hiding behind torn down, and she was no longer immune to his charm.

The attraction was becoming a major problem—because she knew it could never go anywhere. No matter how much she was coming to admire him, to want him like crazy, she had to hold firm. Somehow. Yet it was increasingly difficult to maintain a distance. There was so much more to Frazer than she had first expected, and she believed Annie was right, that the rumours about his reputation were grossly exaggerated. Not that she imagined he'd ever been a monk. He was too sexy, too intelligent, too much fun not to have a bevy of women attracted to him. And, despite all her warnings, she was one of them. No matter how much she wished she could deny it, the sexual chemistry between them was palpable. But impossible.

The doorbell rang, startling her from her reverie and increasing her nervous tension a hundredfold. Sucking in a steadying breath, she walked down the narrow hallway and opened the front door, her stomach clenching at the sight of

Frazer looking heart-stoppingly gorgeous in a temptingly soft leather jacket, chunky black jumper and faded jeans, the well-worn denim clinging to his hips and leanly muscular thighs in a way that made her pulse race and her mouth water. Disconcerted, she raised her gaze, her throat closing at the slow, dimpled smile, and the liquid chocolate eyes darkening with the unmistakable heat of desire.

'Hi, Callie.'

Two words and his throaty voice seemed to wrap around her. 'Hello.'

'You look good.'

'Thanks.' His appreciation brought a flush to her face, although she didn't think her ankle boots, grey jeans and lavender fleece were anything special. 'Um, I'll just fetch my coat and things,' she mumbled, cursing her awkwardness, backing away as Frazer stepped inside and closed the door behind him.

Retreating, foolishly breathless, she gave herself a stern talking-to as she pulled on her coat, and gathered up her bag, cellphone and keys. She discovered Frazer in the sitting room, getting reacquainted with Pecan and Maple. Usually aloof and cautious with strangers, the two felines seemed no more immune to the man's lethal charm than any other female, she noticed with a sigh, halting as he looked up and saw her.

Her heart thudded as Frazer closed the gap between them, her whole body trembling as he reached out to straighten a kink in the collar of her coat, his hands lingering, drawing her inexorably closer. She couldn't breathe as his head bent and his lips, warm and supple, brushed her cheek. Her skin tingled. His subtle sandalwood aroma, earthy and sensual, teased and tantalised her. And she yearned to turn her head the scant distance necessary for their mouths to meet. Frightened at her weakness, the lure of temptation, she stepped back, feeling every throb of her pulse in her veins.

Frazer released her, long dark lashes veiling sultry eyes, a sexy smile playing at his mouth. 'All set?'

'Of course.' She cleared her throat, trying to portray a cool unconcern she was far from feeling. 'We should go.'

Callie was thankful for the diversion supplied by Hamish, who greeted her with customary enthusiasm when she climbed into Frazer's car. The little dog was a dynamo, and devoted to his human companion. The perky Border terrier seemed to have two speeds—sleeping and warp—with little leeway in between, and he was never happier than when he was the centre of attention and being fussed over. A trait for which she was grateful as concentrating on Hamish allowed her time to attempt to get her emotions back in check and distance herself from Frazer.

The wheels crunched through the frozen top coating of new snow as Frazer drove slowly to the outskirts of town and a building which was surrounded by a large garden filled with shrubs and edged by mature trees.

'What is this place?' she asked, looking around with interest as Frazer found a space in a small but crowded car park.

'It started out as a home for disabled children and those with special needs, but several years ago they opened a new wing as a children's hospice,' he informed her, hopping out and moving round to the back to take out some supplies. 'I help out with the decorations each Christmas if I can. The children love it.'

Moved to discover yet another side to Frazer, she helped him carry the things to the front door, Hamish bouncing eagerly ahead of them. Their welcome was warm, and the interior of the home bore no similarity to the bland and depressing places she had been made to live in as an abandoned child. Everywhere was bright and clean, the staff were caring and friendly, and it was clear, as she met one child after another, that all their needs were catered for, and each was treated as an individual with respect and kindness.

It was a joyful few hours. Aside from helping put up decorations and strands of coloured lights in the public rooms and the children's bedrooms they sang songs—Frazer surprising her anew with his talent playing the piano—and then they went outside with the more mobile children to build a snowman and indulge in a snowball fight, Hamish running excitedly around them. Cold and breathless, they trooped back inside to be warmed with cups of tea and piping hot homemade mince pies.

The final task was to move a huge tree into place in the common room. 'The children decorate it themselves on Christmas Eve. I just climb the ladder to set the angel on the top,' Frazer explained, stepping back from ensuring the tree was fully secure, before casting a last, satisfied gaze over their efforts.

'It looks great.' Callie couldn't believe how quickly the time had passed, nor how much she had enjoyed herself. Turning round, finding herself looking into Frazer's eyes, she swallowed, feeling vulnerable. 'Thanks for inviting me. I've had a good time.'

'I'm glad. You've been wonderful...and I enjoy your company,' he added, eyes darkening as he took a step closer.

Oh, help! Rattled, horribly aware of him, she took a step backwards. 'Frazer, I—'

Her words were cut off as several of the older children

giggled and then a chant began, increasing in volume as more of the room's occupants joined in. 'Kiss, kiss, kiss, kiss!'

Confused, Callie glanced around, then followed Frazer's gaze upwards, realising they had inadvertently come to a halt under a generous sprig of mistletoe. Her breath lodged in her lungs and her heart started hammering as Frazer smiled, raising one hand to cup her face, his touch igniting a flame of fearful anticipation as leaned towards her.

'Wouldn't want to disappoint them,' he murmured, seconds before his lips settled on hers.

This was no brief, casual peck. A tremor rippled through her at the feel of Frazer's mouth claiming hers for the first time. Shocked, she found herself returning the kiss, savouring his warm male taste as the tip of his tongue teased the seam of her lips, encouraging them to part before dipping boldly inside. Her hands clenched in his jumper and she swayed against him. Everything around them faded away—the chanting, the laughter, the cheeky comments. Nothing mattered but this unexpectedly erotic stolen moment. Almost as soon as it had begun Frazer was pulling back, regret and searing need in his eyes as he looked at her.

'Next time we won't have an audience, and we'll do this properly,' he whispered huskily.

Callie felt helpless, laid bare, scared witless. Shaking, sensitised from his kiss, she wanted to tell him there couldn't be a next time, that it was impossible, but words refused to come. They stared at each other for endless moments, then Frazer turned aside, and she realised he was sheltering her from the rest of the room, giving her time to get herself back together.

Her emotions were in a whirl. This should never have happened. She had tasted forbidden fruit and now she wanted more, wanted everything, and she couldn't have it. A shiver ran down her spine…regret, fear, anger, disappointment all bringing a chill to her blood and dampening her mood. Ignoring Frazer, she concentrated on clearing up, managing a smile for the children and staff, thankful it was time to say their goodbyes and leave. She needed time alone to shore up her breached defences.

It was dark when they went outside, frost descending, and she snuggled deeper into her coat. Once in the four-by-four, Hamish circled a couple of times on the back seat, then curled up to snooze, and Frazer wasted no time in firing the engine and switching on the heater.

'Cold?' he asked.

Callie shrugged, increasingly uncomfortable at what had happened between them. 'A bit.'

'It will soon warm up.' She could feel his gaze on her for a moment before he turned his attention back to the road and pulled out of the car park. 'We have one more stop to make.'

'OK.'

She didn't know what else to say. All she wanted was to go home, to try to decide how to cope with this latest disaster, but she didn't want Frazer to know how deeply affected and disturbed she was by their kiss.

'We're here.'

Frazer's words drew her from her thoughts, and she looked out into the darkness as he turned up a wide driveway near the broad expanse of loch that edged the town, moonlight casting a shimmering glow across the stillness of the water. He drew the vehicle to a halt outside a modern building. Callie climbed out, curious despite her distracted mood. Hamish jumped out, too, and, having collected a couple of bags from the back of the car, Frazer disconcerted her further by taking her hand in his, linking their fingers as he walked around the side of the building along a lighted pathway bordered by evergreen shrubs. For a moment all her awareness centred on the point where his flesh touched hers, then he released her and inserted a key in the lock of a numbered front door, ushering her in ahead of him. Hamish bounded inside the warm, bright flat and disappeared. Closing the door, Frazer turned to face her.

'Can I take your coat?'

Callie slipped it off and watched as he hung it up, along with his leather jacket. 'Where are we?' she asked, a flicker of concern tightening her nerves.

'I promised the other most important woman in my life that I'd bring you to meet her.' His dimpled smile in no way blunted the shock she felt at the words—shock that made her slow to react when he took her hand again and led her down the hall. 'Come along.'

The very last thing she wanted was to meet one of his women. And she was scared to know what he meant by *'the other most important woman in my life'*. Callie tried to protest, to dig her heels in and insist he take her home, but they were already in a small but attractive sitting room, and her arguments died in her throat as she looked at the woman sitting in a comfy armchair by the fire, Hamish in her lap. The little dog jumped down and the woman rose stiffly to her feet, opening her arms to Frazer, a broad smile of pleasure on her face.

'Frazer, darling!'

'Hello, sweetheart.'

Callie watched as he enveloped the elderly grey-haired lady, who was as round as she was tall, into a bear hug. When she was released, the woman turned with a smile, blue eyes twinkling with enjoyment and kindness.

'You must be Callie,' she greeted, holding out a hand in welcome. 'Frazer has told me so much about you, my dear.' Her eyes twinkled with mischief. 'You've made quite an impression.'

His hand resting at the small of her back, Frazer urged her forwards. 'Callie, this is my grandmother, Lily McInnes.'

Swept along with the introductions, Callie found herself sitting next to Lily, Hamish curled in front of the fire at their feet, while Frazer made them all tea and then busied himself with some festive decorations for the woman who was unmistakably his beloved gran. Discovering there was so much more to Frazer than the casual playboy was dangerous. It would be so much safer if she disliked him. But she didn't. Indeed, she was becoming more drawn to him by the hour.

'How are you finding Strathlochan, Callie? Are you settling in and enjoying your job?'

Although unused to such attention, Callie found herself relaxing. The elderly lady was marvellous. Full of life and humour. 'I really like it here, and the job is all I hoped it would be,' she answered honestly, conscious that Frazer was nearby and listening in as Lily continued to bombard her with questions.

'And what are you doing for Christmas, dear?'

Surprised, Callie looked down at Hamish to hide her discomfort. 'I'm not sure. I…'

'You must come and spend the day with us,' Lily insisted, patting her hand. 'No one should be alone at Christmas.'

'Oh, no, I couldn't. I'll be fine. Honestly.'

She saw Lily share a look with Frazer before speaking again. 'Well, we'll see come the time. It's going to be our first year without the rest of the family, so we'd love your company. Frazer's sister, Fiona, married an Australian. Steve is a chef. He was working over here but they live in Melbourne now. My son and daughter-in-law, Frazer's parents, retired eighteen months ago, and last January they moved out there to be closer to their grandchildren.'

'I see,' Callie murmured, taken aback by all she was learning.

'Frazer, be a darling and check the cauliflower cheese I put in the oven. It should be ready soon, and then we can eat.'

Glancing round, she saw Frazer leave the room to follow his grandmother's bidding, but she had no opportunity to protest about staying for a meal as Lily was speaking again, chuckling as she gently rubbed Hamish's tummy with the rubber end of her walking stick as the dog rolled on to his back.

'Frazer had been working in London, mostly in A and E, but with a six-month stint on the helicopter with HEMS. He came back to Strathlochan when his parents left—he said it was time, but I fear it was so I wouldn't be here alone. Silly boy! He wanted me to live with him but I'd have none of it— even though we're so close.' Callie couldn't help but return Lily's effervescent smile. The woman was a real character. 'I moved to this warden-assisted retirement place. As I said to Frazer, living with him would cramp my style.'

A laugh sounded behind them, a rich, attractive sound, and Callie turned to see Frazer's eyes sparkling, twin dimples creasing his cheeks, his affection for his grandmother obvious.

'You're a wicked woman, Gran,' he teased. 'Goodness knows what you'd get up to with all the single gentlemen here without me to keep an eye on you.'

Callie tried not to be affected, to harden her heart to this warm and endearing side of him. Concerned for his grandmother, he had given up a lucrative job and exciting lifestyle in London to come back here and make sure she was all right and had company. That, combined with his skills as a doctor, his kindness to patients and colleagues alike, meant her view of him had changed drastically from that first unfortunate meeting.

Unlike Frazer, she had never had any family—had never known her parents, had never had a happy Christmas. Her childhood had been one of loneliness, of never belonging, of having no one to depend on or trust but herself. Life's lessons had been hard.

Anything beyond friendship with Frazer was out of the question, but day by day she was realising what might be possible here in Strathlochan…if she could just open up enough to reach out and allow herself to be drawn into the warmth of this community, to grasp the friendship offered by Frazer, Annie, Francesca and her other colleagues.

CHAPTER SIX

'RELAX between contractions, Moira,' Frazer instructed, glancing up to see Callie holding the woman's hand, encouraging her to rest before the next effort was needed.

With the helicopter grounded due to adverse weather conditions, they had answered an emergency call to this isolated farmhouse because their all-terrain vehicle was the only one that could reach the property through the deeply lying snow. A road ambulance, local GP Hannah Frost and a midwife had all been forced to turn back. It had immediately been apparent when he and Callie had arrived in the early evening that there was no way to evacuate the mother-to-be before the baby was delivered. Thankfully, she was only a week short of full term, this was her fifth child, and she had experienced no problems with this or any previous pregnancy. Baby number five was being born at home in the middle of a blizzard, with a power cut thrown in for good measure.

'I know my others have come quickly,' Moira murmured now, panting for breath, 'but I never expected this! Oh…here comes another pain!'

'You can do it, Moira,' Callie reassured her, adjusting the

Entonox. 'You're doing really well. Wait for the next contraction and push with it.'

'The head's showing, Moira,' Frazer told her with a smile, thankful for the battery-powered lights her husband, Dougie McStay, had been able to rig up for them.

The contraction subsided and Moira flopped back, taking a break from the gas. 'Remind me never to do this again.'

Frazer chuckled. 'Rest for a few moments. Has the pain gone?' he asked, and Moira gave a weary nod.

The pause didn't last for long before another contraction came and Moira cried out, reaching again for the Entonox.

'I need you to push hard now. Big push,' Frazer encouraged.

'I can't,' Moira sobbed. 'I—'

Callie soothed her. 'Yes, you can. You're nearly there now. Take a big breath.'

'Come on,' Frazer insisted, as more of the head and face appeared. 'Come on, keep going.'

'Well done, Moira. It's hard work but you're doing well,' Callie praised her, moving aside so Dougie, who had been to check that the other four children were safely sleeping in their rooms, could take her place and hold his wife's hand through the final stage.

The labour continued, and Frazer looked towards the window, unable to see out in the darkness but fleetingly concerned that the winter weather had taken another turn for the worse. They hadn't expected to be delivering the baby here, and now the deteriorating conditions threatened to prevent them driving back to Strathlochan that night. The wind whistled around the windows and snow continued to pile up outside. Who knew when the power might be restored?

Under the Entonox, Moira was sleepy between contractions, and Frazer had to call to her to keep her focused. 'Moira, I need you to push now.'

'Push, Moira.' Callie's voice joined his own, urging the weary woman along.

'Come on, love.' Burly and awkward, but surprisingly gentle, Dougie wiped the beads of perspiration from his wife's face with the cloth in his free hand. 'You can do it.'

'I want it over,' Moira wailed.

Frazer remained calm and understanding but authoritative, as he helped to bring her baby safely into the world. 'Not long now. Pant for a few moments. Good. Now, take a big breath—that's it. Come on—and again. Big push…wonderful.'

Moira cried out with the effort of her labour.

'Good, good.' Focused on what he was doing, Frazer altered his position. 'Another big breath, and then a really good push with the next contraction.'

'Nearly there, Moira, the baby's head is free. One more big, big push,' Callie extolled.

Frazer checked that the cord was not around the neck and carefully rotated to ease the shoulders out. 'Biggest push you can. You can do it. Any second now.'

'It's a boy!' announced a delighted Dougie a few moments later, leaning down to plant a kiss on his wife's flushed cheek. 'After all those girls, we have a son!'

Frazer noted the shimmer of tears in Callie's stunning eyes as she gave the exhausted mother an injection to stimulate the uterus to contract and aid the delivery of the placenta. He put the clamps in place and encouraged Dougie to cut the cord, the gruff farmer beaming with pride. Smiling himself, always moved at a birth, Frazer handed the baby to Callie, who cleaned and checked him before wrapping him gently, rubbing his chest and clearing his airway. She glanced up, and he met her gaze when the first thready wail turned into a furious howl, shocked by the look of wistful longing and edge of pain on her face.

'Apgar scores seven and nine at one and five minutes,' she informed him, and he breathed a sigh of relief that all was under control. 'Baby is doing well.'

A short while later the placenta was delivered intact, and Callie made Moira comfortable in a clean bed before settling the baby in his mother's arms.

'Sorry about this, Doc, but it looks as if you are stuck here for the night.' Dougie grimaced as he returned to the room. 'It's wild out there. The warmest place in the house is the living room. I've made up the fire and put mattresses, pillows and duvets in there. There's a downstairs bathroom, too. And I've left torches and candles in the kitchen. The stove is solid fuel, so the kettle is on if you want a drink. Help yourself to anything you need.'

Frazer glanced at Callie. She looked nervous, but he couldn't deny a moment of delight at the prospect of being stranded with her for a while. He looked back at Dougie and smiled. 'We'll be fine. I have my mobile phone, so I'll contact the base and let them know what's going on. Be sure to call us at any time if you are worried about Moira or the baby,' he instructed, shaking the proud father's hand.

'Will do, Doc. Thank you both for everything. See you in the morning.'

Downstairs, in the dark, Frazer sensed the building tension between himself and Callie. While she disappeared to the bathroom he made them mugs of hot chocolate, then went to the living room, lighting some candles and moving the sofa back so he could set the mattresses in front of the fire. Tossing a few more logs on, he waited impatiently for Callie to arrive. In the days since the decorating party and taking her to meet his grandmother, he hadn't been able to stop thinking of their impromptu kiss. It had been far too short and far too public, but it had been like a taste of paradise and he couldn't wait to do it again—to kiss her properly. And more…much more. He wanted to taste her all over, love her for hours.

He looked round as the door opened and Callie came into the room. She had removed her flight suit, but she was covered from neck to toe in a layer of thick baggy jumpers and a pair of loose jogging bottoms. Frazer bit back a smile, over-whelmed by a wave of affection and desire. She looked so cute, impossibly appealing…and apprehensive. He saw her eyes widen as she looked at the mattresses close together by the fire, and he took her arm, leading her forward before she had a chance to voice the protests he knew were building inside her.

'I've spoken to Archie and updated him on the situation. All being well, the weather will settle and the helicopter can pick us up in the morning. We can come back for the vehicle when the roads are open.' Encouraging her to sit in the warm, he handed her a mug. 'Here, have some hot chocolate.'

'Thanks.'

'It really ought to be champagne, to mark the occasion.'

Her expression was thoughtful in the flickering light from the fire and candles. 'Dougie was so happy at having a son. And he was great at the birth.'

'He's an old pro at this.' Thinking of the large and happy family upstairs, he felt a pang of envy grip him—one that would have shocked him mere months ago. 'I didn't mean that, though. I meant it should be *us* celebrating.'

'Celebrating what?' she asked with a frown, sipping her drink.

'Our first baby together!'

He'd hoped to make her smile, for this to be a bonding experience, but he was horrified when the colour drained from her face and she turned away. Clearly he had unwittingly touched a raw nerve.

'Callie, what's wrong?'

'Nothing.'

Damn. It was like taking a couple of steps forward and several back with her. He had seen how affected she had been by the birth, but the tears now shimmering in her eyes revealed such hurt and disappointment he felt as if he'd been kicked in the gut. The urge to comfort and protect her was too strong to ignore. He gave in to his instincts. Despite being stripped down to his boxers and T-shirt, he took the empty mug from Callie's trembling fingers, set it aside, then sank down next to her and drew her gently into the circle of his arms.

Shocked, Callie held herself stiffly within Frazer's embrace, trying to resist the impulse to let go. She knew he hadn't meant anything by his remark, but it had affected her just the same, because she had worried since her treatment about whether she could ever have babies. Her oncologist had told her there was no reason why she shouldn't have children once she'd had the all-clear and was off the medication. No reason except never finding a man who would fancy her now she was damaged goods—even if she could ever bring herself to risk trusting one again.

All too conscious of Frazer's nearness, his warmth, the steady beat of his heart as he cradled her head against his chest, she sucked in a steadying breath, alarmed at the hiccuping sob that threatened to break free. She tried to pull away but Frazer wouldn't let her.

'Relax, sweetheart. Let me hold you, care for you.' His voice, soft and husky in the near darkness, sent a quiver through her and she found her resistance melting away. 'Talk to me.'

'W-what about?'

One hand gently stroked the feathery strands of her short hair. 'The day I took you home from the hospital you told me you had no family, that you had always been alone.'

'What else did I say?'

'That your creep of a husband had left.' He paused a moment, and she felt him inhale and exhale deeply before he continued. 'You said he'd told you that you weren't desirable.'

'Right.'

'Wrong.' Frazer's fingers sank lower, setting up a nerve-tingling caress on her bare neck. 'You do know Ed was crazy, right?'

Callie shrugged, unable to answer. Frazer had no idea what had happened to her…and she could never tell him. If he found out, he'd reject her, too.

'You seriously believe you are undesirable?' he prompted now, shifting their positions so his lips could whisper across the sensitive hollow behind her ear, his breath warm against her skin, his tongue-tip teasing and tickling. 'I'll just have to prove to you how wrong you are.'

'Frazer…'

Callie heard her own uncertainty as her protest died in her throat. She hesitated, torn between her constant need to be guarded and the temptation to give in to the madness of this night out of time and seek comfort with Frazer. Trembling, she curled into the erotic touch of his mouth. She wanted him so badly, but she was scared. Maybe tonight was her one chance to indulge her feelings, to know what being with him was like. In this place, huddled for warmth, he wouldn't see, wouldn't feel. She could take this one chance. It would have to last her a lifetime, because she wouldn't be able to repeat it, but she would make a special memory. And she was sure it would be better than she could ever imagine. She had never felt with anyone the way she did with Frazer. Ed's touches and kisses had never stirred her the way Frazer's did. He only had to look at her to set her aflame, make her ache with a desperate need. But what she was thinking was crazy. How could she carry it off?

Outside, the howling wind rattled the windows of the old farmhouse and she shivered. Frazer's arms instinctively tightened around her. 'Cold?'

'A bit,' she allowed, although she was bothered by far more than the chill of the air.

'Come here.' Pulling the other mattress closer, he drew her down with him in front of the fire, then covered them with the cosy duvets. As she lay on her side, he snuggled up behind her, wrapping his arms around her and spooning her back against him. 'Better?'

Callie didn't trust herself to speak. She felt ridiculously small and vulnerable next to Frazer's athletically muscled frame, with his heat surrounding her, making her all too conscious of his maleness, his raw sexuality. The temptation to succumb to the driving need to turn over and ask for what her body craved was unbearable.

'Tell me about Ed.' His words diverted her from her wayward thoughts even while his lips nibbled along the back of her neck, fanning the flames of her need. 'How long were you married?'

'Five months.'

His surprise was obvious. 'Not long.'

'We were never good together. We made a mistake.' She certainly had—trusting Ed, believing in him.

'What happened?' Frazer asked now, the palm of one hand distracting her as he stroked slowly back and forth across her abdomen, and she tensed, anxious that he would try to touch her breasts, knowing she couldn't let him.

'Lots of little things,' she managed to reply. 'A couple of big, insurmountable ones.'

The hand caressed lower, easing her concern. 'Is one of those insurmountable issues why the baby upset you tonight? You wanted children?'

'Yes.'

His insight was a surprise. Pain lanced inside her when she thought about it. Somehow it was easier talking in the dark while Frazer couldn't see her. The silence lengthened, but he didn't push her for explanations, simply waited, holding her, while she made up her mind whether to trust him with more of herself. His acceptance and understanding helped, and she found herself telling him a bit about Ed's betrayal when he had left her—not the health reason, or his hateful words, but the second secret which had meant her marriage was over.

'Ed knew I yearned to start a family straight away. I thought he agreed. He gave every impression of consoling me when each month went by and nothing happened.' Unconsciously, she cuddled closer to Frazer's warmth and protection. 'It was only when we broke up that he told me he'd had a vasectomy years ago and he'd never wanted children.'

'And the bastard let you go on wondering and wanting

and worrying when he knew all the time you would never get pregnant?'

Callie nodded in response, hearing the incredulity and anger on her behalf in Frazer's voice. 'I'll never forgive him for that. All that agonising, fearing there was something wrong with me. But he was right about one thing,' she continued, bitterness lacing her tone. 'It probably was just as well. He would have been as lousy a father as he was a husband.'

As it was, Ed would have left her alone with a child to support, playing no role in their lives. She knew that. At times she would have liked to have had one anyway, but the rational part of her knew she would never have coped with a pregnancy or a baby at the time of her surgery. Especially alone. And she *was* alone. She always had been and always would be.

She sucked in a shaky breath as Frazer's hand slid under her jumpers. The touch of his fingers against her bare skin was amazing, terrible, wonderful. She ought to stop him. In a minute she would. Maybe. Biting her lip, she felt her stomach muscles tauten as one fingertip traced smaller and smaller circles around her navel, making her quiver.

'And you're divorced now?'

Callie bit her lip, struggling to follow the conversation. 'Nearly. It would have come through sooner, but Ed did a disappearing act with his new woman and it took my solicitor time to track him down. He's signed the papers now, so it's a formality. It will be over by the New Year,' she finished, her voice a mere whisper as she lost herself in the magic of Frazer's touch, heady from the hint of his earthy male aroma.

'You deserve better, Callie.' His hold tightened, as if he was trying to enclose her, keep her safe. 'You'll have your own family. And a man who loves and cherishes you.'

She cursed the silent tears that spilled between her lashes, unable to explain to Frazer why his prediction was never likely to come true. To do so would mean confiding about her problem. And she couldn't. She felt too ashamed, too physically imperfect, knowing he would be disgusted and that any attraction he thought he now felt for her would die. So she kept silent, wishing that things were different, that Frazer could be a fantasy man who would love her. Yet reality intruded, and she knew this would be the only night she ever spent in his arms. Dared she take advantage of that fact? For long moments she lay still, revelling in being close to him, seeking the courage to turn and face him, wondering what would happen if she did.

Frazer sensed there was much more about Ed and what had happened in her marriage than Callie was prepared to tell him. It hurt that she still didn't trust him enough to share what was hurting her, especially what it was that made her believe her idiot of a husband was right about her not being a desirable woman. He'd like to track the man down and take him apart piece by piece. The pain in Callie's voice had been unmistakable. And after all she had clearly been through as a child, without parents or a family, no doubt what Ed had done to her had felt like the final betrayal. No wonder she found it hard to trust. She was fiercely independent and determined to stay that way, which didn't bode well for his efforts to get closer to her and find a niche for himself in her life.

Sighing softly, he closed his eyes and relished holding her close. She felt small and delicate against him, yet he knew she had amazing strength, both in body and spirit. Every time he breathed in he was teased and tantalised by her sultry coconut scent. And why had he always been keen on long hair on a woman when he was just discovering how Callie's short, soft, feathery strands allowed him uninterrupted access to her neck? The short strands felt like satin under his fingers and the softness of her skin was extraordinary. He loved touching her. Never wanted to stop.

With the wind and the blizzard still raging outside, he buried his face against Callie's neck, dreaming of all the ways he wished to be spending his nights with her in his bed. His fingers resumed their exploration, and her flesh quivered in response to his touch at her navel, but as he gradually inched higher, towards her breasts, she caught his wrist, her body tensing. Worried he'd gone too far, he stilled, letting her guide him, disappointed when she pushed his hand back down. He was about to apologise— but all thoughts, all words were forgotten, when, instead of removing his hand as he'd expected, she slid it beneath the waistband of her jogging trousers…and lower. His breath lodged in his throat. His heart started to thud beneath his ribs.

'Callie?' Voice hoarse, he whispered her name.

He had to be dreaming. Unable to believe this was true, he cautiously accepted her unspoken invitation, growing bolder as she pressed back against the growing fullness of his arousal, moving one leg to give his hand better access. Losing himself in the silken feel of her, warm and moist in welcome, he nipped at the lobe of her ear before he sucked on it, matching the rhythm of his stroking, exploring fingers. It wasn't long before the change in her breathing, the rapid rate of her pulse and the arousing whimpers she made, told him that she was close to release, and he redoubled his efforts, matching the rhythm of her hips as he rubbed himself against her and pushed her over the edge.

Gasping, she turned in his arms, burying her face against his neck, panting hot breaths against his skin. It felt right to have her in his arms. He slid a hand down to cup her rear, drawing her closer, knowing from her movements and the little purr that escaped her that she was more than aware of his own need.

'Frazer…'

Her voice was a shaky whisper as she pulled a few centimetres away. He wished he could see her properly in the dimness of the room, could read her expression, but he only distinguished the glimmer of her eyes, the shape of her lush, rosy lips. They were so close, so tempting. He touched his mouth to hers, finding her pliant—hot and demanding. She tasted amazing, honey-sweet, and he couldn't get enough of her. Groaning, he took more, meeting her questing tongue with his, sucking on her, drawing her into his mouth, inflamed further by her soft moans as she pushed him onto his back and wriggled on top of him.

Again his hands slid under her jumpers, glorying in the feel of her satin-soft skin beneath his palms, but as he moved up her ribcage she caught his wrists once more, urging his hands away, linking her fingers with his as she pinned them by his head. A frown creased his brow, and he wondered why she didn't want him to touch her breasts. But her mouth was urgent on his, the deeply erotic kiss making him mindless, and the way she rubbed against him threatened to blow away the last shreds of his sanity.

Somehow her jogging trousers and his boxers had disappeared. His hands were shaking as he pulled one of their medical bags towards him and rummaged inside, praying he'd find what he needed. He did. And, from the speed with which she plucked the condom from his fingers, her relief was as great as his own. For a moment the fog in his mind became less dense, and he worried that they were rushing this. Yes, he wanted her. More than he'd ever wanted anything. But a ripple of unease ran down his spine—a warning he couldn't grasp that something wasn't right.

'Callie?' He cupped her face, halting her movements as she ripped open the foil. 'Are you sure this is what you want?'

'Just give me tonight.'

The words were so soft he had to strain to hear them. Tonight? He wanted to give her for ever. Concerned about what she meant, he opened his mouth to clarify things. But all thoughts evaporated as she closed one hand around him and took him towards paradise. When he didn't think he could stand it any longer she quickly sheathed him with the protection, then her hips straddled his and their sighs of pleasure combined as she slid down and united them, lost in a daze of unimaginable pleasure. His hands stroked the silken skin of her thighs, gliding up to grasp her hips, guiding her movements as he rose to meet her. It was amazing…hot, urgent, incredible. Her hands clenched in his T-shirt, fisting on his abdomen. She bent to kiss him, and he met her demand for demand, stroke for stroke. When she had to drag her mouth away to draw in a ragged breath he tightened his hold, knowing he wasn't going to last much longer. She shifted position and he groaned as she took him even deeper. They moved together, chasing the ultimate fulfilment, clinging to each other as they finally spiralled into oblivion, her soft cries joining his as they were caught up in an indescribable vortex of pleasure.

Callie collapsed on him and he wrapped his arms around

her shaking, trembling body, needing to hold her, to keep her close. He couldn't breathe, couldn't speak, couldn't think…had never experienced anything so perfect, so unforgettable, so extraordinary before. In that moment, as his breathing and his heartbeat gradually slowed, he knew a sense of utter peace and rightness—knew without doubt that even though he had only known Callie for a short time he was in love for the first time in his life. Whole-heartedly. Completely. Irrevocably. And he wanted to spend the rest of his life with her. A smile on his face, he followed her into sleep.

When he woke, he sensed at once he was alone, and the peace he had known during the night was challenged by a return of doubt and worry, of his unease that what had happened between him and Callie, while magical, had been too fast.

'Callie?'

It was still dark outside, but he could tell the room was empty. The wind had dropped in the night, and now the noises were from inside the house. Anxious to find Callie, to speak with her, hold her, he quickly dressed and used the bathroom, before finding Dougie and some of the children in the kitchen. The power was still off, but the man had already been out to the stock and was making tea and a big pot of porridge on the range.

'Everything all right, Doc?'

'Fine, thanks.' He hid his personal concerns and enquired after the family. 'How are Moira and the baby?'

'No problems! We've decided to call our son Frazer Callum, in honour of you both being here to help us. Callie is up with Moira now,' he added, his smile broad.

Frazer nodded, managing a smile in return. 'I'll just check on them.'

Before he could leave the kitchen, his mobile phone rang.

It was Archie Stewart. His boss had good news. The helicopter could fly, and one of the pilots was on his way out to collect them. More nervous than he wanted to admit, Frazer went up the stairs to see Moira and the baby…and Callie. He wanted more than anything to get her alone, to tell her how he felt, but his heart sank when he walked into the McStays' large, airy bedroom. Callie wouldn't meet his gaze, her movements jerky as she tried to keep a distance between them.

Hurt pierced him, and he felt sick to his stomach. He was confused, bitterly disappointed, scared. Callie's rejection was a physical pain, searing inside him, destroying the joy and hope that had filled him when they had been together. It had been so special between them. How could she not feel that? How could she switch off the passion and the closeness? Did it mean nothing to her?

Swearing profusely to himself, he knew he deserved a good kicking. These last weeks he had been so patient, trying to gain her trust, her confidence, and last night he had allowed himself to lose control, to lose sight of the bigger picture, taking what she had offered, what he had needed, when a part of him had known it was too soon. Callie had been emotional, reacting to the baby, to her painful memories, to making herself vulnerable by telling him what he knew was only part of the story about her marriage and her bastard of a husband. Now he had undone all the progress he had made. She had retreated back into her shell, and he knew instinctively that it was going to be harder than ever to break down her barriers again.

Somehow he managed to draw on his professionalism as he talked to Moira and examined both her and the baby. Reassured that both were fine, and content for them to remain at home, he held on to his composure and informed Callie of the news that the helicopter was on its way, his gut knotting at the relief evident on her face. As they packed up their gear and took what they needed from the four-by-four, leaving the rest in the vehicle for collection later, he tried to breach her defences.

'Callie—'

'Don't, Frazer. Please.' The shakiness and distance in her voice broke his heart. 'Last night shouldn't have happened. I'm sorry. It wasn't your fault, it was mine. But it was a one-off. It can't happen again.'

Before he could reply, he heard the sound of the helicopter approaching. Moments later they took their leave of the McStays, and Frazer wondered if he was ever going to know the joy the family shared. He wanted what they had, that close, happy bond, a house full of children and laughter and love.

And he wanted it all with Callie.

Losing his head last night may have cost him whatever chance he had of realising that dream…of winning the heart of the only woman he had ever loved.

CHAPTER SEVEN

ON CHRISTMAS EVE, Callie sat in her car in the snowy parking area outside the air ambulance base, plucking up the nerve to do what had to be done. Her hands clenched on the steering wheel. How could she have been so stupid? Her selfishness in throwing herself at Frazer had ruined everything.

Disturbed from her thoughts by the sound of the helicopter firing to life, she watched as the crew on duty climbed on board and the aircraft lifted off on an emergency call. Which meant the base would be quiet, and this was a good time to talk to her boss.

Feeling ill, her legs shaking, she barely noticed the biting cold wind as she walked towards the building. Inside it was warm, and bright with festive decorations. She paused a moment, realising how much she had come to feel she belonged with her new colleagues. In the short time she had been in Strathlochan she had made more friends and felt more at home than at any time in her life before. It made it even harder to leave, to give all this up. For the first time she had felt a buzz about Christmas, had been looking forward to spending it here. Now it was over—and it was her fault.

'Callie!' Archie Stewart's voice made her jump. 'Can't keep away from the place even on your day off, I see.'

She could hardly manage a smile in response to his teasing. Nerves tightened her stomach. 'I wondered if I could have a word with you?'

'Yes, of course.' Her boss's smile faded and he looked at her with concern before leading her along to his office. 'I heard today that Desmond Pollock, your patient who had the chainsaw accident, is doing well. They saved his arm, but he'll have a long recovery.'

'That's good news. It was touch and go for a while whether he would survive at all.'

Talking about the incident made her think of Frazer, and her nervous anxiety returned—along with the crushing inner pain that had been with her since she had woken up in his arms at the McStays' yesterday morning. Aware Archie was watching her, she tried to control her expression and took the seat he offered, clenching her hands in her lap.

'So, Callie, what can I do for you?'

'I'm really sorry, but things aren't working out as I'd hoped,' she began, unable to meet his gaze.

'I thought you loved working on the helicopter—that it was what you had always wanted to do?'

'So did I.' She bit her lip, her nails digging into her palms. 'But I can't do it. I have to leave.'

Archie frowned, his gaze assessing, and he leaned forward, steepling his hands beneath his chin as he considered her. 'Callie, your work has been exceptional. Everyone likes you. Tell me what's wrong, what's making things difficult, and I'll do all I can to help sort things out.'

'It's not that.' She fought down a wave of panic, hating that she was lying to a man who had been nothing but kind to her. 'I can't settle here. I need to go back to Glasgow.'

'Are you sure?'

'Yes,' she whispered, feeling she was betraying the trust he had placed in her.

'I'm very surprised…and disappointed.' Her guilt increased tenfold at his words. 'Will you at least think about it again? Let me have your final decision after the New Year.'

It wasn't what she wanted, but it would take a while for Archie to find a replacement, especially over the holiday season. She felt bad enough as it was, without leaving him even more in the lurch. 'All right. But I have to say I won't change my mind.'

'What's the matter, darling?'

Frazer sighed and turned from staring sightlessly out of the window, trying to paste a reassuring smile on his face as he looked at his grandmother. 'I'm fine.'

'I don't think you are.' Lily patted the sofa and he reluctantly sat down beside her. 'Tell me what's wrong. Is it Callie?'

'Why would you say that?' he prevaricated, just hearing the name enough to twist his insides with pain.

'I'm not blind, darling. I saw how you looked at her, and I've heard the way you speak about her.' She took his hand and squeezed it. 'Callie is a lovely young woman, I liked her immediately, but she strikes me as being very lonely.'

He let out a huff of breath, remembering how alone she had been when he had first met her. 'She has no family—has always been alone, has never had anyone to care for her, to love her. And she's been hurt. She doesn't trust easily.'

'You want to be the man to change that?'

His gran's perception had always been scary. 'I'd hoped that might happen. Now I think I've blown it. I made a stupid miscalculation—and I'd been so careful, so patient until then. Callie has retreated, and she won't talk to me.' Frustrated, he ran his hands through his hair.

'You have to try, Frazer. She needs you. I was really hoping Callie would spend the day with us tomorrow, that we could give her a happy, loving Christmas,' his grandmother admitted sadly.

'I wanted that, too.'

Now he wasn't sure it was going to be possible. How could it be when Callie had shut him out so completely since they had parted unhappily the previous morning? Sighing, he leaned forward and absently stroked Hamish, who lay relaxed and untroubled in front of the fire. Frazer's own mind was distracted as he wrestled with the Callie problem and how he was going to solve it.

The sound of his mobile phone ringing permeated the thoughtful silence in the room.

'Sorry, Gran, I have to take this.'

Her smile was understanding. 'I'll go and put the kettle on. Maybe a cup of tea will help aid our thinking up a plan.'

Grateful to have someone on his side, he answered the phone. 'Frazer McInnes.'

'It's Archie.'

'Hello, boss.' He frowned, concerned there had been some major incident that required him to go in to work. 'Is anything wrong? Do you need me?'

'I'm hoping you can help solve a problem. Is there something going on with Callie that I should know about?' his boss asked without preamble.

Frazer's stomach lurched. 'Excuse me?' Surely Archie hadn't found out about the other night at the McStays'?

'Callie came to see me today.'

Frazer stilled, his mind in turmoil.

'She's resigned.'

Shocked and hurt, it took him a moment to find his voice. 'She's done what? Why?'

'I don't know. That's why I rang. I wondered if Callie had said anything to you—if she's been unhappy. She says this isn't what she wants after all and she's going back to Glasgow.'

The news was devastating. Frazer didn't know what to say. Why? That was the question that kept pounding in his brain. After hanging up, assuring Archie he'd do what he could, he stared at the decorations, the presents under the fragrant tree. Some of them for Callie. Happy Christmas. Yeah, right. He'd never felt less cheerful. His insides were knotted and fear weighed heavily upon him. He had to see Callie, talk to her, find out what was going on and why she was running away. Because the more he thought about it the more he was sure that was what was happening. For whatever reason, she had panicked about that night. She'd been denying it from the moment they had woken up, saying it didn't mean anything, that it was a one-off. The hell it was.

She'd been swaddled in clothes against the freezing temperature, but all he'd been aware of was the amazing heat between them, the unique feeling of being inside her, joined so completely, and of the searing intensity of pleasure that had been so much more than he had ever known before. He wanted more with Callie, wanted everything, but she was spooked and he needed to know why. No way could he let her go. Not without a fight.

He wanted to spend hours lovingly exploring every inch of her body, listening to those arousing sounds she made when she surrendered to pleasure. And he wanted to bring her endless pleasure in every way he could. He wanted her to let go of her rigid control, as she had that night in the dark, and he wanted her to trust him to take her to paradise and bring her safely back again. To trust him not to hurt her or ever let her down. So much had happened between them in the few weeks running up to Christmas, and he couldn't let it end here—not when he knew in his heart and soul that Callie was special and that he wanted to spend the rest of his life showing her what she meant to him.

His mind made up, he walked through to the kitchen. 'Gran, I'm sorry, but I have to go.'

'Callie?'

'Yes.' He swallowed, finding it hard to say the words out loud. 'That was my boss. Callie resigned today. I have to see her—talk to her, try to stop her.'

'Of course you do, darling. Do what you have to. And bring her here tomorrow if you can.' She smiled, resting a hand on his cheek, warming him with her kindness, her faith, her understanding.

'I'll do my best.'

Calling Hamish to him, he kissed his grandmother and went out into the swirling snow. Dusk was upon them as he climbed into his vehicle, the hills behind the town shrouded in cloud. He stopped at the local bakery, open until late before closing for the holiday, then headed to Callie's house, hoping that he wasn't too late.

After seeing Archie, Callie had walked until she was exhausted, hoping to forget. Now she lay back in a hot bubble bath, the fragrance of coconut filling the small room. Frazer loved the scent. She closed her eyes, wondering why every little thing made her think of him. It hurt so much. She had been so incredibly foolish. How had she ever imagined she could steal that night out of time and think things would go back to normal afterwards? Making love with Frazer had been the most incredible thing she had ever experienced. That she would never know such ecstasy again made her cry, and it was as if something had died inside her. Worst of all, she had hurt him. She had never meant to, had somehow persuaded herself that it wouldn't mean that much to him, but the pain and confusion in his eyes had been unbearable.

Annie was away, visiting her mother for a few days over Christmas, so she wasn't able to talk with her. Not that she had ever had a friend to confide in before, or to ask for advice. And what would Annie say? She would encourage her to tell Frazer the truth, and she just couldn't. He would be appalled, would no longer find her remotely attractive. So either way it was over. There was no option but to give up her dream job and her new-found home and friends in Strathlochan—and all thoughts of belonging somewhere. It was impossible to stay here now. She couldn't go on working with Frazer, not loving him as she did and knowing all was hopeless. Nor could she stay if he knew the truth. It would be too awkward, too painful.

As the water cooled, she rose, averting her gaze from the reflection of her damaged body in the mirror. She hated looking at herself, felt so incomplete. Breasts were so much a part of being a woman, and—

The insistent ring of the doorbell intruded on her painful thoughts. She pulled on her robe, her skin dewy and flushed from her bath, and went downstairs, horrified to find Frazer on her doorstep. Before she could stop him, he slipped inside,

Hamish at his heels, and carried a bag through to the kitchen. Shaking, she watched him, seeing the sadness in his melting chocolate eyes, the dark circles beneath, the shadow of stubble darkening his jaw.

'W-what are you doing?' She cursed the tremor in her voice that threatened to give her away.

'I've brought you some pecan and maple Danish.'

It was so incongruous she didn't know what to say. 'How did you know I liked them?' she asked at length, wary and confused, wrapping her arms around herself to resist the overwhelming urge to go to him.

'Given the names of your cats, it wasn't such a stretch.'

The full-on dimpled smile stole the very breath from her lungs. Danger signals clanged inside her. She couldn't weaken. Not even when his voice dropped and sent a tingle down her spine.

'Callie…'

'You shouldn't have come here.'

'Archie rang me. He's worried about you. So am I.' His smile faded and his eyes held confusion, hurt and regret. 'Why, Callie? You're putting down roots here, you have friends, you love your job. Why are you running away?'

Tears scalded her eyes and she fought to keep them at bay. 'I can't stay here.'

'Tell me why.'

She shook her head, backing up as he moved towards her. 'Don't, Frazer.'

'I want to understand. I need to know.'

'Why?' She moved into the living room, trying to put more distance between them. 'What difference does it make to you?'

Dark brown eyes filled with an emotion she had never

expected to see. 'I love you, Callie. I care what happens to you and I want to be here for you.'

She thought her heart was going to stop. He couldn't love her. He *wouldn't* love her if he knew. 'You can't,' she whispered, feeling broken inside, wishing this wasn't happening.

'Why not?'

There was only one way she could explain. Without words. Now the moment was here, Callie didn't think she could do it. With a mix of defiance and resignation, she forced violently trembling fingers to undo the tie of her robe. Watching his eyes, she waited for the moment of realisation, the revulsion and rejection which she knew would come. She fought back tears as she slid the robe from her shoulders and allowed it to slither down her arms, leaving her naked, exposed…the truth revealed.

Shock darkened his eyes and she heard his indrawn breath. For a moment he just stared at her, apparently incapable of speech or movement, and her bravado deserted her. This had been another foolish mistake. Unable to hold back her whimper of distress, she snatched up the robe and turned away, commanding hands that seemed paralysed to refasten it, legs that refused to move to get her out of here. Desperate, humiliated, she stumbled from the room.

'No!' The negative was rough, taut with emotion. Hands caught her before she made it halfway up the stairs, arms locking round her to subdue her frantic struggles for freedom. 'No, Callie, don't.' Frazer's voice was raw, his breath warm on her neck as he nuzzled against her. 'Please, sweetheart. Trust me.'

Her whole body shook from head to toe. Despite his words, she could only think of escaping. 'Let me go. Let me go.'

'I can't do that, Callie. I'm never going to let you go.'

'Frazer…'

His hold tightened. 'Did you think this would matter to me? Did you think that I would desire you less? I've been crazy with wanting you since the first moment we met… I still want you.'

'No.'

He pressed close behind her, one hand splaying low over her belly as he pulled her against him, making her intensely aware of the hard length of his arousal. Disbelief, excitement and fear all swirled inside her. Disbelief that he could still bear to touch her, could still possibly find her attractive. Excitement because she ached for him and wanted him more than she'd believed possible. Fear because she found it so hard to trust, couldn't bear to have him look at her or touch her. Was she just a novelty? A challenge? Did he pity her? Whatever it was, she knew she would never walk away intact if this went any further.

'You have to go.'

'I'm not leaving you, Callie. Not ever. So you'd better get used to it.'

Before she could reply to his determined words, he picked her up in his arms and carried her the rest of the way upstairs and into her bedroom. He drew back the duvet and set her in the bed with exquisite gentleness, quickly dispensing with his clothes before following her down. Pulling the covers over them, he turned her towards him and cupped her face with his hands. Tears squeezed between her lashes at the care and the sincerity and what did indeed look impossibly like love in his incredibly sexy eyes.

'Frazer…'

'Shh.' Cradling her head against his shoulder, he wrapped an arm around her waist, drawing her closer, one deliciously masculine leg slipping between hers. 'Just let me hold you, sweetheart.'

Unable to hold back her tears, she allowed herself to relax against him, seeking his comfort and his strength, hardly daring to believe that any of this was real.

Choking back his own emotion, Frazer held Callie tight and let her cry out her hurt. So much now made sense to him, like a morning fog clearing under the heat of the sun to reveal the view. He realised now why she hadn't wanted him to touch her there, why she had been scared to go to the hospital when she was hurt or to let him examine her, why she always wore baggy clothes. Annie had discovered Callie's secret, but had been duty-bound not to break her confidence. That was something else he now understood. No doubt this was why Callie had believed herself undesirable, never likely to have a relationship or children. Why she had thought one night in the dark with her clothes on was all she could hope for. Her bastard of a husband had clearly given her no support, had shredded her fragile self-image, left her when she'd needed someone most. And, having no one else, she had been through everything alone. His heart ached for her.

There was so much he needed to know. What had happened, how she felt, if she was on medication, what the prognosis was. Not that it made any difference to how he felt about her. He would be by her side from now on whatever happened, and she wouldn't be alone ever again. It was time she knew that. And time she knew just how sexy and desirable he found her. As her tears subsided, he tipped her head up so he could look at her, leaning in to lick the salty tears from beneath beautiful but bruised purple eyes.

'I love you, Callie.' He saw her swallow, saw rosy lips tremble. 'I'm going to say it every day for the rest of our lives and prove to you in every way that it's true.'

'I'm not perfect.'

Her whispered words brought a lump to his throat. 'You're perfect to me. The person you are, inside and out, your courage, your compassion, your strength, your humour, your kindness. I see all of you, Callie. I love all of you.' Carefully, he slipped a hand inside her robe and gently covered her mis-shapen right breast with his palm, hearing her gasp as her breath hitched, feeling her body tense. 'Even this. It's part of you. I ache for what you have been through, but this doesn't make me love you any less. It never will.'

Callie struggled to come to terms with all Frazer had said, unable to doubt his sincerity. When his mouth brushed hers, his tongue teasing each corner before whispering along the seam of her lips, her response was instinctive.

'Let me show you how much I love you, Callie, how sexy I find you.'

She whimpered, her lips parting to meet a kiss that was slow, drugging, deeply seductive. Her arms slid round him, her fingers exploring the broad expanse of his back, lean muscles flexing under warm, supple skin. Every particle of her being quivered with sensations she had never expected to know again. His touch electrified her. Fear slowly vanished as he pulled back and stripped the robe from her body, his hands unsteady, nothing in his eyes but desire, and love, and hot, sexy passion. It made her want to cry again. This time with happiness.

His fingertips explored her with heart-stopping gentleness, and she caught her breath as they moved to her right breast. 'Do you have sensation here?' he murmured, lost in concentration.

'Y-yes.' She was surprised just how much she *could* feel—

and how incredibly good it was. She hadn't known. Her heart pounded, and she arched off the bed as his lips and tongue caressed her imperfect flesh, setting off a storm of need inside her. 'Frazer…'

'Mmm?'

'I—Oh!'

Callie squeezed her eyes shut, her hands clinging to him as pleasure speared inside her. Oh, God! She had *never* expected anything like this. It was wonderful. Impossible. She wanted more. And Frazer seemed to know, anticipating her needs even before her brain had processed the hazy thoughts. His skilled hands and clever mouth left no part of her untouched or unexplored. Time ceased to have any meaning. Again and again she thought she would expire from sheer tortured bliss as he took her from one unbelievable pinnacle of ecstasy to another, keeping her on the brink, the ache inside her building and building to unbearable proportions. When she could stand it no longer, he caught her hands and linked their fingers together. Scarcely able to breathe, she wrapped her legs around him, desperate to feel all of him inside her, her hips moving restlessly to his.

'Please,' she sobbed.

'Look at me.' Somehow she forced heavy eyelids open in compliance with his heated demand. She met his fevered gaze, in little doubt of his need, his feelings. 'I love you, Callie.' Her hands clung to his as he groaned and united them…thoroughly, but with torturous slowness. 'Will you marry me?'

Stunned, she stared at him, filled with warmth, an unknown peace seeping through her. And she knew. At last she knew. Without doubt. 'Yes, Frazer, I will. I love you, too.'

His smile captured her heart, made her believe in for ever,

in belonging. His mouth came down on hers in a searing, branding, possessive kiss, one she met and matched with equal enthusiasm. Who cared if she couldn't breathe? Breathing was vastly overrated when the rest of her was zinging with electricity and on the cusp of a climax the magnitude of which she'd never experienced before. Tightening her legs around his waist, she matched his rhythm, her body moving with his, meeting every demand, giving everything, taking everything, and she cried out as they soared together, tumbling in freefall over the precipice as an explosive release ripped through them.

Smiling as Callie snuggled against him, Frazer trailed the fingers of one hand down her spine, watching as the first light of the Christmas dawn peeped through the curtains. After the amazing night they had shared he wasn't sure he would ever move again. But he didn't care. Nothing mattered but winning Callie's heart. He didn't know how it was possible, but he loved her more every moment. What they shared was special, amazing. It was something he had never imagined would happen to him, but now that it had he welcomed it with open arms. He would never cease to be thankful to fate for bringing Callie into his life, for letting her love him even a fraction as much as he loved her.

She made that little purring sound of contentment that always got to him. 'Morning, sweetheart. Merry Christmas.' He dropped a kiss on top of her head.

'Merry Christmas,' she murmured, and a tremor ran through him as she set her mouth to his neck and sucked on his skin. 'I have a present for you downstairs.'

'You've already given me the only gift I ever want. Yourself. Your love. Your trust.'

'Frazer…'

He saw moisture shimmer in her stunning eyes, and drew her in for a thorough, breath-stealing kiss. When he was finally able to speak again he rolled her over, cupping her face with his hands.

'We can't change the past, Callie, but we can make the present and the future whatever we want it to be. Together. I'll spend the rest of my days loving you. And we'll have as many children as you want, making every day special, making Christmas and family traditions all our own.'

'I can't believe this is real.' A tremulous smile curved her lips. 'I must be dreaming.'

Sliding one hand down her delectable body, he gave the curve of her rear a gentle pinch.

'Ouch. Frazer!'

'Nope. You're not dreaming.'

Laughing, she wrapped her arms around his neck. 'Then I'm the luckiest woman on earth.'

And he was the luckiest man who'd ever lived. He couldn't wait to tell his gran. To share this special day with her…the first day of the rest of his life with Callie.

EPILOGUE

Christmas Eve—twelve months later...

THE sound of cheers filled the air as Callie and Frazer made a run for the car, finding themselves showered with rice in the process. Laughing, Callie turned her back on the crowd and tossed her bouquet. Made up of ivy for fidelity and marriage, holly for domestic happiness, snowdrops for hope and white roses for eternal love, it encompassed the spirit of the season and all her dreams and feelings for her new husband and their life together.

When she peeped over her shoulder she was thrilled to discover that the bouquet had landed squarely in the reluctant arms of A and E doctor Annie Webster. Annie scowled at her, but Callie only grinned. There was nothing she would like more than for her best friend to be as blissfully happy as she was at this moment.

Frazer trailed his fingers down her cheek before closing the passenger door and walking round to slide behind the wheel. As he started the car and drove them away—brightly coloured tinsel, banners and tin cans streaming and clattering behind them—Callie leaned back and closed her eyes, wanting to hold the memories, to relive everything about this glorious day…a day she had never expected to know.

It had been the most amazing year. A year in which she had said goodbye to her lonely past and embraced the future. Frazer had kept all his promises, proving to her every day that she could trust him, that he loved her, that her heart was safe with him. After their Christmas and New Year of discovering each other and announcing their engagement, to the delight of grandmother Lily, Frazer had presented her with a glorious platinum ring set with a heart-shaped purple sapphire he insisted was the exact same shade of her eyes. She had swiftly moved into his spacious, cosy cottage on the wooded hillside above the town and instantly felt at home. Her cats, Pecan and Maple, had taken longer to settle and establish a truce with Hamish and with Frazer's floating band of feral misfit cats who roamed the garden and outbuildings.

In June, Frazer had been by her side when she was given the final all-clear by her oncologist and had come off the medication for good. He had then whisked her away to beautiful Tuscany for a week to celebrate. They'd made love, walked and talked, eaten far too much delicious Italian food, especially ice cream, and then made love some more. With every day that passed her love for him grew more intense, and—even more amazing to her—he continued to love her, too, despite her flaws, continued to desire her despite her imperfections.

'We're home, Mrs McInnes.' Her eyes opened, and the first things she saw were Frazer's sinful smile and sexy eyes. 'I can't tell you how long I've been waiting to say that.'

'If I say I can't believe I'm not dreaming, will you promise not to pinch me?'

Chuckling, he cupped her cheek with one hand, and she

pressed her face against his warm palm. 'How about I kiss you instead?'

'A much better idea,' she agreed, revelling in the raw, hot, intense meeting of mouths.

'Indoors.' His throaty voice was hoarse. 'Before we scandalise the wildlife.'

Happier than she had ever been, she slipped out of the car, her hand seeking his as they walked together to the cottage, Hamish scampering at their feet, a tartan ribbon around his neck. 'For a Border terrier, he made a great ring bearer.'

'He did,' Frazer agreed, mischief in his eyes. 'And he didn't do anything unforgivable in the chapel.'

Smiling, Callie leaned against him as he opened the door, reaching up to kiss his cheek. 'It was a beautiful wedding. Thank you.'

'You made it beautiful.' He manoeuvred them inside and closed the door, linking his arms around her waist and drawing her close. 'You're beautiful. My Christmas bride.'

'It was a perfect day. I don't know how you managed it, but it was a wonderful idea to have the ceremony in the private chapel at Strathlochan Castle.'

Callie hadn't wanted anything big and fancy. She just wanted Frazer. And, knowing that her first brief, unhappy marriage to Ed had been conducted in a soulless register office, with just a couple of strangers as witnesses, Frazer had done everything and more to make this day unforgettable. Archie and all their friends and colleagues from the air base, the hospital and the other rescue services, had been there to share it with them. Lily had been ecstatic, and in her element, while Frazer's parents, sister and her family had all flown over for the occasion.

She sighed, thinking of the magical ceremony and the fun-filled, happy reception which had followed it, with the bride and groom leading the way from the chapel to the castle's function room behind a lone piper, the music sounding hauntingly beautiful in the crisp winter air. Even the weather had been kind. Certainly kinder than the previous year, when Strathlochan had been hit by Arctic conditions for weeks. Today the sun had shone in a pale blue sky, glittering off the waters of the loch and the hills beyond, the peaks of which were dusted with a coating of snow.

Now they were home. They had decided against an immediate honeymoon, just wanting to be together, in their own space, with the animals, in the place they loved best. The cottage felt warm and welcoming, decorated as it was with fresh holly and ivy. A too-big Christmas tree, which she and Frazer had cut from the surrounding woods, dominated the living room, and a log fire smouldered in the grate. Christmas was now her favourite time of the year. It marked when she had come to Strathlochan, when she and Frazer had fallen in love, and when he had asked her to marry him. Her first ever happy Christmas had been spent here, with Frazer and Lily. And now her second heavenly Christmas saw her joined with Frazer. For ever. Every year they would have something even more special to celebrate and appreciate.

She looked down at her beautiful engagement ring. It was teamed now with a platinum wedding band, set with sapphires the same shade of purple. Frazer had insisted on wearing his own platinum band, telling her he wanted to proclaim his love and commitment to the world. Just thinking of his words brought fresh tears to her eyes. How could she be this lucky? She, who had always been alone, had found her soul mate, a man who loved and cherished her, who had taught her how to trust and had given her a place to belong. He was a special doctor and a special man. Someone to trust in.

'We've come full circle, haven't we?' Smiling, he led her to their bedroom. 'I thought last Christmas had brought me all I could ask for, but today has surpassed everything.'

'You say the loveliest things.'

She smiled as a faint tinge of colour stained his cheekbones. For a tough, rugged, outdoor kind of man, he could be wonderfully romantic. But she wouldn't tease him about it. Not now. Not when she had another special gift to give him.

'How do I get you out of this thing?' Frazer murmured, as he stood beside the bed. 'It's a stunning dress, and you look sensational in it, so I don't want to ruin it. But it has to come off. Now.'

As always, a fiery ache of need tightened inside her as he growled his impatience, and she anticipated the wondrous excitement of the earth-shattering lovemaking she knew was to come. They still could never get enough of each other. Sliding the jacket of his dress suit off his shoulders, she went to work on his shirt.

'You look gorgeous, too.'

He grunted, his fingers struggling with the line of tiny pearlised buttons that held her unconventional purple dress together. 'At least you didn't make me wear a kilt.'

'Your knees are worth showing off,' she told him, biting back a grin, 'but I didn't want any important parts freezing off before you'd performed your marital duties!'

'Heaven forbid.'

The rich sound of his laughter sent a shiver of awareness

down her spine. Hungry for him, she dispensed with his shirt, trailing her fingertips down his leanly muscled, hair-brushed chest and lower, smiling as his stomach muscles contracted in response to her touch. Urgency increasing, she turned her attention to the fastening of his trousers, swiftly releasing the button but having trouble sliding the zip over the obvious evidence of his arousal.

'I think someone's pleased to see me,' she provoked, leaning in to set her mouth to one male nipple. He swore roughly and she giggled. 'How are those buttons coming along?'

'Damn it, Callie!'

Taking pity on him, she moved her own fingers to help, heat searing through her when the task was completed and he sensuously peeled the fabric from her body. She heard his breath hiss out, and for a moment she thought he might faint on the spot when his gaze fastened with satisfying greed and hunger on her matching barely-there lacy purple bra and panties.

'You're going to kill me,' he groaned, his eyes darkening with hot passion.

He shrugged out of the remainder of his own clothes and her breath locked in her lungs, her heart thudding erratically as her gaze devoured the male perfection of him. She'd never tire of looking at him. Closing the scant distance that separated them, Frazer tipped her unceremoniously onto the comfy four-poster bed that had seen a considerable amount of activity this last year. She opened her arms, welcoming the familiar, yet always exciting feel of his body against her own.

One look in his eyes and she knew she wasn't going to be slowing this down! What she had to tell him would have to wait until afterwards. Not that she was complaining or anything. She smiled to herself as his mouth and hands took possession of her body. And then she couldn't think any more…

'Frazer?'

'Mmm?' It was about the only reply he could manage.

He felt Callie's fingers comb through his tousled hair, but he didn't even have the energy left to open his eyes—not after the tumultuous, wicked, but glorious time they had spent in bed since the wedding. Breathing deeply of her sexy coconut scent, he nuzzled against her neck.

'I want to give you something,' she murmured, turning in his arms.

'Have mercy. Let me get a second, third, fourth or fifth wind first.'

Her breath huffed against his skin as she laughed. 'I didn't mean that!'

Managing to prop himself on one elbow, he looked down at her, seeing stunning purple eyes dark with lingering passion and bright with happiness and love. God, he was so lucky. 'I don't need anything else, sweetheart. You're all I ever want,' he told her, his fingers brushing some feathery strands of hair back off her forehead.

'Well, I can't really take it back now. It's too late.' She nibbled her lower lip, and as his gaze followed the motion he wondered how on earth he could possibly be getting aroused again already. 'Only you can't exactly unwrap it just yet.'

'Why's that?' he asked, his fingers travelling down the line of her cute little nose before he brushed his thumb over her kiss-swollen lips.

Catching his hand, she smiled and kissed it, then drew it

down her body until his palm rested over her navel. 'Because it's going to be another seven months until it's ready.'

Emotion closed his throat as her meaning sank in. 'We're having a baby? Seriously?'

'Seriously.' Happy tears shimmered on long sooty lashes. 'Happy Christmas and happy wedding night, Frazer, my love.'

'God, Callie.'

He didn't have the words to express how happy and thankful he was. Not only did he have his Christmas bride at last, but he'd been blessed with more than he'd imagined possible. His precious wife, who had once feared she would never belong, had now put down deep, strong roots and made a home with him, sharing the promise of a long and happy future with a family of their own. Wrapping his arms around her and holding her tightly against him, he vowed to keep her safe, wanting her, cherishing her and giving her the moon. For Christmas and always.

Together, he and Callie shared the greatest of all gifts. A love to last a lifetime.

REQUEST YOUR FREE BOOKS!

2 FREE NOVELS FROM THE ROMANCE/SUSPENSE COLLECTION PLUS 2 FREE GIFTS!

YES! Please send me 2 FREE novels from the Romance/Suspense Collection and my 2 FREE gifts (gifts are worth about $10). After receiving them, if I don't wish to receive any more books, I can return the shipping statement marked "cancel." If I don't cancel, I will receive 4 brand-new novels every month and be billed just $5.49 per book in the U.S. or $5.99 per book in Canada, plus 25¢ shipping and handling per book plus applicable taxes, if any*. That's a savings of at least 20% off the cover price! I understand that accepting the 2 free books and gifts places me under no obligation to buy anything. I can always return a shipment and cancel at any time. Even if I never buy another book from the Reader Service, the two free books and gifts are mine to keep forever.

185 MDN EF5Y   385 MDN EF6C

Name _____ (PLEASE PRINT)

Address _____ Apt. #

City _____ State/Prov. _____ Zip/Postal Code

Signature (if under 18, a parent or guardian must sign)

Mail to **The Reader Service:**
IN U.S.A.: P.O. Box 1867, Buffalo, NY 14240-1867
IN CANADA: P.O. Box 609, Fort Erie, Ontario L2A 5X3

Not valid to current subscribers to the Romance Collection,
the Suspense Collection or the Romance/Suspense Collection.

Want to try two free books from another line?
Call 1-800-873-8635 or visit www.morefreebooks.com.

* Terms and prices subject to change without notice. N.Y. residents add applicable sales tax. Canadian residents will be charged applicable provincial taxes and GST. Offer not valid in Quebec. This offer is limited to one order per household. All orders subject to approval. Credit or debit balances in a customer's account(s) may be offset by any other outstanding balance owed by or to the customer. Please allow 4 to 6 weeks for delivery. Offer available while quantities last.

Your Privacy: Harlequin is committed to protecting your privacy. Our Privacy Policy is available online at www.eHarlequin.com or upon request from the Reader Service. From time to time we make our lists of customers available to reputable third parties who may have a product or service of interest to you. If you would prefer we not share your name and address, please check here. ☐

BOB08R